"*Come with me,*" *Adam said urgently. "I want you with me.*"

Kerry drew a breath. "I can't."

In his eyes she saw the kind of need she'd always wanted to see. The kind of open vulnerability she was afraid to reveal herself. Her breathing quickened. Her lips parted. Her heart responded, *I love you.*

"Say it. Just say it," he urged.

There was a roaring in her ears, a tidal wave of fear.

Her hesitation was too long. As if from a distance she heard him say bitterly, "It's not in you, is it? God, what a joke. For years I've suffered from loving you, and you don't even feel the same way." He turned from her, preparing to leave.

"Adam . . ." Kerry's voice was shaking.

He glanced back at her.

I love you, she thought again, her throat dry as she worked up the courage to lay bare emotions she'd kept hidden for most of her life. Perspiration sheened her skin. Her stomach clenched.

But the words would not come. . . .

Dear Reader,

Welcome to the Silhouette **Special Edition** experience! With your search for consistently satisfying reading in mind, every month the authors and editors of Silhouette **Special Edition** aim to offer you a stimulating blend of deep emotions and high romance.

The name Silhouette **Special Edition** and the distinctive arch on the cover represent a commitment—a commitment to bring you six sensitive, substantial novels each month. In the pages of a Silhouette **Special Edition**, compelling true-to-life characters face riveting emotional issues—and come out winners. Both celebrated authors and newcomers to the series strive for depth and dimension, vividness and warmth, in writing these stories of living and loving in today's world.

The result, we hope, is romance you can believe in. Deeply emotional, richly romantic, infinitely rewarding—that's the Silhouette **Special Edition** experience. Come share it with us—six times a month!

From all the authors and editors of Silhouette **Special Edition**,

Best wishes,

Leslie Kazanjian,
Senior Editor

NATALIE BISHOP
Dear Diary

Silhouette Special Edition

Published by Silhouette Books New York

America's Publisher of Contemporary Romance

SILHOUETTE BOOKS
300 East 42nd St., New York, N.Y. 10017

ISBN: 0-373-09596-1

First Silhouette Books printing May 1990

Printed in the U.S.A.

Books by Natalie Bishop

Silhouette Special Edition

Saturday's Child #178
Lover or Deceiver #198
Stolen Thunder #231
Trial by Fire #245
String of Pearls #280
Diamond in the Sky #300
Silver Thaw #329
Just a Kiss Away #352
Summertime Blues #401
Imaginary Lover #472
The Princess and the Pauper #545
Dear Diary #596

NATALIE BISHOP

lives in Lake Oswego, Oregon, with her husband, Ken, and daughter, Kelly. Natalie began writing in 1981 along with her sister, Lisa Jackson, another Silhouette author. Though they write separate books, Natalie and Lisa work out most of their plots together. They live within shouting distance of each other and between them have published over thirty Silhouette novels. When Natalie isn't writing, she enjoys spending time at her mountain cabin at Black Butte Ranch, where she catches up on her reading.

Dear Diary...:

September 10, 1967
I met a new boy at school today. He's in the third grade in my room. He got hit by those mean sixth graders. He saved my life!!!! His name is Adam.

June 2, 1975
Tonight I'm going out with Adam. He just broke up with Vicki Fischer, and he needs a friend. It's amazing we're still friends after all these years.

April 18, 1979
Okay, it's honesty time. I was stupid. I thought I was in love. Ryan and I seemed to really hit it off. I should have known better. I'm just dumb, dumb, dumb. But it won't happen again.

May 1, 1990, a.m.
There's a 10:00 meeting today with owners about possible buy-out. Should I be worried? To Do between now and eternity: return Adam's phone call, if I have the nerve.

May 1, 1990, p.m.
Some things never change. Take a look at Adam. He's still gorgeous. Can I seriously survive having him for my boss? At least our friendship can pick up where it left off.

May 24, 1990
I made a mistake. I can't work for Adam. He absolutely will not listen to me about the insanity of taking our relationship a step further! He insists we have dinner together tonight. I suppose I should be glad he's given up on the idea of running away to the San Juans together, but I don't trust what's on his mind....

Prologue

Kerry Camden sat on the edge of the pier, her knees drawn to her chest, the sun-bleached boards beneath her smelling of heat and salt and seaweed. She turned her face to the dusty afternoon sky and inhaled deeply, wrinkling her nose. Adam would be returning any minute. Her pulse beat rapidly. She didn't relish the idea of having to bare her feelings, to admit how much she cared, but the time was now or never.

She drew several quick hard breaths. Her insides were a mass of quivering jelly. It was difficult to cast all her old doubts aside.

Kerry shivered in spite of the heat, rubbing her arms. It was strange to think of Adam as anything more than a friend, yet she'd been forced to these last few weeks. *He'd* forced her to!

And the truth was, she loved him. Oh, yes, she'd faced it, though it had been very hard for her to do so.

For years she'd hidden her emotions deep inside, behind a protective wall of indifference. Not for her, the
same miserable tangle of hatred and bitterness that both
her mother and her sister had suffered. No way. Kerry
Camden would never trust her heart to a man.

But then she hadn't counted on Adam.

Adam. She shook her head, glints of red shimmering in her shoulder-length black tresses. The movement
caused her sunglasses to slip down her nose. She pulled
them off, concentrating on the horizon, searching for
an approaching black dot. John Marsden's yacht should
be pulling into the marina any time now. Adam had
asked Kerry to go fishing but she'd declined, and her
refusal had led to their argument. He'd demanded that
she admit her feelings for him, and she hadn't been able
to. Even when he'd told her he loved her, Kerry's throat
had frozen. Fear had won out. She'd looked at him with
all the love she felt, but it hadn't been enough. He
hadn't believed her, and she couldn't muster the words.

Then he'd coldly walked out.

Leaping to her feet, Kerry dusted off the back of her
jeans, grinding her teeth together in self-disgust. What
a fool I've been! she railed herself for the hundredth,
thousandth, millionth time. Running away from her
feelings hadn't changed them. It never would. Good
Lord, hadn't she learned *anything* from her parents'
divorce?

Faintly, she saw the outline of a boat. Its hull was
white and there was a bit of blue. Kerry's heart jumped,
and she shaded her eyes with her hand. The *Mary Lou*
would be docking soon.

The sun's rays beat into her scalp and perspiration
dampened her throat and hands. Kerry began pacing the
weathered dock. This was no time to be faint-hearted.

When Adam arrived she was going to hit him with the truth, and after that . . . well, it was up to him.

Kerry stopped, lifted her chin and waited. The breeze off Puget Sound blew strands of hair across her face, but she didn't notice. Her hands were clenched at her sides—a brave soldier facing an uncertain future.

The yacht grew closer and Kerry's shoulders slumped in half relief, half disappointment. It was not the *Mary Lou*. She stood nearby, watching as *Camille's Folly* bumped and rubbed squeakily against the pilings. The captain, if one could believe his rank by the insignia on his hat, leaped inelegantly from the boat's bow, landing a few feet from Kerry.

He turned toward her as if he'd been expecting her. "Has the Coast Guard left?"

"The Coast Guard?" Kerry repeated blankly.

"Have you seen them?"

"No, I, uh . . ."

He wasn't listening. He turned and yelled back to someone on board. "They didn't pass through here. Are you sure the message got through?"

"Positive," the man on board declared.

"Well, hell." He sucked air through his teeth.

Kerry didn't miss the urgency. "What's wrong?" she asked, dread creeping up the small of her back.

"We got a mayday call from the *Mary Lou*. She sank about one-thirty this afternoon."

"*Sank?*" The blood left Kerry's head.

He nodded, not really looking at her. If he had, he might have been more gentle, but instead he reported the facts tersely, as a newscaster might. "It went down so fast we barely got a word of warning. We radioed the Coast Guard, but no one knows for sure where they were."

"The *Mary Lou*'s captain sent a distress call to you?" Kerry asked in horrified disbelief.

"Not the captain. Sounded like a hysterical passenger. She said the captain was dead. I got the impression a lot of people had died. Something about the boat filling with water." He glanced back, his brows pulling into a line of consternation. "Say, you don't know anyone on board, do you?"

Only Adam, Kerry thought through a sick haze of disbelief.

Adam. She pressed her hands to her mouth, covering a silent scream.

Adam.

She hadn't had a chance to tell him she loved him.

Chapter One

1967

I met a new boy at school today. He's in the third grade in my room. He got hit by those mean sixth-graders. There was lots and lots of blood. He saved my life!!!! His name is Adam.

Kerry Camden narrowed her eyes at the sight of Tommy Whitlock and Sean Prior poking something on the ground with a stick. The boys' chuckles were deep and malicious. Hate and injustice filled Kerry's nine-year-old heart. There was only one reason those awful sixth-graders would be enjoying themselves: they were torturing something!

She dropped her book bag and ran up behind them, too incensed to care that there was no one else on the footpath that wound through the Scotch broom behind Brentwood Elementary.

"Stop that!" she yelled. "You stop that!"

Tommy's head jerked up and Sean jumped. They both whipped around to glare at Kerry. The dirt-encrusted frog lying on the dusty ground leaped upward, one leg dragging a little as he headed unerringly toward the stagnant pond on the north side of the trail.

"You hurt it!" Kerry cried, her small hands fisting at her sides.

"Get lost, kid." Tommy turned his back on her. He jabbed his stick at the frog, missed, and drew back his arm to jab again. Kerry launched herself at him like a flying missile, hitting him squarely in the middle of his back.

"Hey!" he bellowed.

She flailed and kicked with all her strength, prudence lost beneath a blinding anger. Tommy swore a word that singed Kerry's ears. Then Sean grabbed her by her hair and yanked so hard it brought tears to her eyes.

"Get outta here!" Sean screamed, dragging her off Tommy and shoving her backward.

Kerry tripped over an exposed root, breathing hard. She could hardly see for the tears welling in her eyes. Her hair had been pulled free of its ponytail and fell in front of her face in a riotous tangle. "Leave it alone!"

"Mind your own business, you stupid...slut!" Sean hissed triumphantly.

"Go play with yourself," added Tommy.

"I'm gonna—I'm gonna—" Kerry choked. "I'm gonna tell!"

"Oh, I'm scared. I'm really scared." Tommy made a face at her, then picked up his stick again. Sean stood right in front of Kerry. He kept shoving her shoulders with his hands, short, vicious thrusts that sent her stumbling backward.

Her spine suddenly connected with a warm body.

"What's going on?" a boy's voice asked from behind her.

Kerry turned swiftly, so thankful for a witness she could scarcely speak. "They're hurting that poor frog! It's half-dead already. And they've been pushing me around and calling me names." She wasn't quite sure what slut meant, but it couldn't be good.

She recognized the boy right off. He was new. He'd started school that morning, and he was in her third-grade class, she thought with sinking hopes. The sixth-graders would kill him.

"Beat it, twerp," Tommy snarled.

"Leave that frog alone."

Kerry glanced sideways at her newfound friend, filled with horror-tinged admiration. Did he know what he was inviting? Tommy and Sean would have been happy to pulverize her into the ground. What would they do to *him*?

"Who's gonna stop me?" Tommy taunted. His eyes grew smaller and meaner as he glared at the boy.

Adam. Kerry suddenly remembered his name. He was tall for a third-grader, over a head taller than Kerry. But he didn't have the meat or muscle of the two bullies. He was doomed to lose.

"Don't you have anything better to do?" Adam asked. He was tense and sober. Kerry realized he didn't know what was going to happen to him. She longed to leave before he got hurt.

"Come on," she said, moving closer to him.

But Adam had thrown out a challenge. Tommy smiled a horrid smile, swung his stick around, then crashed it down on the frog.

Kerry screamed. The frog leaped, unscathed. Tommy swore a blue streak. And Adam hurled himself against Tommy in a flying tackle that sent the older boy tumbling into the scum-covered pond.

The smell of rotting vegetation filled the air. For a moment there was utter silence.

With a roar of rage, Sean pounced on Adam, slugging him with the power and experience of three extra years. Adam fought back, but Sean kept right on beating like a boxer. Scared, Kerry jumped on Sean, digging her fingers into his scalp and pulling on his hair the way he'd pulled on hers. He shrieked with pain.

Tommy staggered, dripping, from the pond. "My shirt!" he bellowed. "My new shirt! I'm gonna kill you, you—" He growled in fury, unable to come up with an insult that could top Sean's.

"Get her off me!" Sean howled, and Kerry was jerked away and tossed aside like a rag doll. She staggered to her feet.

Adam lay completely still on the ground.

Tommy, too infuriated to notice, savagely kicked the toe of one soggy tennis shoe against Adam's thigh. Adam's eyes stayed closed.

Sean was breathing hard, looking down at him. Blood trickled from the corner of Adam's mouth.

"You killed him," Kerry sobbed. "You killed him."

"Come on, let's get outta here." Sean's face was turning white.

Tommy was still red and angry. "No, I—"

"Come on, man!" Sean shouted, grabbing a fistful of Tommy's shirt. "He's probably dead. I killed him!"

"Let go!" Tommy roared.

"The hell with you! I'm leaving!"

He tore down the trail, disappearing in the plume of dust kicked up by running heels. Tommy stared down at the unmoving Adam. Fear crawled slowly across his bulldog face. He followed after Sean, racing faster and faster as if from the devil himself.

Kerry felt ready to faint. She didn't do well with the sight of blood. She never had. Little sobs were issuing from her throat as she bent down to touch Adam's unmoving form. "Adam, are you dead?" she asked, scared.

"No." He squinted open his eyes. "Are they gone?"

Kerry bobbed her head in relief.

"I thought playing dead was safer." He tried to sit up, groaned and managed to prop himself on his elbows. "My chest hurts."

"Maybe you have broken ribs."

Adam thought that over. "Maybe."

"And you're bleeding—" Kerry pointed in horror at the thin trickle of blood drying on his lips and chin " —from your mouth "

"A lot?" he asked hopefully.

"Yeah, a lot."

He examined the damage with his tongue, wincing a bit. But his expression lightened. "My lip's gonna swell up."

"Your whole face is gonna swell up."

He bent forward and Kerry decided it was time to help. She grabbed part of his arm and half hauled him to his feet. He was covered with dust. His black hair had turned a strange gray color. One eye was starting to shut.

"Did he kill the frog?"

"No. He missed."

"What a dope." Adam shook his head.

Kerry agreed. "The frog got away. I think he's back in the pond."

"What's your name?" Adam asked. "Aren't you in my room?"

She nodded. "Kerry Camden. You're new. Do you live around here?"

"Over that way." He pointed toward the far ridge where the more expensive homes in Piper Point lay, then sucked air between his teeth and winced with pain.

"Hurt?" Kerry asked, grimacing in sympathy.

"Not too bad."

"My house is right over there." She swept her arm toward the tract homes nestled at the bottom of the hill. "You want to come over and get fixed up?"

Adam pondered that seriously for several moments. "Yeah, okay," he said at last.

Kerry led the way down the trail to where it ended at the small neighborhood roadway. She asked curiously, "Have you still got all your permanent teeth?"

"I think so."

He was beginning to look really terrible. One side of his face had swollen up as badly as when Kerry's little sister, Marla, had gotten stung by a wasp. Kerry began to feel anxious. She wanted her mom to make sure Adam was okay.

Kerry's house was the third one on Maple Street, it was white with black shutters. She took Adam around the back and opened the kitchen door. Her mother was standing at the sink, peeling carrots. "Mom? I brought a friend home. He got beat up by some older kids."

Mrs. Camden glanced at Adam and tsk-tsked. But she hardly changed expression.

Kerry's chest tightened. She recognized her mother's look. Mom had gone silent again. She was always doing that. Kerry had learned to walk softly when Mom went silent, because otherwise her mother would scream or burst into tears. Only Marla, in kindergarten, could still be her spoiled childish self when Mom went silent. Mom didn't seem to care that Marla didn't understand.

"Come on in the bathroom," Mrs. Camden said to Adam, "and I'll take care of that. Then I think you'd better call your mother."

"I can do it myself," he said.

Mom looked skeptical but gave in easily. Kerry saw the telltale smudges of mascara around her eyes and knew she wasn't really thinking about Adam. Afraid she might be the one to send her mother into tears again, Kerry led Adam to the bathroom.

He stared at his reflection in the mirror and looked infinitely happier. "Wow."

"You're gonna have a black eye."

Adam grinned and glanced her way. "So are you."

"I am?" Kerry crowded into the bathroom, staring at her own face. Her cheeks were streaked with grime and her black hair was the same dusty shade as Adam's. There was a small cut above her eye and now that she could see it, she felt the swelling.

Adam started laughing and so did Kerry. It was great! From the other room she heard a funny hiccupping sound and blocked it out. It was Mom crying. Kerry shut her mind to the sound. She wasn't going to think about that now or wonder at its cause. She wasn't.

She slung her arm around Adam's shoulder and declared with forced cheerfulness, "We need a picture!"

"Do you have a camera?"

"Dad does."

Kerry ran into her parents' bedroom. The camera was in the closet. Her footsteps crunched on glass. She looked down and her heart lurched. One of her parents' wedding photos was smashed on the ground.

Kerry squeezed her eyes shut, besieged by nameless fears. Something dreadful was going to happen. She just knew it. Once more she blanked out her mind, though it was difficult with Mom sobbing quietly in the other room.

In the hallway Adam took the camera from Kerry and held it in front of them, as far as his arm could reach, pointing the lens their way. "Get in close," he ordered. "Make sure we're both in the picture."

Kerry squished up next to him. He wrapped an arm around her shoulder. *Flash.* "Better take another," she suggested. "Just in case."

Flash. "How about one more?" he asked.

"Sure."

Flash. He handed her back the camera and grinned.

"You want to be friends?" asked Kerry.

"Sure. Why not?"

Kerry managed to grin back. Adam was so cool! He hadn't made fun of her once for being a girl. She grabbed his hand and pumped it hard. "Pleased to meet you, Adam . . . what's your last name?"

"Shard."

"Pleased to meet you, Adam Shard. Whenever I need help, I'll call on you."

"Same here," he said, and they both laughed at the sight of each other's battered faces.

It was the beginning of a beautiful friendship.

Chapter Two

1975

Tonight I'm going out with Adam. No big deal. We're just going to see a movie. I think Adam is bored. Why else would he ask me out? He just broke up with Vicki Fischer and he needs a friend. It's amazing we're still friends after all these years.

Mom?" Kerry called, pushing open the kitchen door. It was hot. Way too hot for June, but then, sometimes the weather in Piper Point could be unpredictable. She felt scratchy and sticky all over. "Mom?"

There was no answer and the house was so quiet she could hear the hum of the refrigerator. Kerry could tell she was alone. It was just as well, she supposed, taking the stairs two at a time to her room. Mom wouldn't appreciate her coming home from school at noon even though she only had study hall and pep assemblies the rest of the day and the end of the school year was just a few days away.

She stripped off her hot sweater and pants, stood beneath the needle-sharp spray of a cooling shower, then donned a pair of white shorts and a pink tank top. Later she planned to wear something a little more sophisticated. Why, she didn't analyze. It was just Adam she was going out with, but she wanted to look better anyway.

Her hair lay hot on her shoulders so she sat down at her vanity and wound it into a French braid, staring hard at her own reflection as she did so. She really didn't like looking at herself. All her flaws were there to see. She was too gangly; her arms and legs didn't seem to fit with the rest of her. Her nose was too pugged, her lips too wide, her eyes too direct. More than one guy had complained about her sarcastic sense of humor, which Kerry preferred to think of as wry, and she'd spent most of this year watching the boys hover around her sweeter, more well-endowed, precocious thirteen-year-old sister, Marla, rather than take a second look at her.

Kerry leaned her elbows on the vanity top, propped her chin on her hands and sighed deeply. Not that she *really* cared whether she had any dates or not, she reminded herself. The boys at Piper Point were all geeks. Except for Adam. And anyway, none of them would look at her. Oh, sure, she bore a passing resemblance to Jenny Sutcliff, Piper Point High's brightest star, but she didn't possess Jenny's long silky hair, or her deep brown mysterious eyes. Kerry's hair was too wiry, her eyes a cross between green and brown, which her mother termed hazel for lack of a better word. She was just okay looking, and she was too smart to believe her mother's assurances that she would someday be a real beauty.

Thinking of Mom, Kerry frowned. Something was going on between her parents, the same something that had ebbed and flowed in waves of tension for years. Sometimes Kerry thought they should divorce, but deep down she didn't want them to. She'd do almost anything to keep them together.

Still, the last few months had been worse. The atmosphere around Mom and Dad was thick and hostile. Her father was hardly ever home, and when he was, he was short-tempered, anxious and dissatisfied. Kerry tried to stay out of his way. Her mother had grown even more remote and there were lines of discontentment drawn beside her mouth. The one time Kerry had brought up her parents' problems she'd been cut off by a sharp response. It was all too weird and unnerving to consider. Best to forget it.

Her bedroom was suffocating, so Kerry walked down the hall to the bathroom she shared with Marla. The window was open and she could see into the backyard. A shimmering layer of heat made everything seem unnaturally bright and artificial. She wished suddenly that Adam had skipped out, too, and the two of them could be on their way somewhere—anywhere—else.

She heard a car pull into the garage. Mom was home from some errand. On the heels of that thought came another: Mom was visiting her friend Sara in Seattle today. She couldn't be home already.

Kerry frowned. Yes, it was definitely today that Mom had said they were on their own for dinner. So who was pulling into the garage?

Some sixth sense warned her to wait. She listened to the soft drip of the shower and heard the hum of a bee hovering around the rhododendrons outside. The kitchen door opened. Feminine laughter rippled through the quiet house. Sultry laughter, followed by her father's low-pitched voice saying something indistinguishable that had his partner giggling girlishly.

Kerry froze. Who was with her father?

The heavy scent of an expensive perfume drifted all the way upstairs, rising with the heat. Kerry heard murmured voices and then one clear comment by the unknown woman.

"Your house is so beautiful, Griffith. I wish I could share it with you."

Kerry didn't remember moving. She couldn't have said later how she'd gotten downstairs. She was drawn to that voice and the terrible messages slamming across her brain.

They were still in the kitchen. Kerry heard a cork pop and the hissing fizz of champagne. More feminine giggles. Deep masculine chuckles. Her heart was pounding so loudly she was half deaf.

She stopped in the archway between the kitchen and dining room. They didn't know she was there. Her footsteps had been muffled by the carpet. Her father's back was to her, but it was definitely her father: Griffith Camden, salesman extraordinaire, quick with a smile and a wink, full of laughter and outrageous stories, model father, loving husband.

Adulterer.

The woman's arms were draped casually around his neck, the champagne glass balanced in one hand. She was kissing him, trying not to spill the bubbly liquid, giggling all the while. As Kerry watched, the glass tipped, sending a sparkling stream to the floor as the kiss became more passionate, the lovers heedless. Her father's arms tightened perceptibly around the woman's waist. The woman's hands clutched his shoulders.

"Stop!"

It was her voice that cut through the air, and it had instant effect. The woman gasped and her father straightened as if someone had burned him. They both turned to look at Kerry.

"Kerry!" he choked out.

"Oh, my God," the woman said.

"Get out," Kerry stated in a shaking voice. "Get out of my mother's house."

There was no immediate reaction. Both her father and his paramour looked too shocked to move. But Kerry was fast regaining the use of her limbs. Injustice and pain swept through her like a brushfire. Tears stood in her eyes. She turned toward the phone. "If you don't leave I'll call the police."

"Kerry, stop it." Her father's face was white but determined. "Your mother knows about Eileen."

Eileen couldn't quite help the astonished look that crossed her face.

Kerry stopped. "I don't believe you. You're lying."

"She knows there's someone else in my life."

"Oh, you . . . you bastard," Kerry choked out, her throat tightening. She couldn't see for the wash of tears in her eyes, and she turned blindly, stumbling. Her father's hand on her arm was a mistake. She shook him off with all the rage she felt. "Get away from me! I never, *never*, want to see you again!"

"Would you just calm down? There's no need to be so damn hysterical."

"I'll leave," Eileen said quietly, heading for the door.

"Get your hand off me," Kerry ordered through her teeth, heedless of the tears that rolled down her cheeks.

She was shaking so hard she could hardly stand, but all she could think about was the feel of her father's cheating hand on her arm. She yanked herself free.

"I'm going to take Eileen home, but I'll be back. Don't leave. What the hell are you doing here anyway?"

His anger was at getting caught, Kerry dimly realized as she ran upstairs. She heard the door slam. Long moments passed before the engine revved. She clapped her hands to her ears, seared by a pain so intense she felt incapable of moving.

So many things made sense now. Maybe her mother knew, maybe she didn't. But she'd guessed. Kerry was swept by the strongest aversion to the opposite sex she'd ever felt. Cheating, lying, treacherous men. By God, she was never going to fall for one. Not her.

Adam Shard eased his mother's sedan against the curb in front of Kerry's house. The car was a relic, he thought, amused. All it needed was a few fins off the back to be a classic Fifties vehicle. How long she'd owned it, he couldn't tell, but he liked driving it better than the new compact. After all, it had a wide bench seat across the front. A necessity, as far as Adam was concerned, if you wanted to kiss a girl.

Not that he expected to kiss Kerry. She was his friend, and she'd made it clear in a hundred different ways that she found most of the guys in the class stupid, boring and generally consumed by lust to the exclusion of any sense. Adam felt it was a gift of providence that she didn't seem to feel the same way about him. Considering the state of his hormones these days, he was sure she simply hadn't noticed.

Adam grimaced. It didn't help that Vicki Fischer was an unbearable tease. He'd started dating her in spite of her reputation. She was simply fun and bright and cheerful, as far as he could see. And he'd ignored the knowing jabs in the ribs by his friends and the sly winks and smiles, thinking them just as Kerry described. But in the end he found out that Vicki enjoyed leading a guy on, then shutting him down. He was glad he'd broken up with her.

Which brought him to Kerry. She was the one female who didn't play head games. He could trust her to be totally honest, totally fair. Thank God he didn't have to suffer through several hours of torment wondering what his date was thinking, worrying how the evening would end. Kerry Camden was a relief to be with. Kind of like being out with the guys.

Adam jumped out of the car, strode up the Camdens' driveway, then glanced down at his tan shorts and the disreputable pair of running shoes he wore without socks. Not exactly proper attire for an evening out, he thought with a grimace, straightening the gray T-shirt emblazoned with the University of Washington logo tucked into his shorts. He wondered if Kerry was expecting to be taken somewhere special.

He raised his hand to knock and was surprised when the door opened. Kerry, in a tank top and shorts, a white canvas bag slung over her shoulder, her usually mobile face strangely set and distant, appeared as if by magic.

"Ready?" she asked, not quite meeting his eyes.

"Sure."

She strode toward his car without another word. Adam, faintly concerned that he'd done something to make her angry, followed after her.

The way she moved caught his attention. Long legs propelled her forward determinedly, but the sway of her hips was entirely feminine. He could see no bra line beneath the pink cotton top, and his mind's eye thought about how she must look from the front.

Hormones, he thought, gritting his teeth as the familiar, frustrating first heat of desire swept through him. Good God. He was with *Kerry*, for crying out loud!

In the car he hazarded a glance at her profile. She was staring straight through the windshield, refusing to even look at him. He noticed her eyes were faintly reddened. "Have I done something wrong?" he asked, uncertain how to deal with her like this.

She drew in a sharp breath and glanced his way. It was an effort for her to smile, but she managed it. "Not a thing. Where, er, are we going tonight?"

"What are you in the mood for?" His gaze skated over her shorts and top. Good God, she looked good. He'd never noticed before quite how smooth and golden her skin was. How firm yet feminine the muscles of her thighs were. How pink her lips were.

He dragged his gaze away, conscious of a tightening in his own shorts. With an effort, he said lightly, "Neither of us is dressed for a fancy restaurant."

"Good. I—I want to go somewhere I can relax. Where I don't have to think. Can we go see that horror flick everyone's talking about?"

Adam glanced at her, amused. "You want to relax at *Swampthing*?"

"I just need something mindless."

"Okay." He started the engine. "But it's only playing at the drive-in."

"No problem."

Adam drove automatically, all his senses attuned to the woman beside him. He was too conscious of her. Her scent was soft and light, the gentle movement of her breasts beneath her tank top sweetly seductive. His mouth was dry. Not Kerry, he reminded himself uselessly. Not Kerry.

With an inward groan he clamped down on his runaway emotions, wishing fervently he could be different from the stupid, lustful clods Kerry disdained. Unfortunately he didn't think he was. His mind was on a definite track. The next few hours, he realized fatalistically, were sure to be an experiment in torture.

Kerry stared blankly at the screen, watching as another unsuspecting female fell victim to the supernatural evil of the dreaded Swampthing. The show was meant to be taken seriously, but it was too campy to inspire any real fear. And Kerry could scarcely remember a single frame anyway. The screen of her mind played another scenario over and over again. Sparkling champagne and passionate kisses. Tension and desire. Lust and deception.

Her stomach was clamped in knots.

Adam shifted in the seat beside her. "All right, what's wrong?" he asked, turning his gaze from the terrible, bone-crushing mass on screen to examine her troubled face.

"Nothing."

He snorted, laying his arm over the back of the seat. "Give me a break. You've been about as much fun as a case of the flu."

Since Adam had just suffered through a real, heavy-duty bout of the flu, Kerry had to acknowledge she must be a real drag. "I'm just preoccupied."

Heat eddied inside the open windows in a whirling gust. Kerry tried to inhale but the air felt weighted, heavy and suffocating. She was hot, sticky and uncomfortable. Sweat beaded on her throat and between her breasts.

"Well, what is it?"

She shook her head. "Maybe you should just take me home."

"Is it school?"

"No."

"Some guy?" he suggested with stirring aggression.

"Hardly."

"Then what?"

She glanced his way, her mouth twisting. Adam's gray eyes regarded her soberly between thick black lashes. She rarely saw him looking so serious. He was usually fun-loving and easygoing. Open, outrageous, and brilliant without seeming to have to study, while studious, cautious Kerry hid behind a wall of sarcasm. They were oil and water. Fire and ice.

To Kerry's surprise he suddenly lifted a palm to her face, cupping her cheek and chin. It was the only time he'd ever done such a thing. She blinked in shock.

"Tell me," he urged. "I want to know."

She stared at his familiar face and her heart pumped hard and fast. She *could* tell Adam. He would understand. She opened her mouth to do just that, but the enormity of her father's infidelity washed over her in a cold wave. Instead of responding, she could only look into the dark pools of Adam's eyes and fight back a thundering wave of emotion.

What Adam read in her face must have been something entirely different. His gaze suddenly fastened on her trembling lips in a way that made Kerry's breath catch. Then his thumb slid across her cheek and rubbed against her mouth, begging for entry.

"Adam," she protested softly.

He shook his head and closed his eyes. Belatedly Kerry realized what was happening. Too late she understood the tremor that consumed him. She wasn't ready for this, she thought wildly. Not from Adam. Not today!

A heartbeat later his mouth found hers.

At first she was frozen, too stunned to do more than sit utterly still. His breath was warm and moist, his lips firm and pressed to hers in a way that made her head spin. She could smell his clean scent, could feel the increased pressure of slanting lips, could sense his tense fingers at her nape drawing her closer to him.

"Kerry," he murmured, breaking contact for one millisecond, his eyes heavy-lidded. Passion simmered between his lashes like a flickering blue-gray flame. Kerry's eyes were wide. She was scared to death.

But even while every nerve screamed in warning, another feeling stirred inside her. Like some long-hibernating beast, her emotions finally yawned and stretched and awakened. Desire swept through her limbs, turning them liquid. She wanted to crush herself against him and block out the terrible memory of champagne and kisses and her father's treachery.

But when Adam's mouth found hers a second time, crushingly demanding, the shock of its wet warmth brought her to her senses. She reared back, thrusting shaking palms against his chest, her arms rigid with fear, her mind filled with images of her father and the woman called Eileen.

A terrible moment passed. Adam straightened in his seat, his gaze steady on her white face. Kerry's blood pounded in her ears. She trembled like the proverbial leaf.

The muscles in his neck were rigid. She understood he was fighting for control, but she couldn't help him. Couldn't explain that it had nothing to do with his kiss. That it was a matter of timing, nothing more.

"I'm sorry," he said crisply.

"Adam, you're my friend," Kerry choked in a small voice "I just want . . . a friend."

"I understand."

To her humiliation, she felt fresh tears gather behind her eyelids. She felt battered and tossed by her emotions, and she couldn't deal with one more stressful scene.

Adam saw her tears and misunderstood. "God, Kerry," he muttered in self-deprecation. "Don't make me hate myself more than I already do!"

"It's not you."

"Right."

"I mean it, Adam. It's not you."

Of course he didn't believe her, and she had no strength left to convince him. When he dropped her off at her house, she was scared she'd lost his friendship, too, and the thought was unbearable.

She tried one last time to put things back together. "I've got some problems at home. I really need a friend right now." Her voice cracked and she drew a breath. "Just a friend."

In the half light of the dashboard his face was shadowed and more alien than she remembered. But then he leaned forward, searching her gaze as if trying to fathom her secret. "You still want me as a friend?"

"More than ever."

His lips twisted painfully. "Okay. You got it. See you Monday at school."

Relief lightened her heart a little. "Adam?" she called anxiously when he pulled back.

He leaned forward once more, frowning slightly. "What?"

"Don't ever stop being my friend."

The inclination of his head was the only answer he gave. She watched him leave, the car's taillights winking out around the corner. She hoped with all her heart that Adam was as good as his word.

Chapter Three

1979

> *Okay, it's honesty time. I was stupid. I thought I was in love. Ryan and I seemed to really hit it off. I should have known better. I should have known there'd be a Diane out there somewhere. There always is. Even Adam can't manage to stay faithful. His list of women would fill a phone book. But at least he knows what he's doing. I'm just naive and dumb, dumb, dumb. But it won't happen again.*

Kerry tightened her grip on her shoulder bag as she locked the door to her beat-up blue car, a 1969 relic she'd purchased with some of the money she'd earned last summer working at Nordstrom's. Unfortunately lately she'd heard this grinding sound coming from somewhere near the front left wheel. She was certain the car's death was imminent, and she had no funds left to repair it. For the time being, however, it still managed to wheeze and throb from Washington State U. all the way to Seattle, so here she was, on the University of Washington campus, in search of Adam.

It was spring term and the weather was cloudy and cool. Kerry glanced around the parking lot. This *was* the lot where Adam had told her to meet him, wasn't it? In the three years since they'd both started school at different colleges—Adam at U. of W.; Kerry at W.S.U. near Pullman—she had only been to visit Adam once, when he was a freshman living in the dorm. It was too expensive for Kerry to take off for a whole weekend; she simply didn't have the money. Besides, she'd spent most of her free time studying anyway. That was until she'd met Ryan, but that was over now....

"Come on, Adam," she muttered, climbing onto the hood of her car, her sneakers propped on the near-rusted fender. She swept her thick black ponytail over her shoulder. She wasn't going to think about Ryan now, or why Adam's invitation to visit had seemed like a godsend. She was out of her mind to be here when she had so much to do. There would be hell to pay on Monday, but damn it all, she needed to get away.

Beep. Beep. The sound of a tinny horn caught Kerry's attention. She looked around to see Adam astride a metallic-blue ten-speed, grinning at her, his fingers squeezing the rubber bulb of a toy horn attached to the handlebars.

His legs were tanned and muscular beneath a pair of khaki shorts. A thin, white sweatshirt was zipped to his neck, its back billowing in the breeze, the sleeves shoved back to his elbows. His dark hair rippled, and his gray eyes seemed to laugh. Kerry hadn't seen him since last summer at Piper Point, and she was struck by how much older he looked.

"Kerry, my love," he said. "You made it."

"Hah. Just barely. Seattle traffic's a killer." Jumping off her car, she asked, "So, are you going to tell me why we met here and not your house, hmm?"

"Because I wanted you all to myself," he teased. "I live with a bunch of fraternity buddies. I figured there must be some reason you've stayed away so long. I wasn't going to let you meet them unprepared and give you another!"

"Are they that bad?"

"They're total lechers. I'm kicking them out while you're here." He turned his bike back the way he'd come and said, "Ready?"

Actually Kerry wasn't even close to being ready. Adam's casual remarks about his roommates made her realize how unprepared she was. Whatever had possessed her into coming? She had nowhere to stay, and she was reluctant to sack out at Adam's regardless of the sleeping bag she had stowed in her trunk.

"You didn't have to kick them out. I'm not spending the night."

He turned around slowly. "What do you mean?"

"I've got to get back, Adam. Finals are next week, and I'm crazy to be here."

"You're not driving all the way back to Pullman tonight!" He stared at her incredulously. "You said you were coming for the weekend."

"That was stupid. I can't stay. I just wanted to...see you, I guess. But I didn't think it through."

"What is it, Kerry?" he asked, gliding the bicycle her way until he was inches from where she stood. "Are you in some kind of trouble?"

"No!" His perception amazed her.

"Well, you haven't visited in years and you've always been busy when I've tried to see you. Now you're going to be here—what?—two hours, maybe? Come to the house. I promise I'll get rid of everybody. You can have my room. I sleep on the couch half the time anyway. Just don't leave." Twisting the bike around, he called, "Follow me!"

He took off before she could respond, apparently unwilling to listen to any more excuses. Muttering to herself about his incredible pig-headedness, Kerry slid behind the steering wheel and turned the ignition. The engine groaned and chugged. "Come on, you turkey," Kerry said through her teeth, pumping the accelerator. "Come on. Come on!"

The engine turned unwillingly and finally caught, pinging loudly. Kerry didn't give it time to quit on her. She hit the accelerator and reversed rapidly, then cruised quickly in the direction Adam had taken.

His bike was whisking along the sidewalk. She could see his white sweatshirt and his khaki-clad, muscled buttocks in the distance. He turned right at the edge of campus and headed for Queen Anne Hill. Though she'd never been there, she knew the house he and his buddies lived in was about three miles away. It was built circa 1910, had three stories and was in a fairly respectable neighborhood, although Adam's home had gone to seed. Or so he'd told her.

Expecting to have to pace herself, Kerry was surprised how quickly Adam rode. She kept an even speed behind him, chafing when she got caught at the light, frantic when he seemed to have vanished into thin air.

But then she saw his bike starting to climb the hill. She saw now why he'd chosen to ride a ten-speed than drive; it was faster. Keeping him in her sights, she tailed a dismally slow driver, finally cutting free just when Adam disappeared onto a residential street about six blocks away.

Kerry followed quickly, turning onto a street of small older homes, some kept up, others having let time and the elements erode their once elegant structures. Adam was waiting on the sidewalk in front of a rambling blue house.

"Took you long enough." He grinned as she rolled down her window. "Well, here it is—home, sweet home."

The driveway was two fir-needle strewn ruts, the center of which sported foot-high dandelions. As Kerry cautiously turned in, the dandelions brushed the underside of her car.

Music, heavy and throbbing, poured from an upstairs window as she pulled to a stop behind another car, this one sleek, gray and expensive. Adam's, she knew, because she'd seen it last summer when he'd dropped by her mom's apartment.

Kerry yanked on the emergency brake and cut the engine. Her mother and Marla lived by themselves now; her father had moved to Chicago. The divorce occurred right after the incident in the kitchen. Kerry hadn't told her mother. She hadn't had the nerve. But it wasn't necessary. Her parents' marriage had been crumbling for years and it had ended in bitterness and anger.

"Hey, Shard!" a male voice yelled above the music. "Jenny called. Twice. She's gonna be here in ten."

Kerry stepped uneasily from her car, slinging her bag over her shoulder. Adam was just finishing locking his bike to the rail that ran around the front porch.

"Yo, Adam? Ya hear me?"

"I heard you," Adam responded.

The voice belonged to a blond guy hanging out of an upstairs window. He was shirtless even though the temperature wasn't even sixty. The male is a strange animal, she decided with a shake of her head.

"Who's Jenny, or should I even ask?" Kerry inquired with a knowing smile as Adam walked back to her.

"Jenny Sutcliff."

"Jenny Sutcliff?" Her jaw dropped. "From Piper Point?"

"That's the one. Have you got anything else? Like an overnight bag, or something?"

"Uh, no." She shook her head though there was a bag in the trunk along with her sleeping bag. Jenny Sutcliff! "You're dating Jenny Sutcliff?"

"Mmm-hmm. You sure you didn't bring anything? I can't believe it. You drive almost all the way across the state just to say hello? Are you nuts?"

"I could ask the same thing of you. Did U. W. run out of women or something? Why Jenny Sutcliff, Piper Point's cheerleader extraordinaire? Even you didn't much like her in high school!"

"Now that hurts. That really hurts." He slid her a look as they headed for the front door. "I'm more discriminate than you give me credit for."

"Oh, sure." Kerry laughed.

"I am. You don't know everything there is about me, even though you think you do."

Kerry could have argued the point, but she didn't. She merely smiled, her eyes filled with suppressed amusement. Adam glared at her as they walked inside the house. It smelled musty, as if mildew had taken over in a big way, and the front hall was dusty with foot-prints. The furniture was ripped and worn; garage sale rejects.

"Well?" Adam asked.

"Nice."

He laughed.

Around the corner to the kitchen, Kerry could see another male body silhouetted. He moved from the window to stand in the archway, his dark eyes assessing Kerry in unabashed head-to-toe appraisal.

"What have we here, Shard?" he asked, grinning hugely. "Naughty, naughty. What will Jenny say?"

"Drop dead, B.J.," Adam answered without heat.

"B.J." remained very much alive, and Kerry, with an inward grimace, couldn't help remembering her own appearance. She'd tossed on a pair of jeans, cutoff and rolled up a little above her knee and probably in desperate need of a trip to the wash, and a gray pullover sweatshirt. Her hair was scraped straight back from her head, ending in a wild, busy ponytail. She'd run away from the evidence of Ryan's last indiscretion without even bothering to think about what she looked like.

She'd simply wanted to escape.

Footsteps clattered on the steps. Adam's shirtless blond roommate appeared, thrusting his arms through the sleeves of a wrinkled shirt. He gazed curiously at Kerry.

Adam sighed. "Kerry, this is Kirk, and that's B.J. Guys, this is Kerry Camden, my *friend*."

"So you're Kerry." Kirk's freckled, almost homely face broke into a grin. "Here we thought you were a figment of Adam's imagination. We heard a lot about you, but we didn't really believe you existed."

"She doesn't," Adam warned.

"You didn't tell us she had nice legs," said B.J.

Kerry, who rarely ever blushed, felt heat invade her face. A by-product of Ryan's desertion, she thought miserably, struggling to regain the cool control that had become her trademark throughout high school and the ugly nastiness of her parents' divorce.

Another car pulled into the drive, its horn honking loud and long. Kerry could see at least three guys jammed inside the tiny VW bug. "What is this place, a commune?" she demanded. "I thought that went out in the Sixties."

"They're just some more Sig Eps." Adam shrugged. "Fraternity brothers. They don't all live here."

"You could have fooled me."

"Come on, I'll show you my room."

"Whoa," B.J. said on a long whistle, his eyes alive with mischief. "Your room, Mr. Shard?"

To Kerry's surprise, Adam turned so swiftly she nearly tripped on the bottom step and slammed into his broad back. He didn't say a word, just stared at B.J. in a way that made Kerry's stomach clench apprehensively.

If B.J. got the message, he didn't show it, but Kerry's blood turned to ice at the look of pure challenge she could see in Adam's eyes. She'd almost forgotten the attractive blue streaks in his gray eyes, but she saw them now as his gaze bored into B.J.

"Come on, Kerry," he said, starting up the stairs. "Before blood is shed."

She quickly hurried after him, glancing down at B.J. as they rounded the landing. "You don't have to take care of me, Adam," she said in an undertone. "I'm twenty-one years old. I've even passed the legal drinking age."

"B.J. Kellerman can be a great guy, but he doesn't get the message unless you hit him over the head with a two-by-four. Don't even be friendly to him, Kerry, or he'll think you want to go to bed."

She almost laughed at Adam's proprietary tone. He was worse than a big brother! But a part of her responded to the deep caring that went along with it—the same part that wanted to curl up in his arms and cry her eyes out over Ryan.

"I'll remember," she said dryly.

Adam's room was at the end of the hall. A single bed was pressed against the north wall, a chest of drawers against the south. A round straw mat covered the hardwood floor almost wall to wall, and a crude bookshelf and desk were the only other pieces of furniture. A fish tank glowed with green light.

Kerry walked straight over to the aquarium. She felt out of place, and why not? She hadn't seen enough of Adam these last few years to call him more than an old acquaintance, and she didn't know any of his friends. Except Jenny Sutcliff. "Tropical fish, huh?" she said, bending down to look at the exotically colored specimens.

"My ex-roommate's passion. I inherited them when he graduated."

"If they're his passion, why didn't he take them with him?"

"They were just his latest passion. That's how he was. Like everything else he fell in love with, they went the way of the dinosaur." Adam lightly tapped the glass with his fingers, and the fish instantly swam his way. "They're an easy pet," he said, unscrewing the lid from a small bottle of fish food. "Here." He handed the bottle to Kerry. "Just put a little bit on top of the water."

She sprinkled food on the surface. So quick she almost didn't see it, several fish darted upward, then back down to safer waters. "How do you like cleaning the tank?"

"Oh, it's okay. Gives me an excuse to get away when things downstairs start to get too much."

She glanced sideways at him. His gaze was fixed on the fish tank, his expression serious. "What do you mean?"

"B.J. and Kirk and the others. Sometimes they get going on something and I need a reason to escape." He shrugged. "So how about you?"

"What about me?"

He glanced her way. "Come on, Kerry. This is Adam you're talking to, remember? I've asked you to come here a thousand times and you're always too busy. And now suddenly you're here within twenty-four hours of our last conversation."

"Can't an old friend just show up without a reason?" Kerry demanded.

"I don't think so."

Kerry walked to the center of the room, away from Adam. She'd thought she could throw herself in his arms and have Adam take away all the hurt. He was her big brother, her friend, her hero. A part of her wanted him to gallop on a white charger all the way to Washington State, grab Ryan by the throat and shake the life out of him.

But another part of her wanted to cry. Only she hated crying and refused to indulge in it. "I'm just having a tough time at school," she said. "It's been one of those terms."

"Lame excuse, but if you don't want to talk, don't." He grinned suddenly and took two steps to meet her, hugging her so fiercely that it squeezed the breath from Kerry's lungs. Her eyes widened in surprise. "I'm glad you're here."

She hadn't hugged Adam since the night he'd kissed her at the drive-in. She'd hardly even touched him. There was unmistakable strength in the arms that surrounded her. The muscles of his back moved like liquid beneath her rigid fingers. His thighs brushed hers. She could smell his skin, clean and slightly tangy. Her breasts were pressed to his chest. His breathing filled her ears. The hair on the back of his neck lay smooth and silky.

A horn blared outside, long and shrill. Adam inhaled sharply and turned, letting go of Kerry in one quick movement that wasn't meant to repel but did. She was too bemused to even think of a clever remark. Belatedly she realized that although the embrace had knocked the stuffing from her, Adam must not feel the same.

"It's Jenny," he said. A smile spread across his face as he watched from the window. He lifted a hand in greeting. "It's about time she got here."

Dinner was pizza delivered from the Pizza Man, a personal friend of Adam and his buddies, Kerry learned, as a day hardly passed without someone ordering out.

She ate one slice though her stomach was in such knots she could scarcely swallow. What in God's name was she doing here? She had a ton of work at school, and Ryan, though still a gaping wound, was soon going to be just a memory if it killed her.

The beanbag chair Kerry had found in a corner of the living room was straight out of the Sixties and provided a great way to hide. She ate her pizza in near anonymity. More co-eds had dropped by during the course of the evening. Friends of Adam or B.J. or Kirk. Since Adam's attention was on Jenny, no one paid any attention to Kerry. Good. She wanted to be forgotten.

Glancing around the room, Kerry grimaced. She'd never even tried once to fix her hair or makeup the way these girls did. Good grief, it looked as if they spent weeks getting ready just to go to the grocery store! And as far as clothes went, well, who had that kind of money? Kerry had used every dime she'd earned from working to pay for her education.

But Ryan hadn't seemed to care, she remembered ruefully. He'd noticed her in a crowd, had actually picked her out from among a group of much prettier girls. Kerry had been extremely flattered. Stupidly so. She'd responded to his attention like the love-starved woman she was. She'd wanted someone to care for her, to love and cherish her.

Their relationship had started slowly. Kerry, whose only memorable kiss had been from Adam, had been so nervous the first time Ryan's lips brushed hers that her hands sweated. Luckily, Ryan had taken his time. He hadn't pressured her. She thought him incredibly understanding. Here, finally, was someone who'd wanted to know *her*, the real Kerry Camden! He wasn't in an awful rush to get her into bed. He wasn't looking for a one-night stand. He'd wanted something meaningful, something lasting, just as she did.

She hadn't known she was being played by a master.

Over the course of several blind, beautiful months, D day had finally arrived. Ryan wanted to sleep with her. Certain she was in love, Kerry agreed, but she had to fight back the fear of intimacy that plagued her.

It turned out okay. No bells rang and a choir didn't break into song, but then she was inexperienced and embarrassed. What did she expect? It didn't matter anyway. She was in love. So in love that all her defense mechanisms were dismantled, useless, forgotten.

Unaware that she was setting herself up for the biggest fall of her life, Kerry let herself be swept away on a wave of passion and adventure. It never occurred to her to ask why Ryan had chosen her. Not after that first night. It also never occurred to her to ask him what he did on the evenings he didn't spend with her.

She found out slowly. The first clue was a paper she accidentally discovered stuck within the pages of his economics book. Caroline, it said, followed by a number encircled in a heart. Kerry hadn't asked. But she'd kept the note.

Then Kerry received the phone call from Diane. Diane had just found out about Kerry and she was furious. She told Kerry everything, and much more than she'd wanted to hear.

Surfacing from her fantasy was terrible. She fought it like a drug addict who refused help, only wanting the feeling to go on and on. Her innate sense of self-worth was all that had saved her. No matter how much she might have wanted to, she couldn't fool herself.

Diane had called two weeks ago. When Ryan had appeared that night on her doorstep, Kerry had refused to let him inside. She'd told him what she thought of him, and he'd listened without emotion. He didn't even really care, she'd realized later with fresh pain.

Two days ago she ran into him on campus. He was with a beautiful blond. Kerry had coldly ignored him and his vanity finally got to him. He'd made a crack about "making it with a virgin" and how glad he was that "someone had filled that gap in his education." Kerry had made it all the way back to her apartment before she'd started to shake.

Now, safe at Adam's, Kerry closed her eyes and inhaled deeply. *How could I have been so wrong about him? How could I have been so stupid? So naive!*

Miserable, she finally swallowed the last of her pizza. Here she was and she couldn't even confide in Adam. It was too humiliating. But it was better than sitting around her apartment and berating herself for being such a total moron.

Feeling someone's eyes on her, she lifted her eyelids. B.J. was standing near the archway. He lifted his beer, silently asking if she wanted one. Kerry shook her head, her lips twisting wryly. She didn't know what B.J. wanted, but it didn't matter. One thing she'd learned— and it had been a hard lesson—was to never trust men.

B.J., however, wasn't eager to take no for an answer. Through the crush of bodies, loud music and incessant talking, he made his way to Kerry's side. Kerry glanced around for Adam and Jenny. They were nowhere in sight. In fact, since Jenny had appeared, she and Adam had been missing from the festivities. Kerry wondered how serious their relationship was. The thought of them together made her feel slightly sick.

"So you're Adam's mysterious girlfriend," B.J. said, squeezing past a dancing couple to stand over her. He acted as if that topic hadn't been exhausted already.

"We're friends. Period."

Condensation dropped off his bottle onto Kerry's bare knee. "Never anything more? Come on. You can tell your old friend, B.J." He grinned like a devil and squatted down on the floor in front of her at eye level. "Adam isn't the kind of guy to not notice someone like you."

Unbidden, the moment of that one kiss she'd shared with Adam flitted across Kerry's mind. She shivered involuntarily. Amazing. She thought she'd forgotten about it. I mean, after all, it was Adam.

"In fact," B.J. confided, pushing closer until his face was a hairsbreadth from hers, "I think old Adam is carrying a torch for you. I've seen your pictures in his room."

"Oh, yeah? Well, that's understandable. We're friends," Kerry repeated firmly, leaning back as far as she could. Where did guys like B.J. get off? She was tired of men playing games with her.

He made the colossal mistake of cupping his palm around her knee. Kerry glared at him coolly. "Get your hand off me," she said quietly. "Or so help me, I'll kick you where it hurts."

"Whoa." His brows lifted but his smile didn't leave his lips. "Is this how you treat Adam?"

Kerry picked his hand off her knee and flung it aside. "I don't like you. And I want you to leave."

He was astounded. Clearly this wasn't the usual reaction to his overbearing charm. Kerry never moved her eyes from his. Beneath her bravado, her heart was thundering in her chest. She could scarcely breathe. But she'd be damned if she let him see that. She was going to give him five seconds, then she was going to do something drastic.

"What's the matter with you?" Jenny Sutcliff asked, her smile teasing. "I swear, if you don't pay some attention to me, I'm going to get a complex!"

"Sorry." Adam jerked his gaze from the living room doorway back to Jenny. The crown of her head reached his shoulder as she stood in front of him, hands on her slim hips in a pose of mock anger. A wide belt of porcelain chain links cinched in the waist of her long skirt, and her tanned slim arms were shown off well by her white tank top. Jenny was pretty and sweet. Sometimes the way she turned her head or looked at him out of the corner of her eyes, her lips fighting a smile, reminded him a little of Kerry.

Kerry. His chest tightened. Something was going on with her. He didn't know what, but his instincts where she was concerned were unerring. Trouble. Her eyes were full of suppressed emotion. Hurt, anxiety, misery, fury. He wanted to help. Hell, she'd come to him for help! Why else would she be here? But the timing was awful, and there was Jenny.

"Well?" Jenny asked, her dark brows lifting.

Impulsively he pulled her close and kissed her. Eager to please, she tossed her arms around his neck and giggled.

"I've got to check on Kerry," he said regretfully, his lips caught in the dark tangle of her hair.

"What is she—helpless or something?"

"Kerry?" He laughed silently.

Jenny drew back, her eyes narrowed. "Then why do you have to big-brother her?"

"I don't. I just want to make sure she has a good time, and that my roommates don't bother her."

He tried to ease out of her embrace but Jenny was reluctant to let go. "If she's so tough, she can take care of herself. I'm the one who's weak and needs protection."

"About as much as a snake," he teased dryly.

"Adam!"

"You are a woman who gets what she wants." He gently, but firmly, pulled her arms from his neck.

"Does that include you?"

"Of course," he said, kissing her lightly on the forehead. Clasping her hand, he led her down the hallway to the living room. There were people everywhere.

"Hi, Adam," a blonde named Trina greeted him as she squeezed by.

"Is a dark-haired girl in there somewhere?"

"Beats me." She drifted outside to where a soft rain was pattering against the porch roof.

Jenny tugged resistingly on his hand. "Let's go somewhere. These parties are boring."

"In a minute." He let go of her, slipping past dancing bodies to the heat of the room. And that was when he saw her, with B.J.'s hand resting on her knee and her gaze drilling into him in a way that would have intimidated any normal male. But B.J. possessed the sensitivity of a Cro-Magnon. Adam threaded his way toward them.

". . . I don't like you. And I want you to leave."

Kerry's tone was glacial. The power of her personality was stamped on her determined chin. Her lips, normally full and wide, were a thin line of pure fury. The nostrils of her pugged nose were flared in outrage. For a heartbeat Adam almost laughed. Until B.J. daringly moved his hand upward over her thigh.

She slapped him, her hand quick as she thrust his hand away. Only then did Adam see how she was trembling. He lunged for B.J.'s arm before his friend could react.

"Hey, buddy," he said. "Lighten up. We've got places to go. Jenny wants to leave. Kerry, I've been looking for you. You want something besides pizza?"

She didn't even glance his way. If looks could kill, B.J. would be a pile of ashes. It was B.J. who responded. "I'm outta here," he snarled. "She's all yours."

He bulldozed his way through the crowd. Adam looked at Kerry, who regarded him with wide, hollow eyes. He wanted to draw her into his arms but sensed she wouldn't let him. He'd felt the way she'd frozen in his arms earlier. As ever, she erected a shield that no one could pierce.

"B.J.'s an ass," he said.

Kerry didn't answer.

"At least you nailed him," he went on conversationally. "That's worth something."

"He had his hand on my leg."

"I saw. He deserved the slap."

Kerry finally focused on him. Her bottom lip was quivering and she bit down hard on it. Adam's heart went out to her, but when he moved forward she shrank away.

"I need to... get myself together. I think I'll go to your room. Oh, God." Her voice broke. "Is it empty?"

"No one goes in my room but me." He stretched out a hand to help her to her feet. She ignored him and struggled upward by herself.

"Are you coming with us, Kerry?" Jenny asked brightly from behind him.

Adam turned. Jenny had witnessed everything. Her dark eyes were alive with curiosity.

"No," Kerry answered with a shake of her head. "I'm tired." She made a beeline for the stairs.

Jenny looked askance at Adam.

"I'll be with you in a minute," he told her, following after Kerry. "Just give me a minute." Then he bounded up the stairs two at a time after Kerry.

Why did I come? Kerry asked herself, slamming Adam's bedroom door and leaning against it. She squeezed her eyes tightly shut. Talk about jumping from the frying pan into the fire. She needed help getting over Ryan, not a come-on from another weak-brained member of his gender!

Clenching her fists, she gritted back a scream of anguish. Damn it! Damn, damn....

The door opened behind her and she stumbled forward.

"Kerry?" Adam asked in concern.

"Oh, Adam. Go away." She tried to laugh and failed. "I'm fine. Just really, really tired. I shouldn't be here. I shouldn't have come, but I'm okay. Let me go to sleep and I'll be gone by seven o'clock tomorrow morning."

"I don't want you to leave. I'm sorry that B.J.'s such a jerk, and if I could have stopped it, I would have cancelled this party. I tried. I thought they were all leaving, but I was wrong, I guess. It's inevitable. A party just happens every Friday night whether I want it to or not."

"Don't apologize. I didn't really expect you to drop everything and entertain me."

"But I'd like to," he said honestly.

Kerry felt treacherous tears gather behind her eyelids. Even now, she was a sucker for a guy expressing feelings. So few of them did. "I'm just going to unroll my sleeping bag and crash. Take Jenny somewhere. I really would like to be alone." He hesitated, torn between two duties. Kerry pushed gently, "You can bring me something back. I'll have a two a.m. snack, or whatever time you get in."

"Don't leave." Adam was firm.

"Relax. I'm not going to take off for Pullman at midnight. I'm not that crazy."

"I'll be back before you know it," he said, closing the door behind him.

Beneath Kerry's head the floor reverberated with sound. She was certain she would never get to sleep. It didn't help that with her every breath she inhaled Adam's scent from the pillow she'd taken from his bed. She turned her face to it and filled her lungs. God, he smelled good. Had Ryan ever smelled like that? She couldn't remember.

Kerry opened her eyes. The room was dark save for the faint outline of Adam's bedroom window and the glowing aquarium. She calculated Adam had been gone about an hour.

Below her, the party was winding down. The music, though throbbing, was softer; the voices a murmur rather than a deafening scream. Her eyes adjusted to the darkness and she propped her arms behind her head, idly watching the tropical fish.

Maybe this trip had been the ticket after all. Though her thoughts constantly touched on Ryan, the ache was less acute. She wasn't in love with him. Whatever insanity had possessed her was gone. She wouldn't be so foolish again.

Footsteps sounded on the stairs, and she braced instinctively. If B.J. walked through that door she wasn't certain what she'd do, but by God, he'd know it had been done!

The door creaked open. Framed in the aperture was Adam. Quickly he shut the door behind him, as if afraid to awaken her.

"I'm awake," Kerry said.

He crossed the room carefully, his eyes apparently not adjusted to the dark. His toe bumped into her leg. "Sorry. I can't see."

"It's all right."

"You could have used the bed. I can sleep on the couch downstairs."

"No. Thanks. This is fine." Kerry sat up, plumped the pillow, then leaned back on her elbows. She was wearing a Washington state T-shirt; nightgowns weren't her thing. Adam crouched down beside her and yawned.

"I've been thinking about you. B.J. didn't bother you while I was gone, did he?" he asked, his voice sharpening as the thought occurred to him.

"I think he left about the same time you did."

"Good." He snorted in disgust. "What a specimen. I'm going to be glad to graduate next year, even if it means joining the 'real world.' "

He started untying his sneakers. Kerry watched, feeling kind of strange. She'd known they were going to be sleeping in the same room, yet it suddenly seemed odd. "You're still majoring in business?"

"Investments. That's what I want. To handle other people's money." His teeth flashed white in the dim light. "I'm expecting you to make a fortune and let me invest it for you."

"Hah. I wouldn't trust you with a nickel."

"Why not?" He was genuinely surprised.

Because you're a man, Kerry thought before the implication struck home. How prejudiced! How unfair!

But it was true. Adam, though he was a wonderful, terrific friend, was just as fickle about love as any other man. She didn't trust the lot of them. Not with her heart, not with her money, not with nothing.

"Well, it's something we won't have to worry about because I'll never make a fortune anyway," she assured him. "I just want a nice, safe job with no surprises."

"Bull. You'd vegetate. You need a challenge as much as I do."

"Since when are you an expert on me?" Kerry demanded.

"I've always been." After his shoes came his socks and then he stood up, undoing his belt. Panic raged through Kerry, and she shut her eyes so tightly they hurt. But did that bother Adam? No way. She heard the soft swoosh and jingle of his pants hitting the floor. Shortly thereafter the bedsprings creaked. Daring a look out of the corner of her eye she saw that he'd tossed a blanket over him. She wondered if he had anything on.

He was watching her, smiling. Damn! He knew what she was thinking.

"This is interesting, don't you think?" he asked. "We're sleeping in the same room together."

"Big deal." Kerry squinched back into her sleeping bag until just her nose and eyes showed.

"Have you every slept with a man, Kerry?"

She was shocked to the soles of her feet. "None of your business. And if you're offering your services, forget it."

Now she'd shocked *him*! His jaw dropped. "The way you talk, Ms. Camden," he drawled.

"Yeah? Well, get used to it. Nobody's going to push me around any longer. I've learned my lesson."

"Is that what this trip to Seattle's all about?"

"Something like that. Good night, Adam." Kerry turned over, offering him a view of the back of her head.

"Kerry." She jumped at the feel of his hand on her shoulder.

"What?"

A long moment passed. His touch, though light, sent strange signals along her nerves. You idiot! she railed at herself. Here she was, shattered and disillusioned, her trust in human beings half dead, and all she could think about was the feel and heat of Adam's fingers!

Not only that, she was beginning to feel the bewildering heat of desire. Where his fingers lay against the thin fabric of her T-shirt, her skin burned. She realized with a twist of her heart that if Adam should suddenly pull her into his arms and ask to make love to her, she might not be able to say no. How stupid! Talk about trading her current problems for worse ones. Did she feel she had to prove her desirability?

These thoughts flashed across her mind at the same moment her breath caught. Suspended, she waited for him to make a move. In her mind she could already feel his body pressed close to hers, could smell his seductive scent, could taste his mouth. Shivering, she waited.

"Kerry, I've asked Jenny to marry me. The wedding will be sometime next spring. I think she's going to ask you to be a bridesmaid. For me."

He withdrew his hand and Kerry stared unseeingly across the darkened room to the fish tank. Her soul cried out in anguish, but she didn't make a sound.

"Kerry?"

"Congratulations, Adam. I hope you're happy."

* * *

There was only one place large enough and nice enough to have a wedding reception in Piper Point—the Piper Point Country Club. It wasn't posh, but it was nice nonetheless. The main building's stone facade made it look like an English country manor. Azaleas and rhododendrons bloomed in brilliant colors of lavender, fuchsia, cream and goldenrod. A sprawling hot pink rock daphne perfumed the air along the front walk and bees droned gently as Jenny Shard stood beneath the portico, clutching Adam's arm and rapturously greeting guests and friends.

Kerry hung back from the proceedings, standing on the small arched bridge at the edge of the grounds. She'd prayed this wedding wouldn't come off. She'd spent untold sleepless nights creating scenario after scenario where Adam begged Jenny's forgiveness and told her he simply couldn't marry her. He didn't love her. It was a mistake.

Kerry had ceased asking herself why it mattered so much. All she knew was that she had deep unresolved feelings about men in general and Adam in particular. Did that mean she loved him? That she wanted to be in Jenny's place? She didn't think so. She hoped not. It was certainly too late now anyway.

Her gaze following the path of the gully beneath the bridge, Kerry ignored the misery that had crowded into her heart. A year after Ryan, she still felt leery and distrustful of men. Except Adam. For some reason, though time and circumstance should have dimmed Kerry's memory of Adam's kiss, it haunted her thoughts, and seemed more tangible now than it had been when it happened.

Or was that merely because it was safe to feel twinges of passion for a man she couldn't have?

"There you are," a familiar voice drawled.

Kerry didn't have to glance around to know it was Adam. She heard the sound of his shoes on the bridge, felt him rest his elbows next to hers on the rail.

"Shouldn't you be with the wedding party?" she asked.

"You're part of it, too."

Oh, yes. What a joke. Jenny's bridesmaid, when Jenny would have preferred Kerry were blasted from the planet. But Jenny put up with Kerry for Adam, and Kerry dutifully played her part as well. Neither woman could really stand the other.

"Hey, Adam!" a voice called. Jenny's brother, camera in hand, waved at them. "Come on over here."

Kerry protested when Adam grabbed her hand, but he quelled her with a look. She followed, nearly ripping the slit in her blue crepe gown as she stumbled behind his ground-devouring strides.

All the bridesmaids, ushers and other members of the wedding party were in a semicircle around Jenny. Glowing, Adam's parents stood to one side; Jenny's mother fluttered anxiously on the other. Only Kerry and Adam were missing.

Adam let her go and she took her place beside Marcia and Allison, two other Piper Point High cheerleaders. The camera flashed. *Flash. Flash. Flash.* More pictures.

The group broke up and everyone went inside. Champagne poured. More champagne. Kerry felt dizzy. She wanted to escape. Before she could, however, Adam caught her around the waist, dragging her onto the dance floor. His face was covered with lipstick marks.

"Aren't you even going to kiss the groom?" he demanded, half-drunk with delight.

Kerry narrowed her eyes at him. "And be like everyone else? Forget it."

"You're too contrary for your own good." With that remark he bent down and kissed her loudly on the lips. *Flash*. The photographer caught them at just the right moment.

They danced together, not well, since Kerry had never focused her energy on anything but school. Adam couldn't have cared less. He was higher than the flag that drifted lazily from the spire above the clubhouse.

The afternoon changed to evening. Kerry tried to escape half a dozen times. Tiny white lights, twisted around the upper balcony's wrought-iron rail, glowed like fireflies as she made one last attempt to find a few moments alone.

But Adam, ever-dogged, found her. He was calmer, quieter, more tired. It was long past the time he and Jenny should have left.

Kerry folded her arms across her chest. "So what are you still doing here?" she asked him.

"We're leaving. Jenny's saying a few goodbyes. So am I."

Years afterward Kerry would wonder if he meant to sound so final. His quiet words pounded like a club, hurting way down deep in a secret place Kerry had kept well hidden, even from herself. He was shutting a door on all they'd shared. Kerry, his "sister," was being cast aside.

"Then goodbye," she said lightly, fighting back the tears gathering silently in the corners of her eyes.

Adam's arms surrounded her. He didn't see her distress, and she would have ducked her head, but his lips found hers. He kissed her again, this time with a kind of bittersweet passion that made her heart ache. Kerry responded woodenly, afraid he would discern her feelings if she let go too much.

"Goodbye, Kerry." He stared at her a long, long time.

Smiling weakly, she gave him a jaunty salute. It was over. All over. The words "I love you" flitted across her mind but were left unspoken.

It was the poignant end to a beautiful friendship.

Chapter Four

Spring 1990

Tuesday: 10:00 meeting with owners about possible buy-out. (This is a surprise. Should I be worried?)
Wednesday: Fund-raiser plans for children's hospital—9:00 a.m. sharp. (What in God's name am I going to donate?)
Anytime between now and eternity: return Adam's phone call, if you have the nerve....

The memos stared up at Kerry. Written in her own handwriting, they seemed to have acquired a personality of their own. Adam. Kerry smiled in disbelief. Apart from an occasional birthday card, she hadn't heard from him in years. Years. She could scarcely believe he'd actually phoned her!

Kerry drummed her fingers on her desk, then punched her intercom button in sudden decision.

"Rachel? Tell me again when the message from Mr. Shard came in?"

"Yesterday. Last night, actually, just before closing," Kerry's secretary answered. "You were already gone."

"Hmm. Okay, thanks."

Glancing at her watch, Kerry pushed back her chair and walked restlessly around the room, stopping to stare out her window, twenty-two floors above Seattle. In a few minutes she had to attend the meeting with Mr. Jacobson and Mr. Kern, the co-owners of Jacobson & Kern, the investment company where she worked, to find out their decision about selling the firm. Both men were in their eighties, had no children or other heirs and were interested in selling lock, stock and barrel. But their reputation in the Seattle financial arena kept them from accepting lucrative offers from businessmen who somehow failed to meet their high expectations. A pending buy-out had hovered like a pall for years. Even so, this meeting was unprecedented.

Kerry watched the traffic far below, her mind not really on the upcoming meeting. She hadn't seen Adam for what?—five years? He'd called her once, during the worst months of his divorce, leaving more unsaid than said about what had happened between him and Jenny. Then he up and moved from Seattle to San Francisco before Kerry even had a chance to commiserate. That was at least six years ago. Probably closer to seven. Kerry wrote him several letters, but he didn't respond. Now, like Adam, she'd resorted to birthday cards. She'd been right to think their friendship ended with his marriage. Even his divorce hadn't resurrected it.

Her intercom buzzed imperatively. "Ron Tisdale's just come from Mr. Kern's office and he's trucking fast toward yours," Rachel revealed in an undertone.

Kerry's lips twisted as she crossed to the phone. "I'm ready," she said.

"Five, four, three, two—"

The door to her office blew open. Ron Tisdale, immaculate in a three-piece gray pinstripe suit, charged forward, his normally perfectly plastered-down hair frayed and standing on end.

"Bingo," Rachel murmured and clicked off.

"I just talked with Mr. Kern," Ron began without preamble. "They sold!"

"What do you mean?"

"I mean, Jacobson & Kern. They sold the company!"

Kerry was astounded. "They couldn't have! We would have known about it before!"

"Oh, yeah? Well, that's what I said. But while all those rumors were circulating about this person or that person, or this company or that company, buying them out, they quietly took care of the matter themselves! Can you believe it?" Ron was beside himself. "They signed the papers last night!"

Kerry sank down into her desk chair, her mind racing. She and Ron had been with Jacobson & Kern only a few years. Before that, they'd worked together at Seattle Financial Bank. Kerry had been lured away by Mr. Kern himself. Ron, annoyed at her success, had applied to J. & K. directly and had eventually won a job. Neither was eager to have new employers, nor did they want to beat the street for an equitable position with another firm.

"I guess it isn't really a surprise," she said slowly.

"Isn't a surprise? Kerry, are you listening to me? The whole damn company's been pulled out from under us!"

"We're still employed, aren't we?"

His face turned so red he looked as if he were about to burst a blood vessel. "But for how long?" he bellowed.

Kerry remained calm. Over the ten years she and Ron had worked together, she'd gotten used to his tantrums and outbursts. "Whoever's bought us out will look at our records and make their decision on that. There's no reason to get hysterical."

"Easy for you to say," Ron muttered, flinging himself into a chair. "You look great on paper."

Kerry ignored him. Yes, her ten years as an investment adviser, first for the bank and later as a broker for Jacobson & Kern, had awarded her a nice job and an enviable career. She did her job well. Not remarkably, perhaps, but soundly. People liked her. They trusted her. She was calm and knowledgeable. Trustworthy. Dependable. Good old Kerry Camden.

Adam had once told her she possessed an adventurous spirit. No way. She was successful and happy and it all came from doing the job right. Period.

"Do you know who bought us out?"

"Oh, come on, Kerry. You don't have to play coy with me. You know damn well who did."

She stared at him, baffled. "Sorry, Ron. I'm in the dark."

"Well, he called *you* didn't he? I saw the message on Rachel's desk. It must have been right before the old codgers signed their lives away!"

A haunting sense of awareness swept through Kerry. "Adam Shard has bought Jacobson & Kern?" she asked, her voice sounding strange and faraway.

"You know he has."

"Oh, God." Kerry started to laugh, at first in small chuckles, then with huge gasps of air until her eyes burned with tears.

"What's so damned funny?" Ron grumbled.

She shook her head, unable to answer. For several hours she'd thought…what? That Adam was about to make a reappearance in her life? That he was lonely and longed for the friendship they'd once shared? That he *wanted* plain old Kerry? How ridiculous! How unbelievably ridiculous! He'd merely bought another investment company. It just happened to be the one she worked for.

But even so, she was looking forward to seeing him again.

"Since you seem incapable of getting your vocal cords in gear again and explaining what's so hilarious about a San Francisco firm buying us out, I'll—"

"Ron, Adam is from the Seattle area. Piper Point, to be exact. He and I were friends once."

Kerry was certain she'd never seen a blanker look in her life than the one on Ron Tisdale's face. "My God!" he blurted. "Why am I talking to you? You're going to make out like a bandit!"

"I have no idea what Adam is like as a boss," Kerry declared. "But I guarantee his success has been because he's hired good people and made wise decisions. I am not going to make out like a bandit. Everyone here will be judged on merit."

Too late, she realized she'd inadvertently hit a sore spot with Ron. "That Marsden fiasco is going to be thrown in my face again," he muttered furiously. "And it wasn't even my fault!"

Ron had talked one of J. & K.'s clients, John Marsden, into investing in a building renovation project on the outskirts of Seattle. Unfortunately that part of the city hadn't taken off as Ron had predicted and now, two years later, the building was still three-quarters empty. Marsden lost a bundle. To break even now would take years. Ten months ago Marsden had moved his J. & K. business investments to another Seattle firm, and though J. & K. had handled only a small portion of the man's vast wealth, it was still a deadly blow to both the company and Ron Tisdale.

And despite Ron's protests, it *was* his fault. Kerry had even tried to talk him out of the investment at one time.

"Well, I'm not going to go down without a fight," Ron muttered, climbing to his feet and smoothing his hair. "If Adam Shard tries to let me go he'll be facing a lawsuit. See you at the meeting. It ought to be a doozy!"

He stalked out of her office, puffed up with injustice. Through new eyes, Kerry looked down at the memo she'd written. *Return Adam's call, if you have the nerve.*

If you have the nerve… And now he was going to be her boss? She wasn't certain how to even feel! What was Adam thinking of, buying a Seattle firm? If the papers had been signed last night, that must mean he was in the city. Yet all he'd done was leave her a message just before closing. She'd been home all evening, and he hadn't rung to deliver the news personally.

"I suppose I'm lucky he even knew I worked here," she said aloud to the empty room. Glancing once again at her watch, she realized the meeting was in less than ten minutes.

Would Adam be there? she wondered nervously.

Insanity. That was what it was. Pure insanity, but it felt so good!

Adam sat at the large, round conference table in the Jacobson & Kern boardroom. He even liked the fact that the table was round. Straight out of Camelot. The whole thing was perfect. And best of all, Kerry Camden was one of J. & K.'s sterling employees.

Kerry. He couldn't think of her without smiling. What was she going to say when she found out? Plenty, he thought with a grin.

In front of him were the contracts he'd signed, along with Paul Kern and Charles Jacobson. He'd never seriously believed they would sell to him. Sure, he was a Washington boy, but he'd defected to San Francisco. A serious charge. But then he'd told them he was moving back, that he'd already purchased a condominium on Lake Washington, and Charles Jacobson had pulled an ancient pen from his breast pocket and signed his name to the bottom of the contract without another word. Paul Kern had followed suit. And Adam became sole owner of the prestigious investment firm.

He would have to sell his San Francisco firm to make the deal, he realized, but he felt little regret. The decision to move to California had been made right after the divorce, when he wasn't thinking very soundly. He'd only wanted to escape. So to come back now felt as right as rain. And to be the owner of Jacobson & Kern.... Why, even his father with his grandiose ideas would not have expected his son to succeed so well.

Adam's smile faltered, and he was attacked by poignant memories. If only his father had lived to see this day. Or his mother. They'd died together in a freeway accident, one of those freak things that changes everybody's lives. He'd still been married then, but Jenny had not understood his utter grief. How could she? She was too self-centered. In his desperation, he'd longed to run to Kerry and pour out his misery. But, of course, since his marriage they'd grown apart, and he'd had a wife who had taken his best friend's place. It was Jenny to whom he should turn, or so he'd thought. But Jenny wasn't Kerry and that, he reminded himself guiltily, wasn't her fault.

Maybe the very fact that she was so different from Kerry was what had started the break-up. Adam slid a paper clip from the contract and absently began pulling it apart. Jenny's lack of compassion had shocked and appalled him. When she realized what she'd done, her attempts to make up had only made a bad situation worse. He'd never felt quite the same about her after that.

Just before his divorce was finalized he'd called Kerry. "I need to talk," he'd told her, then couldn't think of another blessed thing to say!

But Kerry, ever cool, had answered, "I know what you're thinking. You're thinking I'm going to say 'I told you so.'"

"Well, aren't you?"

"Absolutely! But I'm going to wait until I see you in person so I can really rub it in. Until then, hang in there. You'll get over it," she added in a subdued voice. "My father did."

Was there bitter irony in her words? Adam was never quite sure. He knew she'd suffered during the time of her parents' divorce, but she'd never said exactly what had happened. Obviously she blamed her father. Well, why not? The guy had up and remarried almost immediately.

Adam didn't recall the rest of the conversation. It was just soothing to know that Kerry was still there, still irreverent and still sane. She'd written him a couple of letters, but he'd been too wrapped up in marital problems to answer.

Adam grimaced. No, that wasn't the truth. The truth was, he didn't know what to say to her. All he wanted was out. Out of Seattle and out of his marriage. He'd seen her one other time when he'd stopped by the bank where she worked. The meeting had been strained, their rapport not as it used to be. In a way, he'd forfeited Kerry's friendship, and that was his one regret. But now he had a chance to put that right.

A soft knock sounded on the boardroom door. "It's open," he called.

The door widened and Kerry Camden stepped inside the room.

She stared in absolute disbelief at the familiar figure lounging in one of the squashy leather boardroom chairs. Sure, she'd expected to find him here; Mr. Kern had said he was. But even so, she was shocked right down to her toes to see him again.

"Adam?" Kerry asked in a strange voice.

"Right the first time. You haven't lost your power of observation, I see," he drawled.

His long legs were stretched indolently in front of him and crossed at the ankles, and his hands were clasped behind his head. He wore the pleased expression of a sated jungle cat.

Kerry folded her arms across her chest. "I haven't seen you for years, and you just up and buy the company I work for?"

"Guilty as charged."

Kerry shook her head, momentarily at a loss. She'd forgotten how good-looking Adam was. His hair was lush and thick and black. His jaw was strong and determined, and his eyes, his best feature, were an interesting bluish gray and seemed filled with humor. "I simply can't believe it!" she murmured.

"And you're not sure you like it, either," he guessed, his mouth twisting in that sexy way that was uniquely Adam.

"Time will tell. I've been pretty happy here at Jacobson & Kern. Working for you is the great unknown."

His eyes were full of teasing lights. "I'm not a slave driver."

"That's what they all say," she quipped, surprised at her sudden attack of nerves. "Besides, I'm not sure I want to work for my ex-best friend."

"Ex?" His brows lifted.

"You could have been off the planet for the last five years, for all I knew. That's no way to treat a friend."

Adam grinned, climbing to his feet. "God, it's good to see you again." He came around the desk and stopped right in front of her, smiling down into her upturned face. Kerry's pulse jumped erratically.

"It's good to see you, too."

Adam's gaze warmed. "You know, you were one of the biggest factors in my decision to buy Jacobson & Kern. Without you, I don't think the deal would have gone through."

"Give me a break." Kerry took two steps backward, holding up her hands and shaking her head. "Now that's a blatant lie. You'll never convince me that I had anything to do with it."

"Why not?"

"Because Adam Shard is a shrewd businessman. No, it's true," she insisted as he frowned at the compliment. "You were born for this business and a long-term friendship would never enter into any decision you would make for Shard Limited."

"Kerry, you wound me! I'd do anything for you."

She laughed, the sound reverberating throughout the boardroom. "And you have a bridge to sell me, right?"

"Your lack of faith in my loyalty breaks my heart," he said dryly.

Kerry grinned, so happy to see him she could hardly stand it. She'd missed him so much. Missed the lively bantering, the appreciation of each other's wit. She hadn't realized how empty she'd felt until just this moment. Adam might have his faults, but he was fair and intelligent, and a whole lot of fun.

He grinned right back, looking the epitome of the successful male. He'd flung his gray sport coat carelessly across the back of a chair, loosened his tie and undone the top button of his shirt. His black hair shone with vitality beneath the muted lights, his skin a rich California brown.

"You know something?" she said, pretending to give him the once over. "You've aged well." So well, in fact, that she had to drag her gaze from his strong masculine appearance. Careful, Kerry. Remember who you're with.

"So have you," he remarked appreciatively.

"I can't believe I'm going to be working for you."

"Closer than you know," he murmured.

Kerry's moment of pleasure vanished. "Okay, what's that supposed to mean?"

"Well, I've got a slight problem I want you to handle for me. A friend of mine's account. He had some problems with J. & K. about a year ago, but he's willing to come back. However, we'll really need to work together on it."

Kerry stared at him. "You're talking about the Marsden account."

"That's right. Do you know John?"

"Only of him. He was Ron—" Kerry cut herself off. If Adam didn't yet know Ron Tisdale was the man who'd angered Marsden, she didn't want to be accused of pointing the finger.

"I know all about Ron Tisdale," Adam assured her dryly. "John was rather uncomplimentary about him."

"What are you going to do?" Kerry blurted out, unable to stop herself. She might not like Ron personally, and he'd certainly messed up with Marsden, but overall he wasn't a bad investment broker. Other clients trusted him implicitly.

Adam regarded her thoughtfully. "I don't know yet. Like you said, time will tell."

A sound at the door caused Kerry to jump and Adam to glance past her. Charles Jacobson and Paul Kern entered the room followed by J. & K.'s eight other investment administrators.

"Oh, Kerry. Good. You're already here," Jacobson said in his watery voice. "Ron went looking for you."

Ron, subdued and resentful, met Kerry's gaze coolly. Clearly he felt she'd been getting in good with the boss. Exasperated, Kerry tightened her lips. Ron was his own worst enemy. He liked blaming others for his own mistakes.

Adam's eyes followed Ron as he pulled back a chair near the one Sam Wright was holding for Kern. The elderly gentleman laid down his cane and subsided into the chair with a grateful sigh.

Kerry quickly took the chair across from Ron. The stare he leveled at her was full of accusation. She narrowed her lashes in warning. Silently she told him to stop blaming her for Adam's buy-out. His angry gaze said he wasn't listening.

Adam watched this exchange with a growing feeling of uneasiness and resentment. He didn't like Ron Tisdale already and the guy was doing nothing to endear himself to him.

He moved to take the seat at Jacobson's right, looking over the assembled employees. "By now you've probably all heard that Mr. Jacobson and Mr. Kern have sold their company to me. Let me assure you, I want this transition to be smooth and painless." He smiled to ease the tension that had gathered. "This is a great company. But it's only as good as the people who work for it. I'm not going to forget that...."

When he'd purchased his San Francisco investment firm, Adam had been forced to fight for respect. Like Jacobson & Kern, it had a reputation in the community that went back nearly a hundred years. He was considered the upstart. The "boy from up north." He'd had one heck of a time convincing the employees he planned to play fair.

The people at J. & K. were looking at him as if he'd somehow robbed the company! His voice echoed even though the room wasn't overly huge, making him sound like some prophet of doom. So much for the "state-of-the-art acoustic system'' Mr. Kern had bragged about. This wasn't quite the effect Adam had wanted.

In truth, Adam liked things simple and small. The J. & K. offices were almost too resplendent for him. Too much ultra-thick carpet and too many rosewood desks. Too many Impressionist paintings. Too much fluff. Adam had an aversion to fixed overhead. Buy another chair and rent another room and he broke out in hives. In the investment business, prudence in money management was foremost. How could you expect people to believe in you, if you spent money like water with no eye to the future?

Still, he'd learned his clients didn't expect the same frugality from him personally. In fact, they *wanted* to be able to see that he was making money! If Adam wore expensive suits, Italian shoes and a Rolex watch, it somehow proved he was a success. Why, he wasn't sure. It was a cockeyed approach that made little sense, but Adam had found anxious investors sometimes measured success by how a man dressed. Crazy.

Ron Tisdale was still staring at Kerry. It annoyed Adam. There wasn't something going on between them, was there? Kerry looked as cool as a cucumber. Her hair fell to her shoulders, thick and a little wiry, as black as ink but glimmering with red highlights. Her eyes were wide and an interesting shade somewhere between green and brown. He'd always found her attractive. Not as beautiful as Jenny, maybe, but with a strength of character he was drawn to. In a simple, loose white silk blouse and a charcoal gray suit, she looked remote and in control—just like always. But the clothes couldn't disguise her femininity. Her breasts were soft beneath the silk, her waist tiny. When she'd walked to her seat he couldn't help watching the movement of her hips beneath the smooth-fitting skirt.

There was something incredibly sensual about Kerry that time had only magnified. Adam, who'd been susceptible at seventeen and who'd then denied the attraction at twenty-one, realized he suffered unresolved feelings for his best friend at thirty-two. Incredible. Here he stood, soothing the anxious J. & K. employees, and yet his mind was thinking about Kerry.

"I'm still in the process of moving to Seattle, so I won't be in the office on a regular schedule yet. Mr. Jacobson has suggested that Sam Wright be the liaison between myself and all of you until I'm permanently settled."

Ron glanced toward Sam, a man in his fifties who'd worked for J. & K. for nearly thirty years. Adam couldn't see his expression.

"If you have any questions," he continued. "Now's the time to ask."

Kern spoke up. "I might suggest you tell them about John Marsden straight out, Mr. Shard."

Kerry stiffened. Ron nearly came unglued. He jerked in his seat as if stuck by a cattle prod. Damn, Adam thought. He would have liked to ease into this powder keg slowly. On the other hand, there was no reason to delay the inevitable.

"John Marsden is a personal friend of mine," Adam explained. "I've known him most of my life. He and my father were close friends. He moved the bulk of his investment portfolio to my firm almost as soon as I started business. I know J. & K. did some work for him in the past. Now, I'm happy to say we'll be handling one hundred percent of his investment capital."

The room broke into sounds of surprise. Ron went white. Kerry's eyes widened. Adam hadn't told her yet that she'd be handling all of Marsden's account. He hadn't had the chance. At this point he couldn't tell how she felt about it, but he had complete faith in her ability. She made cautious, sound investment decisions— just the kind Marsden liked.

"Who will be handling the Marsden account?" Sam asked.

"Kerry Camden."

More excited chatter filled the air. Kerry looked as if she might drop through the floor.

"The entire account?" Sam questioned, trying hard not to sound as if he thought Adam was out of his mind.

"I'll be working with her," Adam said. "We'll sort of play it as it goes."

Ron's glare at Kerry was so intense Adam was sure it could produce a nuclear meltdown! He eyed the man dispassionately. *Was* there something going on between him and Kerry? God, he hoped not! But if there was, he'd certainly thrown a spanner in the works by giving Kerry the Marsden account. Tisdale looked sick with worry, nearly apoplectic with rage. And he didn't strike Adam as the forgiving, understanding type, either. There was no way he and Kerry could be an item. No way. Their personalities were just too different. And yet . . .

Kerry's eyes met Adam's. Her lashes were so long they left shadows on her cheekbones. Her hair shone under the "state-of-the-art lighting system." She looked so appealing that Adam momentarily forgot the purpose of this meeting. It had been too long since he'd seen her. She was his rock, his touchstone.

It was Jacobson's turn to say his piece. He rose, tall and stately, his hair thin and white and as feathery as cotton candy, his suit at least twenty years out of date. "Paul and I were made an offer we couldn't refuse," he said with the touch of humor he was famous for. Polite chuckles sounded from the table. "We took a damn long time finding someone with the right qualities to take over our baby. We hope you'll all be happy with our decision."

He rambled on, using phrases like "wonderful corporate teamwork" and "the spirit of excellence that has always been such a part of J. & K.," then launched into Adam's own investment history. It amazed Adam how much the man knew about him! After finishing with something about how "Shard Limited's incomparable reputation should speak for itself," he sat down with the unbending regality of his generation. Adam glanced at the J. & K. employees. They all looked slightly dazed but hopeful. All except Ron, who looked downright sick.

"More questions?" Adam asked, after thanking Jacobson for his loyalty-stirring speech.

The woman seated next to Kerry tentatively lifted her hand. "I know this isn't exactly pertinent, but I assume the benefit we're sponsoring for the Puget Sound Children's Hospital will still be held on schedule?"

"Yes. That's in two weeks, right?"

Heads bobbed in assent.

"So everything basically just stays the same?" another man asked.

Adam nodded. "I know there are always bumps during any transition. I'll do the best I know how to keep things running smoothly."

Five minutes later the group exited the boardroom. Several people hung back, however. Kerry was one. Ron another. Trouble already? Adam wondered as he helped Kern to the door. The older man leaned heavily on his cane. "Leave me alone," he said irritably as Sam tried to pick up where Adam left off. He slapped at Sam's hands. Shrugging, Sam let him teeter away on his own power.

Adam turned expectantly to Ron.

"I'm not going to beat around the bush," Ron said aggressively. "I handled the Marsden account before, and I took the heat for a bad move. Marsden blamed me personally. It nearly cost me my job. Since you're his friend, I'm sure you've heard all about it, but before you decide to let me go, I suggest you check my record. I've given out more good advice than bad. Just ask Kerry." He smiled tightly in Kerry's direction.

Kerry's lips parted in surprise. Ron had really put her on the spot! Adam intervened. "I'm not letting anyone go just yet. Let's all try to work together for a while."

Ron wasn't satisfied. His brows descended like a black cloud. With a grunt that could have meant anything, he clenched Adam's hand in one short, aggressive handshake.

Adam next turned to Sam, who glanced pointedly at Kerry. Clearly he wanted to be the last to claim Adam's attention.

Adam inwardly sighed. He would have liked to talk to Kerry alone again.

Kerry looked troubled. She glanced up swiftly, meeting his gaze directly. "Adam, I . . ."

"What?"

Sam, who was hovering near Adam's right elbow, looked avidly at Kerry. Hesitating, Kerry finally shrugged. "See you later," she muttered, walking determinedly out the door and down the hall to her office. This time the gentle sway of her hips reminded Adam of that long-ago moment when he'd watched her walk away in a pair of shorts.

Kerry passed her office and strode to the women's room. She glared at her reflection in the mirror. Her hazel eyes were shadowed with suppressed emotion, and the red highlights in her hair seemed to shimmer with frustration.

After rinsing her cheeks, she took several deep breaths, then patted her face with a paper towel. What had Adam done to her? Ron would never forgive her. Never! Okay, Ron wasn't exactly her buddy, but she'd always managed to get along with him. Now there would be all-out war!

Kerry groaned. As happy as she was to see Adam, she saw problems popping up already. No one was going to understand about the Marsden account. *She* didn't even understand! She could handle part of it, but all of it? Her co-workers would never forgive her.

"Adam," she muttered to her frustrated reflection, "you behaved like a boss from hell."

Kerry sighed and leaned against the counter, closing her eyes. She was torn by feelings she didn't want. She couldn't believe Adam was back in her life! And that he was going to be such a powerful force!

The last time she'd laid eyes on him was six or seven summers ago when he'd dropped in unannounced at the bank. He'd been divorced a couple of years by then. Kerry had been giddy with delight, just like now. But then one of the bank's secretaries had turned on the charm. In those moments while the blond secretary flirted and Adam responded, jealousy had flooded through Kerry's veins, hot and venomous. Shaken, she'd managed to hide her feelings, sick with herself for acting so foolishly.

No matter how much she loved Adam as a friend, she knew better than to want something more. Adam was nothing better than a playboy! He couldn't be faithful to one woman. He probably hadn't even been faithful to Jenny! Over and over again Kerry had seen the way women had fallen at his feet. Just because she hadn't seen him in a few years didn't mean the situation had changed any.

Now Kerry calmly examined the facts. She and Adam could begin their friendship anew. He could even be her boss without too much problem, she figured, but he could never, ever, be anything more. She had to control these other feelings for him now, by God, or she would really pay the price! Hadn't she learned anything over the years?

She had a sudden vision of Adam with someone from the office. Rachel, perhaps. Or Sharon. Or maybe Adriana. Her stomach clenched.

Kerry swore softly under her breath. "It doesn't matter," she said as she left the restroom. "It doesn't matter at all."

Rachel, her blond head glued to her receiver, made frantic eye signals at Kerry as Kerry headed toward her office. Lifting a hand to let her faithful secretary know she understood, Kerry pushed open her door. Ron was undoubtedly waiting inside.

"I didn't want to leave without talking to you again," Adam said.

Kerry's skin broke out into goose bumps. "Well, okay, boss man, but you're taking up my valuable work time."

He was leaning against her desk, glancing down at the pages scattered across its top. Kerry suddenly remembered the memo she'd written to herself about returning his call, and felt uncomfortable. She moved forward.

"I'm flying back to San Francisco tomorrow morning," he said, turning his gaze her way.

"But you'll soon be a fixture around here," she answered lightly.

"Do you want to talk about Marsden now or later? I'd just as soon get started."

"You sure don't let any grass grow beneath your feet, do you?" she remarked.

"No, I don't."

"Kerry?" Rachel asked tentatively from the doorway. Kerry turned to look at her. "Um . . . I didn't want you to forget that meeting with Mr. Levinson. About his stock portfolio?" She gazed at Adam, one hand lightly touching the back of her teased hair.

"I hadn't forgotten."

Reluctantly, Rachel disappeared the way she'd come. Normally her secretary wouldn't have left her chair to deliver that message. The intercom worked just fine.

"Looks like you've already made a conquest," Kerry said dryly.

Adam's eyes were alive with mischief. He bent forward, leaning his face close to hers. "Jealous?"

"Not on your life." A potent wave of musky cologne enveloped her—*his* musky cologne. Kerry had to admit that Adam could be a very powerful force indeed. "Do you have any idea how insufferable you can be?"

"Mmm-hmm. You've told me often enough."

"Well, look. I've got to meet with Mr. Levinson. A small account, but you never know." Drawing on her courage, she added, "You'd better leave before I fall victim to your fatal charms, too."

"Now that would be a first." He stretched lazily and she couldn't help noticing the way his shirt tightened over his chest.

"Get out of here." She made shooing motions with her hands. "Or I'll be late."

"Why don't you skip the meeting? Let's go play hooky."

"Some boss you are. Trying to test my job responsibility?"

He hung his head as if she'd maligned him terribly. "I knew it. You've become a workaholic. You probably need a vacation."

"At least a month," she agreed. The file she needed to bring to the meeting was beneath his hip. She grabbed the edge of it and gave it a yank. The file didn't budge but her fingers accidentally brushed against the fine wool of his slacks. "Move over," she demanded.

"All you had to do was ask." Obligingly he raised one hip, picked up the file and handed it to her. "However, I'm not against your methods."

"Insufferable," Kerry repeated. She curled her fingers into her palm, alarmed at the tingling she still felt.

"Have dinner with me tonight."

The invitation was spoken quickly, almost urgently. Kerry glanced up in surprise. His expression gave nothing away, but she could sense there was something more behind it. "Tonight?" she repeated blankly.

"That's right."

Kerry glanced away, annoyed at her heightened awareness to him.

"If you turn me down I'll think our love affair is over," he added, smiling. "Be ready around seven. If you're still at the same apartment, I'll pick you up there."

Kerry protested, "Did it ever occur to you I might have other plans?"

"Do you?"

"No-o-o."

"Well?"

Kerry sighed. "All right. Seven o'clock."

"You won't regret it," he said, flashing her a smile as he straightened from her desk.

Kerry snorted, not nearly so sure.

Adam disappeared through the door. Kerry's gaze followed after him. It was just one dinner. No big deal. And she did need to know more about Marsden.

Two seconds later Kerry heard Rachel's chair slam into her desk and the rapid-fire sound of her footsteps. She flung open Kerry's door dramatically. "Who was that?" she cried. "The new boss?"

Give me strength, Kerry thought. "Mmm-hmm."

"The one who called you yesterday? Do you know him?"

"We're passing acquaintances," Kerry answered.

"Maybe I can weasel an introduction out of you?" Rachel looked ready to fall to bended knee.

"I'd be delighted."

Spying Mr. Levinson heading her way across the wide reception room, Kerry turned toward the door.

"Is he— Do you know if— Is he married?"

"Calm down, Rachel." Kerry sighed. "He's divorced and as far as I know, unattached. But with Adam anything's possible."

Chapter Five

Some things never change. Take a look at Adam. He's still gorgeous and irritatingly lovable. Unfortunately I have this terrible feeling that disaster awaits around the corner. Can I seriously survive having him for my boss? At least our friendship can pick up where it left off. But I never, ever, want to get any more romantically involved. (I hope I'm listening to myself!)

Kerry tossed down her pen and rubbed her eyes. She hadn't written in her journal in years. Her last entry, in fact, had been right after Adam's wedding. It had simply read "The End." Prophetic, really, she thought with a tired smile. But now he was back, and worse yet, he was in charge! How was she ever going to live with that?

Shaking her head, she slammed shut the spiral note-book she'd had since she was nine years old, and shoved it inside her top dresser drawer, hiding it beneath silky underwear and stockings. Yanking open her closet door, she wrinkled her nose at the small collection of evening clothes. She had two, maybe three, suitable outfits for tonight's "date," and they were tightly stuffed inside the minuscule space. Her apartment was compact and utilitarian; what it lacked in size it made up for in livability. Not that she needed much area, but now, staring at the limp, crushed clothes she wondered if she might be due for a change.

She took out her one black dress and surveyed it critically in her vanity mirror. It was almost too elegant for tonight, but she didn't have anything else. Besides, she felt like dressing up.

After pulling on a pair of shimmery black stockings, she slipped her feet into black, sling-back pumps. Frowning at herself, she wondered if she looked too severe. Maybe that was good. The one thing she intended to accomplish tonight was to put her relationship with Adam on the right track. They were business associates and friends. Nothing more.

"What are you so worried about?" she asked herself irritably as she snapped on a pair of silver earrings. "Adam isn't interested in you anyway!"

She brushed her hair back and held it with a matching silver clip. Then she walked to the kitchen to pour herself a glass of diet soda. She thought of the expensive champagne Mr. Kern had awarded her last Christmas when she'd turned around the limping Moreland account. It had sat unopened for nearly six months. Should she uncork it now?

She went to the cupboard where she'd hidden it and drew out the bottle of Dom Perignon. She had an aversion to champagne. She could still see it spilling in a silver stream from her father's lover's glass.

But it was hardly the champagne's fault. Determinedly, Kerry unwound the wire around the cork, then carefully wedged the cork loose. It exploded with a loud *pop*, hit the ceiling and bounced downward.

"Damn!" Kerry laughed as champagne fizzed over her hands. Shrieking, she jumped backward, the liquid narrowly missing her dress. Champagne poured over the tops of her shoes, and she felt it inside her toes.

The doorbell rang.

"Just a minute!" Kerry hurriedly poured out two glasses and carried them to the door, balancing both in one hand as she twisted the knob. "For you," she said, smiling as she handed a glass to a surprised Adam.

"Champagne?"

"Mmm. Sure to give us both a headache, but who cares. I've had this bottle since last Christmas."

Adam's gaze dropped slowly over her appearance. "My, my, well, would you look at you," he murmured.

Kerry's cheeks pinkened in spite of herself. "Oh, give me a break."

"You never could take a compliment, could you?"

"Never," she agreed unrepentently. "You don't look so bad yourself."

In a midnight-blue, open-necked shirt and a pair of gray slacks, he positively radiated good health and masculinity. Kerry resisted the pull on her senses by refusing to do more than glance at him.

"That's two compliments from you in one day," Adam remarked lazily. "I don't know if my heart can stand it."

"Well, I've been storing them up. It's been six years."

"Seven, but who's counting?"

"Has it been seven?"

Adam inclined his head. "Since that time I stopped by the bank to see you, yes." He glanced around her apartment, and Kerry was suddenly conscious of how small and characterless it seemed. She silently vowed, as she had many times before, to take the time to really decorate the place.

"What," Adam asked carefully, "is that?"

Curled up on one of the kitchen chairs, his slanted blue eyes trained suspiciously on Adam, Kerry's Siamese cat lay as immovable as stone.

"Oh, Problem," she said, smiling. Hearing her, Problem flicked the end of his skinny brown tail.

"Problem?"

"That's his name."

"I suppose I don't have to ask how he was christened."

Kerry laughed. "He roamed around the whole apartment complex creating havoc with the garbage bins until he finally adopted me. My next-door neighbor told me he was my problem."

"Ahhh." Adam walked over to the cat. Problem stretched and yawned and started to purr when Adam scratched behind his ears. "Somehow I never saw you as a cat person, Kerry."

"I never did, either, but as you can see Problem had other ideas." Kerry liberated her black cotton sweater from the closet and started to thrust her arms through it, but Adam suddenly appeared beside her. He plucked the sweater from her grasp and held it out for her. Slipping her arms inside, Kerry felt his warm fingers briefly brush against her nape. Goose bumps appeared on her skin.

"Ready?" she asked, her voice unnaturally tight.

"Whenever you are. Where would you like to eat?" he asked.

"This was your idea," she reminded him. "You choose."

"How about someplace down on the wharf?"

"Sounds fine to me."

"Is there anywhere that has dancing?" he asked, opening the front door.

"Dancing?"

"You know, that thing we did at my wedding?"

Kerry slid him a look. She'd wondered if he would bring up Jenny. Though their divorce was long over, Adam had never wanted, or been able, to express his true feelings about it. "Dancing's not high on my list of priorities," she explained as she walked ahead of him down the stairs from her third floor apartment. The car he was driving was a luxury model. Kerry couldn't help smiling as she settled in beside him.

"What?" he asked, glancing her way.

"Did I say anything?"

"Not in words, maybe, but I sense disapproval all the same."

"Not disapproval. Envy." Kerry ran her hand over the expensive leather seats. "You always did have a talent for getting the best of everything."

"Not everything," he answered lightly as he switched on the ignition. The car started with a roar and settled into a soft purr.

"So what's missing in your life?"

"I can think of a thing or two."

"Such as?" He didn't immediately answer. Watching him, Kerry was conscious of the expensive gold watch peeking from beneath his cuff, a definite sign of success. "Such as?" she repeated when his attention seemed to be solely on the traffic.

"I miss our friendship."

"We're still friends. We just haven't seen each other in a while."

"No." He fiddled with the dials on the radio, and amazed, Kerry sensed that he was trying desperately to change the subject.

"No?"

"Our friendship pretty much ended with my marriage, which, by the way, was the second biggest mistake I ever made in my life." He glanced her way. "You were right about that."

"I don't remember saying it was the biggest mistake of your life!" Kerry exclaimed, embarrassed.

"Don't you? Well, never mind. I'm glad to be back in Seattle and starting over again. The last few years in San Francisco aren't really worth remembering. So I thought I'd start with you, with us."

"There you go again, pretending you bought J. & K. because of me," she teased.

"It's not all pretending."

His tone was serious. Kerry glanced his way, certain he was putting her on. Swallowing, she asked, "What was the first biggest mistake?"

"What?"

"You said marrying Jenny was the second biggest mistake. What was the first?"

"Oh, that." He wrinkled his nose and rubbed it sheepishly. "Someday maybe I'll tell you about it."

They stopped for a red light and Adam glanced her way. "Stop frowning or you're going to have permanent creases between your eyes."

"I'm not frowning."

"Yes, you are. There." He reached over and touched her forehead right above the bridge of her nose. "Just like that. Relax, you still look great."

"Still?"

"For a thirty-two-year-old woman."

She sputtered impotently, and he had the nerve to laugh.

"I'm revising my opinion of you," she said flatly. "You're not insufferable, you're hateful."

She subsided into silence and refused to be drawn into more conversation the rest of the drive, no matter how hard Adam tried. Being with him again was too unsettling, and she had this certain feeling that he could infect her reason. He'd done it to other women. She was smart enough to know she wasn't immune.

The restaurant Adam chose was an informal bistro that cantilevered over Puget Sound. He requested a table by the window and Kerry turned her attention to the view of the water. Ribbons of light from the windows of the restaurant shimmered on the undulating black surface. In the distance, a faint line of burnt orange was all that remained of the setting sun.

The windows were thrown open and the salty tang of the sea penetrated the café. Kerry inhaled deeply, willing the pressures of the week to the back of her mind.

Adam ordered a draft for himself, but Kerry refused another drink. "I wasn't kidding, you know," he said. "You do look great."

"Humph," Kerry snorted.

"Almost as good as your secretary," he added innocently as he picked up his menu. "Of course, she is younger."

Kerry snatched the menu from his grasp. "Okay, wise guy. I'm no older than you are, remember?"

"Yeah, but you told me I've aged well." He snatched the menu back.

"And I haven't?" Kerry's voice rose in spite of herself.

"I just said you looked great, didn't I?"

"Are you trying to start an argument? Is that it? Here we haven't seen each other in God knows how long, and all you can do is bicker?"

Adam's eyes danced. "It's not all I can do," he drawled, his mouth curving.

Kerry made an indignant sound.

"What was that?" he asked innocently.

"None of your beeswax!" Kerry muttered, deliberately choosing one of the silly, childhood phrases she'd almost forgotten.

Adam laughed aloud, drawing glances from other patrons. Kerry buried her nose in her menu. This was a dangerous game they were playing, the kind they'd never indulged in when they were kids. The kind they shouldn't be indulging in now.

The waiter came and took their order, and Kerry refused to make eye contact with Adam. This "date" was not going as planned. She had to stop this nonsense now!

"How's your sister?" Adam asked, making conversation.

"Married. With a pair of three-year-old twins."

"You're kidding." Adam seemed genuinely taken aback. "I always pictured Marla as the footloose and fancy-free type."

"Unlike her sarcastic older sister?" Kerry guessed, more amused than angry.

"Unlike her sensible older sister," he corrected smoothly. "How are you two getting along these days?"

"Terrific," Kerry said and meant it.

She didn't know who was the more surprised: herself or Marla. All the childhood rivalries, jealousies and fights had melted away years before. Somewhere along the line Marla had grown into a real person, one whom Kerry liked, admired and wanted to be with. "One of the benefits of adulthood," she went on, "is that you don't have to hate your sister anymore just because she's your sister. You can actually like her and it's okay."

"Do you see her often?"

"Yeah. She lives in Seattle. Only about forty minutes away from me."

Adam looked pensively out the window as the waiter brought their plates. "I won't be back for a while after this. I've got to wrap things up in San Francisco, and it's going to take some doing." He shot her a look she couldn't interpret. "I guess we'll have to make tonight last."

"I'm not a night owl, Adam. You know that. As much as I'd like to paint the town red, I've got work tomorrow. I've got to get to bed early." She'd been concentrating on cutting her meat but now she looked up—into the sober sensuality simmering in his eyes. Her heart lurched. Quickly she glanced away, frowning. She was not going to think of Adam as anything other than a friend no matter what he did!

Daring a look back, she saw that he was regarding her with amusement. Her pulse slowly returned to normal. Idiot, she berated herself. She'd imagined the whole thing.

"So tell me the truth this time. What made you decide to buy Jacobson & Kern? You could have probably started your own company here," she pointed out, deliberately guiding their conversation.

"Not with J. & K.'s reputation."

"No, but you'd make your own reputation in time."

"Your confidence in my ability is heartwarming," he drawled.

"What is this? False modesty?" Kerry complained. "For as long as I've known you, you've always done whatever you set out to do. When you decided to go into investment, I knew you'd be a success. You had to be. Adam Shard never failed at anything."

"I wasn't so hot as a husband," he pointed out with a touch of humor.

"Well, that's because you're not husband material," Kerry answered blithely. "But you're an outstanding businessman. Your success rate was great even before you bought out that company in San Francisco. When you and Jenny were still married and you worked for Crowe, Weatherby, and—"

"Wait a minute. Who says I'm not husband material?"

Kerry stopped short. "I do."

"Why am I not husband material?"

He sounded so disgruntled that Kerry had to smile. "Well, Adam. What can I say? Your reputation precedes you."

"In what way?" At her short laugh, he demanded, "I'm serious, Kerry! In what way?"

"In every way! You never lasted with any woman longer than a few months, and, like you said, your marriage was short-lived. You can't tell me that you've lived like a monk these past few years," she added. "I won't believe you."

"How do you know I haven't been seeing the same woman for the last five years, hmm?"

"Have you?" Kerry's chest tightened reflexively.

"No-o-o," he admitted.

"I rest my case," she murmured, relieved in spite of herself.

"I'm not the womanizer you seem to think I am."

"Adam, it doesn't matter to me what you are. We've been friends too long for anything you do to surprise me. Forget it." Kerry was anxious to change the subject. "So why did you decide to come back to Seattle now?"

He seemed disinclined to change the subject, but he finally shrugged. "Seattle's my home. When I left for San Francisco, I just wanted to get away. But now I want to be here. It's funny," he mused. "I thought I'd never want to come back."

"Why not? Because of Jenny?"

Adam snorted. "No. That died an unlamented death."

"Then what?"

"Oh, I don't know. Some unfinished business, I guess." He took a swallow from his draft and turned his attention to the meal.

There was something different about Adam, Kerry decided. A change in attitude she couldn't quite put her finger on. It piqued her interest, and she found herself studying him surreptitiously while she picked at her plate, unable to do justice to the luscious seafood.

"You never told me what the first mistake was," she reminded him.

"No, I didn't."

So that was the end of that, huh? Kerry felt Adam was deliberately hiding something from her. She turned her face to the cool evening breeze wafting through the open window. Fine. If he wanted to be mysterious, let him. It wasn't going to bother her.

Strains of music filtered inside, and Kerry glanced around to see a three-piece band tuning up at a small patio to the right. Moist air off Puget Sound had dampened the tile floor, but even so several couples had drifted outside, waiting to dance. Kerry heard soft laughter as the band broke into a slow song.

"Ready?" Adam asked, tossing down his napkin.

"To dance? Not on your life!"

"Why not?"

"Oh, Adam." She tried to evade the hand he reached across the table, but he caught her arm, pulling her to her feet.

"What's wrong with dancing?" he demanded. "What in God's name do you do for fun, Kerry?"

"I don't have any fun. It's not good for the soul." She was distracted by the thought of dancing with Adam. She didn't want to be that close to him.

"Says who?" he laughed. "You?"

"It's a truism of life. One of those things you just learn."

"You know something," he growled, guiding her to the dance floor against her will. "You talk too much."

Kerry stumbled in his wake. "Adam, I really don't want to dance."

"Too bad. I do."

"Well, that's really considerate of you," she complained. "I hope this isn't your usual tactic with women, or you're going to lose popularity."

"I'll take my chances," he drawled in that sexy way. "So who've you been seeing lately, hmm?" he asked, drawing her into his arms.

Kerry tried to wriggle free, but though he held her loosely, his grip was surprisingly hard to break. "No one."

"Oh, come on. There must be someone."

"Well, there isn't. If it's any of your business."

"Beeswax," he reminded her, laughing silently. "What about Ron Tisdale? He looked like a contender."

"Ron Tisdale!" Kerry snorted. "Get real!"

"I can't tell you how glad I am to hear it," he said dryly.

She was suddenly aware that the tune was too slow and romantic for a dance with Adam. She opened her mouth to tell him so the same moment he dragged her against his body.

The shock of hard masculine thighs and steely arms froze her tongue. "I've always wondered why you never married," he mused aloud.

Kerry recovered herself. "I never met anyone worth marrying."

"Really?" He was amused. "How about someone to have an affair with?"

"That's your department, not mine." She bent her head, suddenly remembering that time they were together in college. "You're not offering your services again, are you?" she asked innocently.

For a moment Adam looked blank, then he broke into laughter. "I didn't offer my services before," he reminded her, grinning. "You just wanted me to."

"Hah!" Hard fingers rested lightly against the small of her back. Kerry could feel every single one. She had to escape! "What about you? No repeat performance at the altar scheduled?"

"Not so far, but there's always hope."

"You mean, you'd actually consider marriage again?" She pressed her hand determinedly against his chest, vainly trying to keep some space between them.

To thwart her, Adam grabbed her fingers and wound them around his neck, gazing down sardonically into her flushed face. "Relax. I don't bite. Well, not usually anyway," he amended. "And, just for the record, since you seem to have a rather low opinion of my morals, I never cheated on Jenny."

"So you were faithful, what? A full year and a half? Maybe two? You must deserve some kind of medal."

Adam stopped moving, his hands at her waist suddenly hard and unfriendly. "What the hell is this?" he growled. "God, Kerry! You sound like a bitter old maid. My marriage broke up because Jenny wasn't the woman for me, and I wasn't the man for her. It had nothing to do with my being faithful, which, now that I think of it, is really none of your damn *beeswax* anyway!"

Kerry swallowed, chastised. "Sorry."

"Damn right," he muttered.

Silence followed. They swayed back and forth. She felt his jaw brush her forehead as he glanced down and tried to read her expression. Kerry purposely focused her gaze on his broad chest.

"We were talking about you," he pointed out. "Not me."

"I don't want to talk at all."

Adam inclined his head in agreement. Neither of them spoke a word for the next couple of songs. Kerry wished she'd kept her thoughts to herself. Adam was right. What he did with his life was his business. She had no right criticizing him.

She wished they could just leave. Dancing with Adam—just *being* with Adam—made her uncomfortable. She was overly conscious of his scent and his strength and his disturbing touch. Every breath she took brought her breasts in hard contact with his chest, and the brush of his thighs against hers caused an awareness in her flesh she refused to acknowledge.

She had to get out of there.

"Want to leave?" he asked.

She almost sighed in relief. "It's kind of late," she agreed.

"We didn't talk about Marsden."

Kerry was astounded. She hadn't once thought about the Marsden account! I must be losing my mind, she thought. "Oh, that's right. Maybe we can talk about it on the way home."

"God forbid we might actually stay out past eleven," he muttered, but he led her to the door all the same.

It turned out Adam had very few rules when it came to John Marsden. "Just keep up with what he's got for now. The accounts are already being transferred. If John calls you while I'm in San Francisco, do your best. But remember, he likes to play it safe."

"So do I," Kerry said as he pulled into her apartment complex.

"I know," he answered, and waited until she'd climbed the steps and unlocked her door before he drove away.

Chapter Six

Make sure you've got something ready for Puget Sound Children's Hospital. All of J. & K.'s management team is donating. Ron's putting up his beach house for a weekend, and Sharon's husband is offering a guided fishing tour up the Cowlitz River. Mr. Shard has pledged $5,000 and John Marsden is matching his pledge. Think about what you want to give. This is a great opportunity for us to show Mr. Shard our commitment to Jacobson & Kern.

Sam

Kerry groaned in frustration at the message Sam Wright had left on the top of her desk. What did she have to donate for the auction? Nothing!

"'Great opportunity for us to show Mr. Shard our commitment to Jacobson & Kern,'" she grumbled aloud. Adam had been gone nearly two weeks. She hadn't expected to miss him as much as she did, and it irked her.

Her intercom buzzed and Rachel said, "Are you there, Kerry? Sam wants everyone to meet in his office in fifteen minutes to discuss the fund-raiser."

"What if I have other things to take care of first?" she asked rhetorically.

Rachel giggled. "You could always take it up with our new boss," she said suggestively.

"We're not that close of friends." Kerry's tone was wry.

"Oh, I forgot to tell you. Your sister called while you were out. She said she was going to be in Seattle tomorrow and wants to take you to lunch."

"Good!" Kerry's mood improved. "It's about time she got into the city."

"She said be ready at noon."

"Will do. Thanks, Rachel."

"Any time."

Kerry hadn't seen her sister for several weeks. Everytime she called Marla these days, her sister was involved in one family crisis or another. Last week alone Melissa had fallen out of the top bunk and been rushed to the hospital—it was later learned that her twin, Ryan, had pushed her—and the day after that the car broke down and stranded Marla and the kids on the freeway for three hours. A week later Kerry had called and gotten James, Marla's husband. Marla was in the tub and refused to leave the luxury of a bubble bath—her first free moment of the day, she wanted Kerry to know in loud voice from the bathroom!

So it was great that Marla had actually called her. Now they could finally get together.

Sighing, Kerry grabbed a pad and pencil and headed toward Sam's office. She intended to write down everything the other employees were donating to give herself ideas. She was going to have to think of something for this fund-raiser and fast.

Sam was seated behind his desk, looking exceptionally proud to have been put in this position. Adam, you'd better get here fast, Kerry thought wryly. Or else Sam's head won't be able to fit inside this room.

"Is everyone here?" Sam asked, looking around. They all nodded. "Well, then, let's get right down to business. I hope everyone plans to donate something for the auction. It doesn't have to be much. It's more a gesture of teamwork and good faith."

Kerry spoke up. "I'm afraid I don't have a beach house or a husband who fishes. If anybody has any bright ideas for me, I'm willing to listen."

"I can think of a thing or two," Ron said smoothly.

Kerry glared at Ron. "Why don't you be more specific?" she challenged. "I'm sure we'd all like to be entertained!"

"Now, now," Sam inserted benevolently. "I'm sure there must be something you can give, Kerry." He nodded toward the newest member of the staff. "Tim, there, has got season tickets to the Sonics. Four seats. He's putting two different nights on the block."

"Gee, I'm sorry, Sam. I let my season tickets go this year," Kerry said with a straight face. "And they were right at the half-court line, too."

Sam narrowed his eyes at her, uncertain whether she was putting him on or not.

Sharon was pouring herself a cup of coffee from the silver thermos on Sam's credenza. "I've got a great idea, Kerry. Why don't you offer to cook a gourmet meal for two? Say, in the bidder's own home? That's what I was going to do before Eric bailed me out."

Kerry laughed. "Me? Cook? Sorry, Sharon, I am the bane of the discriminating palate. Budget Gourmet is about as culinary as I get."

"So? It can be funny. No one cares."

"I would," Sam said with a snort of disapproval. "This is a serious fund-raiser. It's not a joke."

Ron smoothed the crease in his slacks. "You'd better believe I wouldn't bid on Kerry's cooking." He gave a mock shudder. "I want to live to see thirty-five."

"If this is reverse psychology, Ron, it's working," Kerry declared. "I might just do it."

His eyes widened in horror and he clutched his throat. The room broke into laughter and even Kerry smiled. She wasn't exactly a horrible cook, but her menus were far from gourmet. Soups and salads were the mainstay of her single-life dinner menu.

"Okay, put me down for dinner for two, cooked to perfection, in the bidder's own home," she said with sudden decision.

Sam uncapped his black pen. "With a starting price of...?"

"How about fifty dollars?"

Ron laughed. "Nobody'll pay that!"

Kerry batted her lashes at him. "Make it a hundred, because I'm worth it."

"A hundred it is," Sam agreed. "I'm sure Mr. Shard will be pleased by our team spirit. Now, is there anyone else who needs help coming up with a donation?"

* * *

Kerry squeezed her way past the throng by the door of the Working Girl Café, a new lunch counter not far from Jacobson & Kern—Shard Ltd. She glanced around the room. Marla was seated at a table in the far corner. Spotting Kerry, she waved eagerly.

"I can't tell you how glad I am to be here!" Marla declared as Kerry scooted her seat into the table. "I got a sitter for the twins and just left. I don't even feel guilty!"

The waiter refilled Marla's empty wineglass. To his look of inquiry, Kerry shook her head. "I've got to be sharp this afternoon."

"What for? It's Friday," Marla said breezily. "You've only got a few hours left."

"I know, but nevertheless..." She smiled. "Besides, my day has just begun. As soon as I get home I've got to try out a new recipe."

"Try out a new recipe?" Marla repeated. "Are you serious?"

"It's a long story," said Kerry dryly, then filled Marla in on her donation for the auction.

Marla's blue eyes sparkled with amusement. Shorter than Kerry by two inches, Marla still possessed the soft, unblemished skin and thick dark brown hair she'd had as a teenager. There was something pink and pretty about Marla that hadn't hardened with age. Yet her sister had aged, Kerry realized with faint uneasiness. The skin across her cheekbones was drawn and there was a telltale redness around her eyes.

"Is something wrong?" Kerry asked.

"You mean with me? No. Why?"

"You look kind of tired."

"Well, I guess! You don't know what it's like chasing after a couple of three-year-olds! Ryan's an absolute monster. He tortures his sister endlessly. Melissa's crying all the time."

Marla fussed with her napkin, and Kerry wondered if she were covering up. "You make motherhood sound so attractive," remarked Kerry.

"Oh, I love them, and I wouldn't have it any other way, it's just..." Her voice trailed off and her lips tightened. "Sometimes I just feel like a single mom. James isn't a lot of help with the kids."

Bingo. James was the problem.

"My psychologist tells me I'm trying to live the ideal life, and it's killing me. I need to back off a little."

"Your psychologist?" Kerry was incredulous.

Marla shrugged, almost sheepishly. "I thought I was falling apart a while back. A friend recommended a psychologist. So I went to her, and things have been better."

"Why didn't you tell me you were falling apart?" asked Kerry, concerned.

"Oh, you know!" Marla laughed, embarrassed. "You're always so together. You'd never let a man get to you like James was getting to me! I was almost afraid you'd talk me into divorcing him."

Kerry gasped. "Marla! I would never do that! For God's sake, I didn't want Mom and Dad to split up even after—" She cut herself off. She'd never discussed with Marla the day she'd surprised her father and his girlfriend, and she didn't feel like bringing it up now. "Have things really gotten that bad between you and James?" she asked instead.

Marla shook her head and swallowed from her wineglass. "No, no. I'm just feeling low. The last thing I want is a divorce," she said forcefully. "Let's talk about something else. How's it going now that Adam is your boss? Is it good, bad, what?"

Kerry reluctantly allowed the subject to be changed. "Too early to tell. Adam is moving to Seattle sometime this weekend. He'll be in the office starting Monday. Then we'll see."

"But how do you feel about it?" Marla pressed, her good humor returning. "I mean, *Adam*! Your best friend. It must be weird to have him as a boss."

"I haven't really gotten used to the idea yet," Kerry admitted.

Marla eyed her sister speculatively. "What's he like these days?"

"Pretty much the same, I guess." Kerry shrugged, feeling uncomfortable. She was glad when the waiter came to take their order.

But Marla was persistent. "I always thought he was so good-looking."

"He still is," Kerry grunted unwillingly.

"Still the same sexy eyes and smile?"

"Yes." She wrinkled her nose.

Marla grinned. "I always wondered why the two of you didn't get together. I mean, Adam was always crazy about you."

Kerry snorted in disbelief.

"It's true!" Marla declared, warming to her subject. "You were his friend, and he was always hanging around with you when all the rest of his buddies were stupidly panting over the cheerleaders and homecoming princesses!"

"You were a cheerleader and homecoming princess," Kerry pointed out dryly. Her sister could be a broken record on the subject of Adam. And she was totally off base.

"You can't tell me he bought out that company you work for without knowing you were one of the employees!" she swept on, undeterred. "I bet he did it on purpose. Just so he could be with you again."

"Oh, sure. And next he's going to buy my apartment complex so he can move in next door." Marla was, and always had been, an incurable romantic!

"Why can't you see it, Kerry?" Marla demanded. "Why are you the only one who can't see how he feels about you?"

Kerry sighed and leaned across the table. In a firm voice she said, "Now, listen. You haven't seen Adam in years, so you don't even know what you're talking about. Why do you always have to play matchmaker for me? Do I ask for it? Hmm?"

"You're not doing such a hot job of finding available men on your own."

"If I wanted an available man," Kerry said, smiling through her teeth, "I'd make more of an effort. Adam and I are friends. That's all. And that's all we'll ever be."

Marla took another sip of wine. Kerry didn't trust the sparkle that suddenly entered her eyes. Oh, God. Marla was plotting something!

"Marla," Kerry groaned, "if you do or say anything to Adam, I swear I'll renounce you as my sister!"

Marla merely patted her hand. "You worry too much," she said, and turned all her attention on her meal.

Kerry sighed. There was no hope for her. Marla was bound to do something totally awful and embarrassing in the name of keeping her sister from becoming an old maid.

Kerry frantically stir-fried the Chinese vegetables in her new wok. Gray smoke swirled upward, stinging her nose. The grease was burning! The temperature was too high!

"I am never going to get this right!" she shouted in frustration, yanking the wok from the burner. Grease popped and splattered, burning Kerry's arm in half a dozen small spots. Furious, she ran to the sink, pouring cold water over her forearm. So much for learning the art of Chinese cooking in seven days or less. She was going to have to settle for an old standby.

Problem yowled to be let out, and paced anxiously on his delicate brown toes like a drunken tightrope walker, hoping Kerry would come to his rescue.

"In a minute," Kerry muttered through her teeth.

The doorbell rang at the same moment she turned off the tap. Examining the bright red spots on her arm, she walked to the front door, throwing it wide open. Trying to streak between her ankles, Problem pulled up short at the sight of a pair of khaki-clad masculine legs blocking his way. Almost in midstride, the cat wheeled around and shot for the outside stairs.

"Adam!" Kerry cried, half-exasperated.

"Busy?" he asked, his nose wrinkling at the scent of burned oil and vegetables.

"I'm cooking. Can't you tell?"

"Cooking what? Barbecue?"

"Chinese food," she said evenly, her mouth quirking. "What in the world are you doing here?" She stepped back, allowing him inside. "I thought you'd be at your new condo, waiting for the moving van."

"I'm already finished. Got everything settled last night by ten o'clock."

"You mean you're here in Seattle for good?"

Adam smiled. "Didn't we just have this conversation?"

Kerry shook her head. "It just seems kind of strange," she said, feeling slightly dazed.

"If you don't stop looking so shell-shocked you're going to give me a complex. You're supposed to be thrilled that your old buddy's come home."

"I am," Kerry said, her voice not quite measuring up to her words. She *was* happy that Adam was back, but at the same time it made things more complicated. In some ways it was too bad Adam was her boss. She would have loved to just gripe as one friend to another. "Maybe having you around will make Ron behave. Working with him since you've been gone hasn't exactly been my idea of a fun time," she said ironically.

"What is your idea of a fun time?" Adam asked, moving into the kitchen. He surveyed the burned mass of vegetables with distaste.

"What do you care?"

Adam shot her a look. "Because let's go do it, whatever it is." Glancing at her ruined meal, he added sagely, "And while we're at it, maybe we should have dinner out."

The line at the theater snaked around the building and spilled into the parking lot. It took twenty minutes to find a place to park, and when they did, Adam stepped outside the car and examined the crowd unenthusiastically.

"Maybe we should have gone to the drive-in," he remarked musingly.

"Think *Swampthing*'s playing?" Kerry asked impishly, coming around to his side of the car.

He glanced down at her, the corners of his eyes crinkling at the memory. There was a flash of something in that look that made Kerry's breath catch, but a second later it was gone. "Do you have room for ice cream?" he asked, indicating the restaurant next door to the theater. White tables with red umbrellas were clustered in an outdoor patio area.

Kerry shook her head. "I'm stuffed." They'd just gulped down huge hamburgers at a local burger joint. "But I could use some iced-tea."

"After you."

The place was packed on a Friday night, but Adam and Kerry were in no hurry and an outside table was finally cleared and readied for them. They both ordered iced-tea. Dusk was slowly settling, shading Kerry's face. Adam lounged across from her, his feet propped on another chair. He was twirling the striped red and white straw in his glass between two fingers.

It was the first peaceful moment Kerry had spent with him. Ever since he'd blown into her life again, she'd been faced with one crisis after another. Her work had changed. The pace had picked up. He'd given her the Marsden account, for pete's sake! Instead of the calm sameness of her everyday existence, there was now another element of risk and adventure.

"So tell me how it's been with Ron," he said, stretching lazily in his chair.

Kerry wrinkled her nose. There were some things a woman understood that a man never could. Like when a guy was putting you down even while he was complimenting you. Try to explain that and you'd be accused of being paranoid, or egotistical, or just plain female.

"It's more his manner than anything he's done. I don't think he likes working with women and, hey, this isn't a new thing. He's treated me, and every other woman in the office, the same way."

Adam grimaced. "Don't worry. I'll keep him in line."

"Well, that's a relief." Kerry smiled. "I hope that's an indication of how good a boss you are."

"I'm the best," he said, grinning.

Though he was teasing, Kerry wondered if that might not be true. No one could argue with Adam's success. And she knew from experience that he was fair and conscientious and possessed remarkable savvy about human nature. As long as his love affairs stayed out of the office she was certain they would get along fine.

"Tell me about Jenny," she said, surprising herself.

"Jenny?"

"Mmm-hmm. I've always wondered what really went wrong between the two of you."

Adam groaned and closed his eyes. "It's a long time ago, Kerry."

"I know."

"And it really doesn't matter anymore."

"Maybe not," she said agreeably. "But I remember how much you wanted to marry her. What happened?"

"I *thought* I wanted to marry her. There's a big difference. I was twenty-two, finishing college. She was there, and she wanted to get married, and..." He shook his head, frowned down at his empty glass and swirled the melting ice cubes with suppressed emotion. "I don't really know what happened."

Goaded by some inner demon, Kerry asked, "Didn't you love her?"

"Oh, come on. You're not going to bring the *L* word into this, are you?" His lips curved into a smile.

"What a cynic! I thought that's why people got married."

"Just an old wives' tale," he drawled. "Marriage and love are two separate issues."

"Are you saying you never loved Jenny?"

Adam arched a brow at her. "At twenty-two, I didn't know diddly. Maybe I thought I loved her, I don't remember."

"Oh, Adam!"

"Well, I don't see you falling in love all over the place!" he defended himself. "You've never even been married once, so how would you know?" He leaned forward, his elbows on the table, regarding her with calm superiority. "You're not even dating now, are you?"

"I date. Sometimes." She bit the words out.

"No heart palpitations? No sweating palms? No pulse in your head?"

"Contrary to what you seem to believe, I've had my moments." Kerry tossed back a gulp of iced-tea. One moment. With Ryan. Hardly a mad passionate love affair but, yes, she'd thought she loved him.

"Oh, you have, have you?" he asked sardonically.

"Not as many as you've had, of course. But yes."

"I find it very hard to picture you with another man," Adam admitted somewhat seriously.

"*Another* man?"

"Any man, then."

"Well, for your information, I find it very hard to picture you with only one woman."

Adam sighed in exasperation. "You've really painted me black, haven't you?" At her look, he said, "Okay, maybe I'm not interested in marriage again, but I'm hardly Don Juan. I'm not keen on seeing more than one woman at a time. I'm not even good at it. But I don't feel like settling down with just one, either." He glanced past her toward where the sun was sinking behind the jagged skyline of buildings. "I think that moment passed me by."

Kerry heard unexpected poignancy in his words. "It sounds like you and Jenny just finally realized you didn't love each other," she said lightly.

"It was a little more complicated than that, but essentially, yes. I haven't seen her since the divorce."

"Do you want to?" Kerry couldn't prevent herself from asking.

"Not really."

It wasn't meant to be a damning statement on his character; Adam was just being honest. But Kerry thought how indicative his comment was of how he truly felt about women in general. They were fine. They were great. But they weren't all that important in life. At least not one single woman was. Maybe as a general sex they were important, but for Adam, the individual didn't count.

"What's that frown mean?" he asked.

"I was just wondering how you and I have stayed friends. We're not alike at all."

"Aren't we?"

She shot him a swift look. "Good grief, no!" She wagged a finger in front of his nose. "There's a little part of you that's too much like Ron Tisdale."

"There *are* some parts that are the same," he admitted blandly.

"Like sexual innuendo," she said forcefully.

He grinned. "And a little bit more."

"You even commented about my cooking the way he did," Kerry complained. "I'll have you know, I'm not half bad."

"Oh, yeah? Did Tisdale sample your cooking?" Adam asked.

"He didn't. I'm making dinner for some unknown lucky auction bidder." Adam stared at her in total lack of comprehension. "The fund-raiser? For Puget Sound Children's Hospital?"

"Is that what the Chinese food was all about?" he asked. Laughter rumbled deep in his chest. "Oh, God! You're kidding! Say you're kidding."

"I'm not kidding," she said. It wasn't *that* funny!

"You're actually doing all the cooking yourself? And cleaning up afterward?"

Kerry narrowed her lashes warningly. "I'm perfectly capable in the kitchen."

Adam hooted with laughter. "But to make a gourmet meal for two? This I've got to see!"

"Well, the only way you're going to see it is if you buy me for a night because I'll be damned if I ever offer to cook you a meal after the way you've maligned my culinary skills!"

To Kerry's intense surprise, Adam leaned across the table, tilted up her chin and kissed her lightly on the lips. "You're on," he said, amusement threading his voice. "I *am* going to buy Kerry-for-a-Night and make you prove yourself. You're going to have to whip up the most exotic meal in town!"

The conference room at the Four Seasons Hotel was filled with chairs. On a low dais at the front of the room was a table covered with scrolls of paper on which were written the donations. But there was also a basketball signed by the Sonics. And someone had actually given a champion blue-point female Himalayan cat who was yowling piteously in a cage. The cat had already been sold to a little old lady with matching blue hair, and Kerry wished someone would remove the poor thing from the room.

Kerry sat at the end of one aisle, three rows back. She hadn't saved a place for Adam because he'd shown up late, but he'd found a place on the opposite end of her row. As the auction progressed, he kept leaning forward to catch her eye. He was waiting to bid on her entry.

Kerry had to resist reverting to junior-high tactics such as making a face at him. By now everyone at J. & K.—oops, she kept forgetting; *Shard Ltd.*, if you please—knew she and Adam were longtime friends, but Kerry didn't want to give anyone the wrong impression. She was quite aware several people, including Rachel, thought there was something more afoot between them.

Hah. As if she'd ever be fool enough to get involved with Adam Shard. She, of anyone, knew better. Oh, sure. She had her weak moments. But if nothing else had cured her, the raft of female calls flooding in from San Francisco ever since Adam had moved to Seattle certainly had. He'd apparently left a lot of broken hearts behind. Which was certainly right in character for Seattle's own playboy of the western world.

Out of the corner of her eye she saw him lean forward again, grinning like an idiot. He really thought he'd gotten her this time. Rachel, seated three chairs down from Kerry, glanced with avid curiosity from Adam to Kerry. Kerry kept her eyes trained straight ahead.

If Adam had been thinking he could ease into his role as boss without making waves, he could think again. He was the hottest topic around the office these days. It fried Kerry that her name should be linked with his romantically. She was *not* like those San Francisco women, and she *never would be*!

Now he was wiggling his eyebrows at her, motioning to his watch. Soon Kerry-for-a-Night—good Lord, even she was calling it that now!—would be on the auction block. Secretly she hoped he did buy it. Then she could burn the damn meal and smirk about it, too!

"Next up, dinner for two, cooked and prepared in your own home, by one of Shard Limited's most celebrated gourmet cooks, Ms. Kerry Camden."

Most celebrated gourmet cooks? Kerry about fell over. She hadn't written that! Narrowing her eyes to slits, she glared down the row at Adam.

"You're gonna pay for this, Shard," she muttered under her breath.

"What?" Rachel asked, all ears. The people seated in between them looked interested.

"Nothing," Kerry muttered tersely. Woe to Adam Shard. If he bought her, he was going to find out he'd gotten more than his money's worth!

"The bidding starts at one hundred dollars, and may I remind you again," the auctioneer added, sounding slightly self-conscious to be uttering the same phrase over and over again, "this is for a good cause."

"A hundred," Adam called out.

"A hundred and twenty," another voice responded.

Kerry suddenly grew cold inside. If Adam didn't buy her dinner for two, someone else would. She groaned inwardly. Then she would have to live up to her press!

"Two hundred," Adam said, unperturbed.

Kerry relaxed a little. There was a buzz of excited conversation. Uh-oh, grist for the mill, Kerry realized with a sinking heart. Her relationship with Adam was bound to be next week's office headline.

There was no return bid. Kerry was staring straight ahead, thinking rapidly. She hadn't purchased anything tonight. There wasn't anything she'd actually desired. But, as the auctioneer had said, it *was* for a worthy cause.

"Three hundred," she said smoothly, calculating how much money she could actually afford to donate. She had some extra cash saved for something special. She would buy herself back!

A roar of excitement rose like a wave. Kerry slid Adam a sideways look, her lips twitching. His own eyes were lazy and amused.

"Better make it five hundred," he answered in a bored tone.

The resulting noise nearly deafened Kerry. Were those her co-workers cheering? Their feet were pounding the floor! Rachel leaped to her feet, reached over and clapped Kerry on the shoulder, laughing like a banshee.

Slowly the room quieted. Rachel sat back down. The auctioneer gazed straight at Kerry. "Any other bids?" he asked hopefully.

Five hundred dollars. Was paying it worth the price of a joke? She could bid him up by as little as a dollar, but he would certainly top her bid. Feeling all eyes on her, her hands began to sweat. How stupid! she berated herself. She'd actually gone out of her way to draw attention to her relationship with Adam!

But on the other hand, the damage was already done and Adam had had it his way far too long. "Six hundred," she said coolly, closing her ears to her own folly.

But this time there was no noise. The room was breathlessly silent. The bidding had taken on a new dimension. Tense moments passed. Moments when Kerry could hear her heart beat in her ears. What the hell was she doing?

"A thousand dollars," Adam drawled. "And that had better be more than you're willing to pay, Kerry."

"It is," she declared in disgust, and the assemblage broke into whoops of laughter.

Life, Kerry decided the following Monday as she made her way to Adam's office, was never going to be the same. The office was a bubbling cauldron of speculation. She couldn't walk down the hall without feeling someone's eyes following her. Okay. She'd been stupid. She knew it. But at least the fund-raiser was a success. And Adam, for his flamboyance, had won himself a place in the hearts of his employees. Most of the women, half in love with him already, were practically ready to sacrifice themselves at his feet. The men thought he had style and panache.

None of them could figure where Kerry fit in. Even when she explained how they'd known each other since the third grade, no one seemed to believe she and Adam could be just friends. He was just too damn good-looking, Kerry finally decided as she walked briskly down the hall toward Adam's office. The women in the office couldn't understand why she hadn't fallen under his spell.

"Door's open," Adam called after she'd rapped loudly on the panels. Before she could enter, however,

Ron Tisdale came through Adam's door, regarding Kerry with a faint smile.

"So what are you planning to prepare for a thousand dollars?" he drawled, then spoiled the effect by coughing and coughing until Kerry wondered if she should clap him on the back. "Damn cold," he muttered, clearing his throat.

She noticed how shadowed and sunken his eyes were. "You look terrible, Ron," Kerry observed. "Are you okay?"

"Hell, no. I feel rotten."

"You sure it's just a cold?"

"Maybe the flu." He shrugged. "Ellen was out last week with it. Better look out or you'll be next."

"I'll watch myself. Why don't you just go home?"

"Can't. I've got too much to do. I'll crash later." He headed past her toward his own office.

Kerry forgot him almost instantly. She had other things to take care of. Sticking her head around Adam's door, she surveyed his lair. He was seated at his desk, frowning at a stack of papers. He'd tossed off his coat, and his tie was askew, which made him look more approachable. As approachable as a Bengal tiger, Kerry amended at the same moment he glanced up to see her.

"Yes?" he asked, hiding a smile.

"I want to know when you want this fabulous gourmet meal," she said, closing the door behind her and folding her arms across her chest.

"How about Friday night?"

"Okay, but since it's going to take me hours to prepare, I'll have to leave work early."

"Don't try to make me feel guilty. You're not chained to your desk here. You can leave anytime you like."

Since that was undeniably true, Kerry switched tactics. "There is no way this meal is going to be any good. I'm going to make certain of it. So why don't you let me take you out instead?"

Adam looked appalled. "Shame on you, Kerry. You're trying to weasel out of this."

"You bet your socks!" she replied fervently.

"No way. I paid good money for this treat. Friday night, you're cooking for me. And it better be good, because I'm bringing a date."

Kerry stared at him, frozen. Of course he was bringing a date. It was dinner for two, wasn't it? There was no reason to feel so betrayed! "I'm sure she would prefer being taken to one of Seattle's finest restaurants," Kerry pointed out woodenly.

"*She* is a *he*. I've invited John Marsden. He's looking forward to meeting you."

"You're bringing Marsden for dinner?" Kerry practically shrieked.

"That's right."

It was one thing to tease with Adam, but it was a whole other prospect to fail dismally in the eyes of one of Shard Ltd.'s biggest clients. One of *her* biggest clients! Oh, sure, Adam and John Marsden were friends, but she'd be damned if they enjoyed themselves at her expense.

"Be prepared to eat the best meal of your life," she muttered through her teeth.

He grinned with unforgivable enjoyment. "I'm absolutely counting on it."

Chapter Seven

I am never going to trust Adam Shard again. Never, never, never! I'm so frustrated I could cry. Why couldn't he bring some woman to dinner? Why does it have to be someone whose opinion about me matters to me? I'm going to kill Adam before the night is over. And he deserves it!

It wasn't really that she couldn't cook. How tough was it? She knew enough basic information to find her way around a kitchen. Good grief, she'd been feeding herself for years. But to prepare a meal for Adam and John Marsden... She couldn't fail. She just couldn't. She would never hear the end of it from Adam. And even though John Marsden was his friend and undoubtedly already knew the details of how she'd gotten herself into this predicament, she couldn't bear to think of the chuckle the two men would have if she didn't pull this off.

Okay, so what was the answer?

Kerry looked around at the circle of cookbooks sprawled across her tiny counters. She'd won the concession: Adam and John were coming here, not to Adam's condo. Of course the only reason he'd given in was because he still wasn't fully unpacked, and God knew what kind of kitchen utensils and bowls and things he must possess anyway.

So here she was, with only a few hours left to salvage her pride, still unsure what to prepare! She glanced out the window, tense and irritable. Hazy clouds scudded rapidly across the sky. The weather had been just plain weird. Sunny one moment, cold and overcast the next, hailing the next.

She supposed she could fall back on bouillabaisse, but she'd be damned if she could think of anything to serve with it. And was fish stew really exotic enough to be worth one thousand dollars?

The doorbell rang. Muttering an expletive, Kerry tore off her apron and stalked across the living room, flinging open the door. Her sister, Marla, wearing jeans and a pullover sweatshirt, stood on the stoop. Since Marla never just dropped by, much less wore anything as casual as her current attire, Kerry was totally shocked.

"Marla! What are you doing here?" Kerry demanded in surprise. "Where are the kids?"

"They're with James. Oh, Kerry." She flung herself onto the couch and burst into tears.

"Marla." Kerry's heart was in her throat.

Covering her face with her hands, she sobbed brokenly, "I'm so tired I can't see straight. The twins haven't been sleeping very well, and if I'm not up with one, it's the other. James came home from work early and I just left. I just left!''

"Are you getting along any better with James?"

"No." She shook her head, dropping her hands. Her blue eyes were pools of misery. "I'm so unhappy."

"What can I do?"

"Nothing. Just let me be with you for a while. I just need some space."

Kerry hated seeing her sister so unbearably miserable. She felt helpless.

Problem peeked warily around the hall corner. He meowed at Kerry, then leaped to the couch, climbing onto Marla's lap. Kerry reached to removed him, but Marla pulled him into her arms, hugging him in an absurdly childlike way. "Don't take him away," she pleaded.

"If you want him, he's yours." Kerry was really frightened by Marla's behavior.

As if surfacing from a deep sleep, Marla focused on Kerry for the first time. "You look frazzled yourself," she said on a half laugh. "Did I interrupt something?"

Kerry grinned crookedly. "I have to create a feast in less than four hours."

"Oh, God. The dinner you're making for Adam! That's tonight?"

"Afraid so."

"I'm sorry," she said in a small voice. "I didn't mean to foul you up."

"You didn't. I don't care about the dinner," Kerry said sincerely. "Not when you're this unhappy. I wish I could do something. Tell me what to do, and I'll do it."

Marla shook her head, fighting back fresh tears. "Let me help you."

"Are you kidding? And be accused of bringing in replacement help? No way."

"So what are you serving?" Marla asked, sniffing.

Since talking about Kerry's meal seemed to help Marla get her mind off her misery, Kerry went to the kitchen, collected one of the cookbooks and brought it back to her. "How about *saumon truite au caviar noir, beurre blanc*? Which, if my French serves me correctly, is some kind of salmon with black caviar and white butter."

Marla grimaced. "Yuk. I hate caviar."

"Me, too. I only thought of it because Adam hates it, too."

She managed a smile. "You're falling for him, Kerry."

"Because I want to feed him something he won't eat? Oh, come on."

"I know you, and you wouldn't be so worked up if this dinner didn't matter."

"He's bringing John Marsden with him. *The* John Marsden. The one with the *millions*."

"How much did Adam pay for this meal?"

Kerry wished she didn't have to answer. "A thousand dollars."

"He wants you, Kerry," Marla said in the tone of one who knows.

"Marla," Kerry began in a long-suffering voice.

"I know what to do about tonight. Just take my advice. And thanks, Kerry, for being here when I need you." Marla stood up and hugged her fiercely. "Now just listen..."

Adam checked his watch for about the twentieth time. He and John had spent the greater part of the last five hours dawdling over lunch, then heading out to the marina to look at his boat, the *Mary Lou*. They'd gone over every square inch of the magnificent craft, but now Adam was anxious to leave. Really anxious. The sun felt hot and itchy on his crown even though the day was cool, cold even, and he was restless and uncomfortable.

"So what do you think?"

Adam pulled his gaze away from the sparkling horizon. His eyes hurt. "Sorry, John. I wasn't listening."

"Well, what do you think of the *Mary Lou*? I've been pointing out her virtues for the past hour and a half and you haven't said a word."

John Marsden was in his fifties and a friend of Adam's father. John was something of a mentor for Adam. He'd encouraged Adam's interest in investments right from the start. When Adam had expressed an interest in moving back to Seattle, John heartily endorsed the idea. They both agreed it was one of the best decisions Adam had made in a long, long time.

Except right now he felt godawful. What the hell was the matter with him?

"The *Mary Lou*'s fabulous. Beautiful," he assured John.

Marsden gently tapped his pipe on the boat's rail. "You've got to come fishing with me soon. No more putting me off."

"When have I ever put you off?"

"I invited you to take a cruise this evening, didn't I?"

Adam inwardly smiled. "I told you, I'm busy tonight." Adam had lied about bringing Marsden with him to Kerry's place for dinner. He just liked seeing her get all worked up; he couldn't help himself! But he'd planned on being alone with her from the first. He wanted her company to himself. In fact, he couldn't wait to be with her.

Except he felt like he might fall over.

"Have you got any aspirin?" he asked when it looked as if Marsden was about to launch into another round of persuasive arguments about the evening cruise.

"You don't feel well?" Marsden squinted against the smoke curling from his pipe.

"I've been better."

"Come on below."

Adam followed Marsden down the narrow steps to his captain's cabin. He was given two tablets and swallowed them without water. Outside, hail suddenly pelted the boat's deck and hull.

"Strange weather." Marsden shook his head, then eyed Adam thoughtfully. "You do look kind of pale, son. Maybe you should give up this hot date, huh?"

"Not a chance."

Thirty minutes later Adam was fighting Friday night traffic back to Kerry's apartment. His head throbbed. Hail rained down in intense, sporadic bursts. Traffic crawled. His wipers slapped rhythmically back and forth.

Through a wet blur, he saw the car in front of him suddenly slide sideways, narrowly miss a collision, then feel the full brunt of about five angry horns. Adam glanced over. The front right tire was flopping around the wheel well. The driver, a young woman with a pale, frightened face, sat frozen in the car.

Through his rearview mirror he saw her open her door. Black heels stepped cautiously into shallow rivers of water running down the road.

"Damn," Adam muttered, pulling his own car over. He sloshed through standing water to where she stood shivering in a sleeveless dress.

Blinking against the now torrential rain, she said, "It's my tire."

"Do you have a spare? And a jack?"

She nodded.

"Then let's get to it," he said grimly, coughing. Dimly he realized he must have picked up some bug. Tisdale's probably.

He wished he was with Kerry.

"When's he going to be here?" Marla asked as Kerry arranged the asparagus vinaigrette and tropical fruit salads on the table. The dishes to be heated were lined up for the microwave.

"Soon. Any minute."

"Oh, God. I've got to get out of here. I look terrible!" Marla was in motion instantly, then stopped. She came back to Kerry and smiled at her a little sadly. "You made me forget for a little while. Thanks."

"You're very welcome," Kerry said lightly. "And thanks for this." She waved an arm at the beautiful array of food that now occupied the counter space where the cookbooks had been.

Marla laughed. "Don't tell Adam the truth."

"Never."

"Have fun," she said, and dashed out the door into the dark and threatening evening.

Kerry glanced at the digital clock on her microwave. Adam was late. Not a lot late, just a little. Traffic, she decided, wrinkling her nose. Seattle was a mess on Friday nights.

She smiled as she imagined his look of surprise when he discovered her "cooking." The caterer Marla had recommended was even better than Kerry could have hoped for. The salads were an aesthetic delight: tender green asparagus spears and bright red cherry tomatoes; exotic mangos and papaya and kiwi mixed with peaches and topped with raspberry sauce. The entrées made her mouth water: something with boned chicken and razor-thin apple slices, and something else with mussels in a savory sauce with flakes of basil and rosemary.

How in God's name was she going to convince Adam and John Marsden she'd cooked all this? They would never believe her! And even if they did, the almond and Gran Marnier tarts for dessert would be the crowning blow.

"Lie," she told herself sternly. "Lie, lie, lie."

She walked quickly to her bedroom, examining her cream-colored dress. It was pretty blah, which was the effect she was trying to create. Briefly she'd toyed with the idea of renting a black maid's dress with a frilly white apron but decided that was going too far. After all, John Marsden would be here, too.

Touching her French braid to make certain it was still in place, she walked back to the part of her apartment that could be construed as the dining room. Her table was tiny. There was only room for two. But that was okay because she didn't intend to eat with them.

She was just lighting the candles when she heard Adam's knock. Pinning on a bright smile that she hoped wasn't too artificial, she threw open the door dramatically. "Good evening, Mr. Shard, Mr. Marsden . . ." Her voice trailed off. Adam was alone and he was soaked to the bone.

He coughed hard and shook his head. "Marsden couldn't make it."

"What happened to you?" Kerry demanded in concern. "Get in here before you freeze to death!"

A burst of wind followed Adam inside, extinguishing the candles. But Kerry didn't notice.

Adam ran his hands through his hair and they came out wet. "I've been helping a lady change her tire."

"You're soaked to the skin!"

"I know, I probably should have gone home first." He sighed. "And I think I might have got Tisdale's bug."

"Wonderful. Sit down before you fall down. Do you want to change your clothes or something?" Kerry asked helplessly. She had nothing for him to put on.

He wiped a hand across his forehead. "I'd really like a shower."

"You're welcome to one."

"No, I probably should go home." He glanced around distractedly. "The place looks nice. I'm sorry."

"Never mind," Kerry said quickly. In the face of Adam's current condition she felt mean-spirited at attempting to deceive him. "Yes, I think you'd better take a shower and get warm. I'm not going to be responsible for you dying of pneumonia. I'll take your clothes downstairs and throw them in the dryer."

With great reluctance Adam allowed her to guide him to the bathroom. He looked as if he was about to pass out. Kerry turned on the taps for him. "Need anything else?"

His lips twisted with amusement. "I think I can take it from here."

"If you change your mind, just yell." She stepped around him and closed the door behind her.

She stood in the hall, listening. She heard the click of the shower door close behind him, and the steady rush of water. She thought of how sick Ron Tisdale had been this week. If Adam had caught the same virus, he wasn't going to be feeling well for quite a while.

She was still standing outside the bathroom door when the taps switched off. She waited, but when Adam didn't appear, she called anxiously, "Adam?"

The door opened so abruptly that Kerry stepped back, shocked. He was naked from the waist up, a towel slung over his narrow hips. Dark hair lay in damp whorls on his broad chest. She stared in mesmerized fascination at the sight of muscles sliding beneath smooth, taut skin as he raked his hands through his wet hair. Then her gaze shifted to the towel. It looked as if one false move might send it skating to the floor.

Adam was shivering. "I should have gone home," he said again on a deep cough.

"You need to be in bed," said Kerry in a voice she wouldn't have recognized as her own. Clearing her throat, she pushed open the door to her bedroom. "Crawl in. I'll see to your clothes."

"What about dinner?"

"Are you hungry?"

"Not really."

"I didn't think so. Go to bed." Kerry smiled. "I'll eat it by myself. And let me tell you, I worked my fingers to the bone, so I hope you feel bad!"

"I do." His gray eyes looked into hers. Kerry's heart softened.

"Go to bed before you fall over," she said gruffly.

He frowned, swaying on his feet. "Where are you going to sleep?"

"The couch. Please, Adam." She practically pushed him into the room.

Luckily her own clothes were picked up and the bed was made. Not that she was a slob, but she'd been running behind all day.

"Are you sure?" he asked, sighing heavily. "I should probably just go home."

"Not on your life. You paid a thousand dollars for Kerry-for-a-Night. I can be a nurse as well as a cook."

She shut the door firmly behind him and went into the bathroom to pick up his clothes. She took them to the downstairs laundry, marveling at how strange it felt to execute such a domestic task for him—strange and a little wonderful. But the feel of his cold, water-soaked jeans and shirt made her shudder slightly. She hoped he hadn't complicated the flu with exposure.

Half an hour later she peeked into the bedroom, relieved to find him asleep and sprawled across her double bed. The sheets were tangled around him, the towel tossed heedlessly on the floor. She could see his broad shoulders and the damp hair that curled at his nape.

He wasn't sleeping well, she realized as he turned over and murmured something unintelligible. Tiptoeing to his side, she look down into his now flushed face. She remembered, suddenly, Adam's bout with the flu when he was in high school. He'd ended up being hospitalized. She also remembered calling him a wimp whenever he got sick, because he really knew how to overdo it. He, in turn, learned to hate hospitals.

Worried, she let herself out of the room, leaving the door ajar. An hour later she checked on him again. This time he was shivering, and she pulled the comforter up to his shoulders, her fingers grazing his skin. His flesh was on fire.

Kerry chewed on her bottom lip. Should she be really worried? Chances were that he was going to be fine in a matter of hours. Still . . .

She left the bedroom and paced the confines of the living room. Finally she phoned her sister for lack of anything better to do.

"Relax," Marla said after Kerry had anxiously explained about Adam. "He's probably fine."

"I just don't want anything to happen to him."

"Nothing's going to happen to him." A note of indulgence crept into her voice. "You really do care about him, don't you?"

"Of course I do!" Kerry answered irritably.

"No, I mean *really* care about him."

"Marla, please!"

"Okay, okay. Look, if it'll make you feel better I'll stop by in about an hour."

"No, Marla. Good grief." Kerry sighed in exasperation. "But thanks. You're probably right. He's going to be fine. I'm just being paranoid."

"You're sure you don't need me?" She sounded almost anxious to come.

"I'm sure. Bye, Marla." Kerry replaced the receiver, a little calmer. Marla was right. Adam would be right as rain within a few hours. Kerry was amazed at herself for overreacting. It wasn't like her.

She cleaned the kitchen, covered the salads and entrées with plastic wrap and stuffed everything in her refrigerator except for a small bowl of fruit salad. This she ate while staring mindlessly at the TV in the living room. The luscious bits of mango and papaya were delicious. Too bad Adam wouldn't be able to enjoy her "gourmet meal."

After rinsing her bowl, she set it in the dishwasher, then wiped down the counters and the table. With a last peek at Adam, she went back downstairs to collect his laundry.

Her neighbor, Mr. Little, glared at her through a pair of trifocals he could never seem to adjust to the right distance. Now his head was tilted back and he looked at her as if she were some noxious specimen. "Dad-blame cat," he muttered. "It's usin' my petunias as a toilet."

"Who? Problem?" Kerry frowned. "How's he getting on your deck?"

"He jumps! Sails through the air like a dang blame bird! Next time I'm takin' the broom to him."

Since Problem had scarcely endeared himself to the neighbors even long before Kerry came on the scene, Kerry could understand the sentiment. But if Mr. Little and some of the other residents really resented Problem they would have had him collected and taken away instead of practically forcing Kerry to adopt him. The Siamese was probably safer than Mr. Little would ever admit.

"Mr. Little, if someone has the flu, what would you do for them?" Kerry asked, pulling Adam's jeans, shirt, Jockey shorts and socks out of the dryer.

"Lots of fluids. Rest. Check his temperature from time to time." The "his" was slightly stressed as Mr. Little bent his head forward and examined the clothes out of the tops of his glasses.

"Thanks."

Kerry smothered a smile as she carried Adam's clothes back upstairs. Mr. Little would have something to talk over with Miss Matthews when he was invited over tomorrow night, as he was every Saturday night, for dinner.

Stacking his clothes on the coffee table, Kerry couldn't resist checking Adam again. I'm as bad as an overprotective mother, she thought. I can't leave him alone for five minutes without worrying.

The comforter was back on the floor and the sheet had slipped to expose Adam's thigh and leg. He looked incredibly masculine and big in her double bed. Kerry stared at him for a full minute, listening to her bedside clock tick quietly as she grappled with feelings she hadn't known she possessed. Deep feelings with deeper roots. There was something so extremely sensual about him that Kerry fantasized about slipping in beside him, covering herself with his warmth, feeling her heart beat against his.

Abruptly she left the room, her breathing fast and ragged. What the hell was the matter with her?

She took Mr. Little's advice to heart, however, and scrounged through the top shelf of her linen closet, which she used as a medicine cabinet, for her long lost thermometer. When she found it she took a deep breath and walked back inside her bedroom.

Adam was in exactly the same position. Unsure if waking him was such a good idea, Kerry tentatively placed one hand on his bare shoulder. "Adam?"

There was a slithery movement under the comforter and Problem suddenly leaped for Kerry's leg. She screamed, a short sharp squeak of fear, then clapped her hand to her mouth.

Adam's head moved against the pillow, then he rolled onto his back. His eyes were still closed. "What the hell?" he muttered.

"Adam, I want to take your temperature."

"Oh, God."

"Please."

He didn't answer and she wondered if he was fully awake. "I'm going to stick the thermometer under your tongue," she warned.

He protested and swatted at her hands, but Kerry got the job done. She held the tip of the thermometer in place. It was the longest minute of her life.

When she finally checked his temperature, her mouth went dry. 104! His fever was sky high! What in the world was she going to do? "Adam, your temperature's a hundred and four," Kerry said, hoping he could hear her.

Slowly he lifted one lid. "So?"

"Do you think you should go to a hospital or something?"

His answer was rude and succinct. Kerry was convinced he wasn't going to expire just yet.

A noise woke her from a sound sleep, and Kerry jumped, disoriented, her arm groping for the bedside lamp. Her fingers smashed into something hard and round that rolled to the floor and crashed. Where in the world was she?

Memory washed over her in a cold wave. Adam! Stumbling to her feet, she switched on the kitchen light. A yellow path of light revealed the piece of modern art that had smashed to smithereens against the edge of the table. She was lucky she hadn't cut her bare feet.

Low moans were issuing from down the hallway, causing her hair to stand on end. Scared, she ran like lightning to her bedroom door.

Moonlight striped the bed. Adam lay on his back, murmuring incoherently. Kerry touched his forehead. His skin was hot and blazing. The fever was still raging.

He suddenly clasped her hand and asked blankly, "Kerry?"

"I'm right here. Let me get a cold washcloth. You're burning up."

"I was dreaming," he murmured, turning over.

She returned to the linen closet, grabbed a washcloth, dunked it under cold water, wrung it out, then brought it to Adam. He was on his side and she gently lay a hand on his shoulder as she sank onto the edge of the bed. "Here," she said, turning him onto his back. She pressed the damp cloth to his forehead.

"Am I at your place?" he asked suddenly, sounding wide awake.

"Uh-huh. Don't you remember?"

In the ghostly light she could see that Adam's eyes were open. But she sensed that he wasn't as awake and clear-headed as he sounded. Moments later his eyelids flickered closed.

Carefully Kerry withdrew her hand, then gasped when his arm suddenly snaked around her waist, drawing her to him with surprising strength. "Don't leave," he commanded quietly.

Kerry felt the heat of his skin. She counted her heartbeats, listening to Adam's breathing, intensely aware of his hot skin through the thin sheath of her cotton nightgown. She suddenly felt self-conscious and wished she'd put on a robe first.

Grimacing, she waited excruciatingly long minutes. Her bedside clock made the only sound. Until she heard a contented purr. Tucked against Adam's side lay a small brown circle of fur. Problem had found a bedmate.

Slowly Adam's grip loosened to where she could extricate herself. He protested sleepily, but Kerry picked up a limp Problem and headed back to the living room. "You're out for the rest of the night," she told the cat, opening her front door.

Problem stretched, paused at the threshold, then trotted out to the windy night. Kerry returned to the couch where she lay tense and wary, her ears tuned to her bedroom.

It was nearly daylight before she fell asleep again. Exhausted, she was in the middle of a dream when she suddenly jerked wide awake, blinking in the gray light of morning.

There was no sound from the bedroom. Not a sound at all. She strained her ears. No, there was a scraping noise of some kind. Could Problem have gotten back in?

Throwing off her covers, she stumbled down the hallway—straight into a warm, hard human body! She screamed.

"Kerry?" Adam's voice was full of confusion.

"Adam! What are you doing out of bed? You scared the life out of me!"

"Why're you here?" he mumbled.

She realized, then, that he was standing in front of her stark naked. Kerry was momentarily speechless. There was something so overpowering about Adam! Averting her eyes, she said unsteadily, "You're at my place, remember?"

"The dinner."

Gently she turned him back in the direction of her bedroom. "We'll settle up about that later," she said with a smile.

Kerry waited until he was back under the covers, flopped onto his stomach. She heard his teeth chattering and dragged the comforter over him once more. "You're going to owe me for this. Just remember that."

"Kerry" he asked as she turned to leave.

"What?" When he didn't immediately answer, she asked quickly, "Are you okay?"

"Hell, no. I feel terrible," he grumbled.

Kerry grinned. "What were you doing in the hall?"

He sighed. "I wanted a glass of water."

"Well, I'll get you one. Just a minute."

Kerry flipped on the hallway light and wandered into the kitchen to pour him a glass of water. She brought it back to the bedroom only to find Adam asleep again. Placing the glass on the nightstand, she turned off the light, so tired she could hardly see straight.

It was nearly afternoon before she awoke again. Too much worry and too little sleep had done her in. Peeking on her patient, she saw he was resting comfortably, so she took a quick shower and changed into her clothes.

Marla called around one and asked how Adam was doing.

"Better," Kerry assured her. "Although he's just lying around and not doing anything."

Her sister laughed. "At least you got out of cooking him dinner."

"Do you have any idea how much food I have at this place? Why don't you come over and take some home for you and James and the kids?"

"Maybe I will. James is taking the twins to the park later this afternoon so I could drop by then. I don't imagine you want two screaming three-year-olds in your apartment with Adam there."

"Uh, no." Kerry chuckled.

"I have to admit, I'm curious to see Adam again," Marla revealed a little wistfully.

"He's not exactly at top form."

"That's okay. See you later."

Marla arrived at four almost to the minute. Kerry was a little reluctant to take her down the hall for a peek at Adam. It seemed like a terrible invasion of privacy, and though Marla's interest was perfectly harmless, it bothered Kerry in a way she couldn't explain.

Marla stood at the door and looked at Adam who was flat on his stomach, his arms stretched out straight across the bed, wrists dangling over the edges. Kerry had replaced the comforter so it covered him to the waist, but it had slipped a bit and the dusky curve of his spine was visible.

"Wow," said Marla as Kerry closed the door. Her blue eyes glinted with mischief. "Hubba, hubba."

"Oh, shut up," Kerry said good-naturedly, pushing her back toward the kitchen. She handed her a cardboard box filled with bowls of food. "Enjoy."

"You, too," Marla said with extra meaning. Kerry just shook her head.

The rest of the day passed slowly and quietly. Kerry had brought home some paperwork from the office, but she couldn't keep her mind on it. She watched TV, stood on her small balcony and waited while night fell, tried to read a novel and finally went back to her paperwork. Her mother phoned around eight. The conversation was a little strained, as they all were. Though Kerry had sided with her mother during the divorce, their closeness had vanished somewhat when she'd remarried. Kerry's stepfather was a widower with three teenage children. They kept her mother too busy to worry too much about her grown-up daughters.

By the time Kerry was tired enough to go to bed it was nearly midnight, and she realized she was starved. She thought about asking Adam if he wanted something to eat, then decided if he was hungry, he'd say so.

She looked in on him once more, just before she changed into her nightgown and retired to the couch. There was a touching vulnerability about him in sleep that she'd never noticed before. The sweep of his lashes was seductive against such hard masculine cheeks, and his mouth was just plain sexy.

Good old Adam, she thought with a smile, climbing beneath the couch blanket.

It was pitch black when Kerry opened her eyes. Her limbs were cramped and her pillow had slipped from beneath her head. Sitting up, she stretched her arms over her head.

What time was it? Padding into the kitchen, she checked the oven clock—3:00 a.m.! Good grief, if she didn't get back on schedule she'd be hard pressed to get to work in time on Monday.

Kerry was wrapping the blanket around her again when she heard a low moaning. This wasn't the restless cry of the night before. This was pain.

She flung off her covers and hurried down the hall to the bedroom. Adam lay on his stomach, shivering again. "Adam?" she asked softly, concerned, swiftly crossing the carpet.

His answer was a groan. "Kerry? God..."

"Are you worse?" she asked, hovering by the side of the bed. "You can't be worse!"

"Stay with me. Please." His voice was muffled by the pillow.

Kerry hesitated, alarmed. Stay with him? Here? Her gaze skated around the room. There was no chair in her bedroom, only the bed. But she didn't want to leave him if his condition was worsening. She supposed she could sleep on the floor if she had to.

"Um . . . just let me get my blanket and pillow," she said.

He flung himself onto his back. "Just sleep with me."

She had difficulty believing her ears, and she stared through the darkness into his face. His eyes were closed. Did he know what he was saying?

"Really, Adam, I don't think I'd feel comfortable in bed with you," she said, laughing a little.

She jumped when his fingers wrapped around her knee, drawing her forward. She had to brace herself with her hands on his chest to keep from tumbling onto him. Unfortunately the pressure caused him to cough, and as she tried to struggle upward she lost her balance completely, sprawling across his chest.

"Sorry," she apologized swiftly, bracing herself on her arms.

"Don't leave," he begged.

His arms were locked around her. Kerry was wide awake now. "Adam, I can't sleep with you."

"Oh, come on, Kerry. I'm too sick to discover whether you're still a virgin, believe me. Just sleep with me."

Kerry narrowed her eyes. This was quite a speech from someone who was supposed to be running a hundred and four degree temperature! "I could never fall asleep," she protested, conscious of the hard masculine angles of his body beneath hers.

"Try it." He slowly released his arms and slid her to the side of the bed next to him, sighing as if the effort had been too much for him.

Kerry lay atop the covers, as stiff as a board. Adam turned on his side. He was so supremely unconcerned it was laughable. And what did that comment about her virginity mean? She was thoroughly annoyed with him.

"This is nuts," she muttered aloud, angry at herself for being manipulated. His even breathing only infuriated her further.

So why don't you just get up and go back to the couch?

Kerry closed her ears to the answer simmering in her subconscious. It made sense that she wouldn't want to sleep on her cramped sofa, didn't it? She didn't want to leave him alone anyway. He was sick and he needed her help.

And he was warm and alive and undeniable attractive.

Swearing under her breath, she rolled the comforter around her, refusing the temptation of curling around Adam's sinewy skin. She laughed softly at herself and her own dismal attempts to make this situation seem reasonable.

"Good night, Adam," she said.

His answer was a deep snore that she thought might be faked.

It was the heat that awakened her the last time. The heat that had dampened her skin with a sheen of sweat. And the unreasonable feeling that her legs were tied down by weights. She couldn't move. Her lids felt heavy, too, and she struggled to open her eyes, blinking several times to chase away the cobwebs of sleep.

A very masculine arm was wrapped around her chest just beneath her breasts, and a hair-roughened leg was thrown possessively across hers. Adam lay snuggled against her back, his face buried in her hair, his naked body surrounding hers like a second skin.

Her first thought was quite calm: how had they gotten under the covers together? Her second was less rational: did she have anything on?

A peek downward reminded her that she had on her nightgown. A minor relief.

Kerry lay perfectly still, too bemused to move. The situation was loaded with humor, and she could just imagine the mileage Adam would get out of this one. She inwardly groaned at the thought of him saying to any future male she might introduce him to, "Did I tell you about the time Kerry and I slept together...?"

As her senses cleared she realized something else. Adam's skin was damp. Not from sweat, from water. He'd gotten up and taken a shower, for crying out loud! And that was why her skin was moist, too.

So that was how we ended up under the comforter together. Kerry frowned. But then that meant he'd purposely climbed back into bed with her without a stitch on.

Her jaw tightened. The drip, drip, drip of the shower mocked her. What in the world did he think he was doing?

She shifted one leg, filled with injustice at the casual way he presumed on their relationship, then gasped as his grip around her suddenly tightened.

"Where are you going?" he asked in a far from sleepy voice.

His low tones, so close to her ear, sent a tingle down her spine. Goose bumps rose on her flesh. "I've got things to do."

"It's early yet. Barely five-thirty."

"You took a shower," she accused.

"Don't you think I needed one?"

"You should have told me!" she said angrily.

"Why? Did you want one, too? If I'd known, I would have woken you up."

Kerry sucked in a breath, sure she'd been duped. "Adam..." she warned.

"What?" Amusement threaded his voice.

"You're well, aren't you?"

"Well enough," he admitted, shifting closer. His fingers were hard through the sheerness of her nightgown and so close to her breasts that she didn't trust herself to draw a breath.

It didn't help when she felt the brush of his lips across her shoulder. Her skin quivered. She tried to jerk free, but Adam was ready for her and succeeded in flipping her onto her back, pinning her arms down and staring at her with ill-concealed amusement.

"What the hell do you think you're doing?" Kerry challenged through her teeth.

"This situation has interesting possibilities, don't you think?"

"You begged me to sleep with you!" she sputtered, aghast. "It wasn't my idea."

To her horror, he leaned over and placed a kiss at the corner of her mouth. "That's true, but then I never dreamed you'd say yes."

"Adam, for God's sake," Kerry protested weakly, turning her chin away.

A part of her sensed he was teasing; he wasn't really serious. But the situation was fraught with pitfalls. Good Lord, she could actually feel a part of herself respond. If Adam ever knew...

She tired to twist away from his marauding mouth, and was infuriated by his deep laughter. Her eyes were slits of outrage, and she would have dearly loved to wipe the mocking smile off his face.

"Get off me," she ordered icily.

"Are you really such a prude? I thought you were going to faint when you caught me in the buff."

"I thought *you* were out of your head!"

"Not that out of my head. Do you have any idea what you look like in that nightgown?"

"Let go of me or I'll scream."

He grinned hugely. "You're too much."

Since anything she said was used at her expense, Kerry subsided into stony silence. She glared at him, and he returned her stare through eyes that dared her to continue making a fool of herself.

The only sound was their breathing, hers light and fast, his even and steady. Kerry could feel every inch of him and through her dazed disbelief, she felt desire creep into her veins. Her breath caught in the back of her throat. This can't be happening, she thought anxiously.

Adam was too perceptive by far. He seemed to sense the change in her even before she did, and stared down at her in a way that made her mouth go dry. Her heart began pounding.

"Kerry?" he asked softly.

She felt him tensing, responding to whatever he could read in her face. For one split second she froze. It was all the invitation he needed. This time when he kissed her his mouth covered hers possessively, suffocatingly. Her body trembled beneath him. His heartbeat was heavy and deep and rang in her ears. His skin was hot and smooth and Kerry's fingers, clenched in protest against his chest, felt the crisp hairs on his skin.

And then his tongue entered her mouth, wet and demanding, stabbing and flicking against her own. Kerry's head spun. Her limbs turned to water. Her palms flattened against his skin. She wanted him so much it hurt.

"Kerry," he murmured breathlessly.

In her mind's eye she saw that silver stream of champagne. The laughter. The kisses. And she remembered Ryan. The way he whispered her name with such longing.

She thrust with all her strength, surprising him as she pushed him away. Scrambling off the bed, she wrapped her arms around her waist, glaring down at him in trembling outrage.

"You tricked me! I thought you were really sick last night!"

Adam's gaze was thoughtful. Kerry's pulse beat in her ears. Slowly, with lithe animal grace, he stretched out on his back and propped his arms behind his head. "You want me," he said bluntly, his lids lowered seductively.

Kerry's jaw dropped.

With charming immodesty, he flipped back part of the covers in silent invitation. "You should have said so before," he said conversationally. "We've wasted a lot of time."

"Go to hell!"

"Come on, Kerry. Don't fight it. It's bigger than both of us."

She pointed a finger at him. "Get up. Get dressed. And get out!"

"I'm already up," he said innocently.

Kerry backed out of the room, nearly tripping in her haste. She slammed the door behind her, then stood staring at it in numb surprise. *Adam* said that?

The door swung open so abruptly that she gasped. She stepped backward only to have Adam grab her arm and drag her forward. Her mind instinctively filled with vicious ways to thwart him, but before she could put thought to action, he warned, "Whoa, Kerry, don't even think it. Now listen. I was just joking, okay? For heaven's sake don't get all panicky. I'm not going to do anything to you!"

Belatedly she realized the towel was tucked firmly in place around his lean hips.

"I'm sorry I joked around," Adam said. "I didn't know you'd be so Victorian about the whole thing. Where's your sense of humor, Kerry?"

"Let go of me."

He stared down at her, looking like some kind of rugged masculine god. Two day's growth of beard darkened his jawline, and his hair was curled lazily down his nape, still damp, silky smooth. "Kerry, what are you afraid of? It was good, wasn't it? That doesn't mean—"

"Shut up. Please. Adam." Kerry backed up, pulling her arms free.

"For God's sake, don't look at me like that. Even you can admit something happened in there between us."

"Nothing happened." Kerry's tone was unusually bitter. "You didn't seriously think I'd fall at your feet like the rest of your women, did you, Adam? You forget. I'm different from them.''

Now it was Adam's turn to be angry. His lashes narrowed and the look he swept over her nearly scorched her skin. ''Not so different.''

''You certainly have an inflated opinion of your own charms! Believe it or not, *I* don't find you irresistible!''

''Stop lying to yourself. Have you ever slept with anyone?'' he asked bluntly. ''Anyone at all? You act like you've never even seen a man naked before!''

Normally Kerry would have flayed him alive for such a personal comment, but her composure was already shredded beyond redemption. Unable to cope, she simply turned and headed to the kitchen. He was right on her heels.

''Hey.'' He grabbed her arm and she shook him off. He swore violently. ''When the hell did you get so sensitive?''

Kerry swept up the neatly stacked pile of clothes and thrust it into his arms. She searched her mind for some killing remark, but was distracted by the deep circles under his eyes and the way one hand was propped against the wall, as if his legs weren't entirely trustworthy. He's still not well, she thought with a pang.

''I'm sorry,'' she said woodenly. ''You're not well.''

He snorted. ''Well enough.''

Kerry was beginning to feel really stupid. What had ever possessed her? She should have never climbed into bed with him. Already their past relationship was on rocky ground. ''I don't want things to change between us. That's all.''

''They haven't.'' His gaze swept over her drawn face. ''Yet.''

Before Kerry could remark on that, a racking cough swept his lean frame.

"You should still be in bed."

"I'm fine," was his short reply.

He chose the bathroom to dress in, and Kerry scurried to the bedroom. She yanked out her rather tattered chenille bathrobe and tied it around her waist. Now that Adam was out of sight, she had a chance to worry about what she looked like. A glance in the mirror made her groan. Her hair stuck out all over, as wild as a witch's, and without a shred of makeup on she looked about ten years old.

Dragging a brush through her hair, she only succeeded in making the black strands crackle and fly with static electricity. In the mirror's reflection she saw the tousled blankets on her bed. Memory washed over her in a wave of incredulity. She had slept in the same bed with Adam. *Adam*. She had let him kiss her. She'd felt a storm of emotion she'd never felt before—and that she never wanted to feel again!

She knew that if she'd let him, he would have made love to her. No questions asked.

The door to the bathroom opened and Kerry jumped. But Adam turned in the other direction, his long strides taking him toward the kitchen. "Kerry?" he called.

Gathering her composure, she tugged once more on the cinch of her robe. She headed toward his voice and found him sliding his feet into water-stiffened leather running shoes. He'd tossed on his shirt but it was still unbuttoned, giving her an ample view of his chest and stomach. His jeans hugged his hips with devastating closeness.

He stood, his gaze taking in Kerry's robe. Before she could say anything, he spoke. "I've got to get home and check on some things."

"I'm not kidding, Adam. You should still be in bed. Besides, it's barely six o'clock," Kerry reminded him.

"If I stay here, Kerry, the situation will only deteriorate," he said in a calm voice.

Her pulse fluttered alarmingly. His blue-gray eyes were all knowing. She would never be able to deny she'd responded to him because he knew! *He knew!*

When she didn't answer, Adam let himself out the front door. He hesitated just outside and demanded, "Just what did that crack about 'all my women' mean?"

"You know." Her tone was dry. "Your effect on the female gender is well-documented."

"But I don't have an effect on you, right?"

She blushed, knowing he could see through her lies, but was unable to tell the truth. "Right."

"What would it take to get it to work on you?" he asked casually.

Kerry slowly shook her head from side to side, warning him with her eyes that she wouldn't play such a dangerous game.

"You haven't changed much, Kerry," he said softly. "But I have. And I'm not going to let you get away with this much longer."

Kerry stared after him, alarmed and a little breathless at his threat. Now what did that mean?

"See you Monday," he said, closing the door behind him. He made it sound like doomsday.

Chapter Eight

...No, I'm not going to say I told you so. I'm genuinely sorry you and Jenny didn't make it. But, Adam, you always pick the wrong type of woman. You're too smart to make the same mistakes over and over again, but you do anyway. Is that an "I told you so"? Maybe it is! Oh, well, next time you're in Seattle, I'll buy you a beer and tell you all your faults. Until then, be good. Or at least be careful.

Love, Kerry

Adam smoothed out the crumpled letter, his lips twisting into a smile. He'd found it in a box of junk he hadn't unpacked yet. Kerry had written it soon after his divorce, but he'd never written back. He couldn't remember why now, but it had seemed important at the time.

There were other forgotten memories in the box. An old photograph album. He flipped it open and scanned pictures from grade school and high school and college. There were some shots of his wedding, too, though most of those pictures were in a separate album that Jenny had taken when she'd left. He stared hard at Jenny and tried to remember what he'd found so compelling about her.

He stopped over one photo. He and Kerry were dancing at the reception and he was kissing her. It was clear he was laughing, but she looked uncomfortable and annoyed. It also reminded him of kissing her in her bed yesterday morning and a prickle of awareness slid over his skin.

Plucking the photo from the album, he suddenly remembered another picture. He set the box on the edge of his bed and searched through the rest of his boyhood junk: old soccer trophies from the fourth grade, baseball cards, a card signed by all his buddies after he broke his arm and had to miss the end of the season soccer party. At the bottom of the box, smudged by years of neglect was the photograph he was looking for: he and Kerry in her bathroom after that fight on the path outside Brentwood Elementary. His eyes were practically swollen shut; Kerry didn't look much better. Her face was putty and her black hair was dusty gray and wild. Their arms were around each other and their chins were both lifted up defiantly, daring the viewer to take his best shot.

Adam slipped the two pictures into his wallet. Kerry would get a kick out of them, he thought, smiling. His smile slowly faded as he remembered her in his arms.

For a few moments he'd lost his head, almost forgetting he was with Kerry. But now, by God, he was fully aware. Kerry. He'd wanted her as long as he could remember. He'd settled for friendship, but it had only been because of her rejection, and now, *now*, with the memory of her limbs stirring beneath his, the taste of her mouth on his tongue, the light, fast pounding of her heart....

Adam shook his head. These kinds of thoughts were counterproductive. He quickly finished dressing, then grimaced at the sight of his reflection in the mirrored closet doors. He looked like hell. The flu hadn't quite given up the ship yet.

After glancing at the clock on his dresser, Adam strode down the condo's thickly carpeted hallway. It was early, but that was okay. He wanted to get to work before Kerry. Grabbing his jacket and briefcase, he headed down the front steps of his home to the private garage where his car waited.

It was another overcast day, typical of Seattle, but the clouds were high and light, promising better weather. June was only two days away. Summer was fast approaching, and Adam was suddenly deeply glad he was back in Seattle.

He had to unlock the doors to the office: he was the first one there. He walked straight to Kerry's office, flipped on the lights and looked around. Inhaling, he was convinced he could smell her soft, light scent. God, what was it about her that stirred him up? He'd known her for years! Yet she was a fire in his blood, and he knew without a doubt that he would never get over her until he doused those flames. He wanted to sleep with her and soon and to hell with what happened afterward.

Growling, he propped himself against her credenza and crossed his ankles, his palms flat on the smooth wood. He frowned out the window to the gray shadowed city outside. He could scarcely remember a time before Kerry wasn't a big part of his life. He'd been attracted to her even since high school. Even when there were other women in his life, she haunted his thoughts.

And now he sensed the time was right to take their relationship a step further. If only Kerry weren't so reluctant. She acted scared to death! Her body responded all right—he hadn't mistaken that—but she was nearly hysterical about keeping him at arm's length. Why? Was she that afraid of ruining their friendship? Or was it something else?

He remembered kissing her that time at the drive-in and almost laughed. He'd been so green! And selfish. The last thing she'd had on her mind was necking, but it was only years later, with the benefit of hindsight, that he could really look at her reaction objectively. He'd taken her rejection at face value and had purposely buried his attraction to her, believing it gone forever. But it had only been simmering, waiting for another opportunity.

That opportunity was now. They were working together. Neither one of them was involved with someone else. They liked each other. No matter what had taken place in the past, he and Kerry were now older and wiser, and *ready*, he reasoned firmly, to break new ground.

He just had to convince her of that.

Adam pulled out the photographs, looking at them in turn. He didn't kid himself that he was in love with Kerry. He cared about her as much, or more, than any other woman in his life. He cared about her more than he'd ever cared about Jenny, he realized now. But his desire for her was merely a passing thing. As with any other woman. He just had to get her out of his system, that was all.

And then . . . ?

He and Kerry had been friends long enough that taking their relationship a step further shouldn't change anything. They were both adults. They had deep feelings for each other. There was nothing to worry about. Nothing at all.

Footsteps sounded in the outer reception room. He could hear Rachel talking to someone else. Ron probably. Adam grimaced. He was going to have to make some decisions about him soon. The guy had a chip on his shoulder the size of Gibraltar, and it didn't look as if anything anyone said or did would knock it off.

"I'll leave a message for her," Rachel was saying. "But she's got a meeting with Mr. Marsden this morning and I don't know how long it'll last."

Ron swore fiercely and stalked down the hall.

"I'll tell her what you said," Rachel sang out as she walked into Kerry's office. Adam didn't have time to alert her to his presence. She stepped through Kerry's door totally unsuspecting and when she saw him standing there she shrieked to holy heaven.

"Mr. Shard!"

"Sorry, Rachel. I didn't mean to scare you." Now how was he going to explain this? "I was just waiting for Kerry," he added lamely.

"Kerry called and said she'd be a few minutes late."

"I'll wait."

The smile that curved her lips was knowing, and Adam felt impatient. He stifled the urge to tell her he and Kerry were just longtime friends. Besides, after the thoughts he'd been having lately, he intended for that status to change.

Rachel set Ron's message squarely in the center of Kerry's desktop. Glancing Adam's way, she asked, "Is there anything I can get you? Some coffee? Or tea?"

"Coffee would be great."

Her hips swayed from side to side as she left. Adam smiled to himself. Was that for his benefit? No matter what Kerry thought, he was not interested in office liaisons. They were too complicated, took too much energy and more often than not ended in disaster.

But Kerry, my love, you're a special case.

He heard her rapid footsteps a few moments later but Rachel appeared first, slipping through Kerry's door and crossing her carpet in slow footsteps, careful not to spill a drop of coffee in the steaming cup she held out to him.

"Look out, it's really hot," she said, turning the cup around for him to grab the handle. Her fingers grazed his as they made the transfer.

"Thanks."

Kerry walked in at that moment. Her gaze centered briefly on their hands. "Well, hi, guys," she said, tossing her briefcase on a chair. She studiously avoided Adam's eyes.

"Morning, Kerry," Adam answered lazily. He felt a rush of longing so intense it startled him. She wore a dress today, moss-green and soft-looking, with sleeves that stopped just below her elbow. A small gold watch with a tiny dangling chain encircled her left wrist. He was mesmerized by that touch of femininity to an otherwise very businesslike appearance. He wanted to walk up behind her and slide his arms around her waist.

"I was just bringing Adam some coffee," Rachel said brightly.

"So I see." Kerry's tone was neutral.

"There's a note from Ron on your desk," she said, taking her cue and heading for the door.

"Oh, joy."

As soon as Rachel left, the temperature seemed to drop a few degrees. Kerry was doing her damnedest to avoid him.

"I've been waiting for you," Adam remarked casually as Kerry picked up the note and read it.

"Mmm?"

"We, um, left on strange terms the other morning." When she didn't answer and didn't act as if she ever planned on answering, he asked dryly, "Aren't you even concerned about my health?"

She glanced up swiftly, her hazel eyes frankly assessing, dark brows arched. "You look fine to me."

"Now that's a lie. I took a look at myself before I came. But since you're so concerned, yes, I do feel better. I should be a hundred percent by tomorrow."

Kerry nodded, her gaze sliding away. Her black hair had been tamed by two clips holding it away from her face. "Was there something else?" she asked when the seconds crawled by and he didn't speak again.

"You're trying to shut me out," he answered softly. "I'm here to tell you, it's not going to work."

A flush crept over her skin, tinting her cheeks a becoming pink. "I don't know what you're talking about."

"You know exactly what I'm talking about."

"Adam, leave me alone. Ron wants to see me, and I've got a meeting with your friend, Marsden, in fifteen minutes."

"Have you talked to Marsden yet?" Adam asked curiously.

"As a matter of fact, I talked to him this morning. I called the office to say I was running late and Rachel told me he'd phoned. So I called him from home." Her brow furrowed. "Adam, he wants to divest himself of all his real estate holdings and become more liquid. I'm going to have my hands full trying to talk him out of it since now is not the time to sell. I thought he was supposed to be conservative. What is this, some kind of test?"

"He's probably pulling your leg."

Her eyes flashed. "Thank you, Adam. That's just what I need. A client who wants to play games."

"He's just breaking the ice. Relax, Kerry. He's teasing."

"Well, he sounded damn serious to me! And it's not something to joke about anyway."

"Good God, woman. Where's your sense of humor?" Adam laughed.

Kerry clamped her lips together. "That's the second time you've asked me that. Don't you think it's revealing that I lose my sense of humor every time I'm around you!"

He moved toward her; he couldn't help himself. But she backed around the desk and glared at him. "I know Marsden's your friend, but I would appreciate it if you stopped acting like you and I have something going, okay?" she finished through her teeth.

Adam was taken aback. "What's Marsden got to do with you and me?"

Kerry regarded him coolly. "You told him you and I had a hot date on Friday! And that you spent the weekend with me. I grant you, that last part wasn't intentional, but you can see how it looks to Marsden!"

"I did not tell him I spent the weekend with you." Adam grew impatient. He hated overexplaining things. "I talked to him yesterday and told him I'd been sick. He'd been trying to reach me. He knows we're friends."

"That phrase is certainly getting overworked around here, isn't it?"

"You're making too much of this," he clipped out.

"And you're not helping by acting like we're seeing each other!"

For a brief moment he glimpsed behind her feminine armor and saw how frightened she was. "I wish we were seeing each other, Kerry. I'd like to start today."

"No." She stiffened.

"Relax, Kerry. Marsden does know we're friends. And for the record, he assumed I had a hot date Friday night, I didn't say that. When he found out it was with you, he probably just felt like teasing you. That's all."

Kerry was silent, her lips tight. Frustrated, Adam realized this little problem had only intensified her resolve to keep away from him. But he wasn't going to let her.

"Adam," she said seriously, regarding him with an intensity that totally derailed his concentration. "I'm happy you trust me with Mr. Marsden's account, but please don't undermine me. Every time you make some kind of remark about us, it only makes it worse."

Her stubbornness was enough to try a saint! Worse, it was wrapped up in rationale that he believed in himself! "I'm not undermining you, Kerry. Stop being so afraid."

"I'm not afraid!"

"You're petrified."

The look she sent him was blistering, but her lips quivered and gave her away. If Adam had been anywhere but where they were he would have pulled her into his arms and kissed her until they were both senseless.

"I want you, Kerry. And you want me. Why is that so damn hard to accept?"

The air escaped Kerry's lungs in a whoosh. Adam stood on the other side of her desk, but she felt suffocated by him. There was passion simmering in his eyes, making them seem more blue than gray. He was so intense it scared her. He was right. She *was* petrified! And she *did* want him!

Her gaze fell before his conviction. Her heart pumped hard and painful. She wished he would just leave.

"I've got to go," she said woodenly.

"I'll see you at the meeting."

"No!" Kerry's gaze jerked upward. "Let me handle this one by myself. Please. I don't want to be your mouthpiece. I've got a reputation in this business, too."

His mouth tightened perceptibly. "I know that."

"And I'm not going to have everyone looking at me out of the corner of their eyes and whispering!"

"For God's sake, Kerry, is this because of the weekend?" he demanded. "No one knows that you and I were . . . in bed together." His lips twisted humorously.

"Watch it, Adam," she warned.

He grinned disarmingly. "I understand friends make the best kinds of lovers."

"I don't want you as a lover," Kerry said succinctly. "This conversation is getting way out of hand." She walked around the desk and stooped for her briefcase, every nerve attuned to the man behind her.

"Why did you choose investments?" he asked, taking her by surprise.

"What do you mean?" Kerry straightened.

"Why did you choose the same field I did?"

"Now what are you trying to suggest? That I picked investments because *you* did? Adam! That's beyond egotistical." Kerry was furious.

"Maybe." He shrugged. "But you and I are on the same track. We always have been. It's only a matter of time until we get together."

"No," she said unsteadily.

"God, Kerry."

"I'm sorry, Adam," she said distantly. "Don't take this wrong, but I'm not just not interested."

He laughed aloud. "The hell you're not, Kerry, my love! And I'm going to prove it to you."

"You'll fail."

"No, I won't."

She'd inadvertently given him a challenge and she could tell by the gleam in his eyes that he was ready and eager to meet it. She felt the first rush of panic freeze her blood. In a stab of honesty, she said, "I can't be with anyone I don't love and don't trust. Your friendship means everything to me, but I'd be a fool to want anything more."

"I'm going to the San Juan Islands this weekend," he said softly, as if he hadn't heard a word she'd uttered. "Come with me."

She'd never received the full force of Adam's sexual energy before, and she didn't like it one bit. That was not the kind of woman she was, and he should know it.

"Adam," she answered, picking up her briefcase from the chair. "Go straight to hell. Do not pass go, and do not collect two hundred dollars."

* * *

She was still steaming by the time John Marsden was shown into her office. In fact she was angrier now than she'd been during the fight with Adam. Just who did he think he was dealing with? She'd managed to thrust the memory of the weekend to the back of her mind; he should be able to do the same!

Was Adam crazy? Did he want to ruin the only lasting friendship she'd ever had?''

"Good morning, Miss Camden," John Marsden said graciously, fingering the pipe in his vest pocket. "Would it be too much of an inconvenience if I smoked?"

"No. Please. Go ahead."

"I suppose we ought to get right down to it, then," he said, eyeing her distracted state with interest.

Kerry nodded, drew a deep breath and looked him straight in the eye. "You said you want to sell most or all of your real estate holdings. I think that would be a big mistake right now. Your properties aren't the kind that are selling. You'd be better off holding on to them for a while."

He nodded. "What would you suggest?"

Kerry examined his face. He wasn't teasing now. She opened the file on his real estate holdings. For just a moment the memory of Adam in her bed superimposed itself on her pages. Damn. "If you really want to sell something, the waterfront property would go for a nice price. But it's so valuable it's bound to go up at a rate that outstrips most other investments."

He nodded again, thoughtfully. "Does Adam agree with you?"

"Actually, I'm not sure what Adam's feelings are," Kerry answered tightly.

Was that a smile hovering on the wily entrepreneur's lips? Kerry surveyed John Marsden suspiciously, but the gray-haired gentleman looked merely interested as he said, "Okay, let's go over it together."

"You've got yourself a handful there, Adam," Marsden said on a wheezing laugh. It was the only truly old quality about him, a chronic condition that actually owed more to Seattle's damp weather than age.

"You mean Kerry?" Adam asked mildly, pushing the elevator button for the lobby floor.

"Seems pretty headstrong to me. When I mentioned your name, her back went up so fast it made me chuckle." He chuckled again at the memory.

"Exactly how did my name come up?"

"I asked her if you agreed with her ideas."

"Ahhh." Adam rubbed his nose to hide his exasperation. He could just imagine how well that went over. "And what did she say?"

"What she said doesn't matter. What she meant was she thought your opinion was, er, nonessential." Marsden was thoroughly amused.

"I can imagine," said Adam dryly.

They walked through the main floor lobby and onto the street. It was drizzling and Marsden made a sound of disgust. "Damn weather," he muttered. "Might as well move to Arizona."

"You'd hate it," Adam said with a smile. "It's too nice and too hot."

"You're probably right."

A black and yellow cab waited at the curb. John Marsden absolutely detested driving. Bending down to open the door, he suddenly patted Adam's arm in commiseration. "Don't give up on her," he advised. "She'll come around."

"Who? Kerry? We've been friends for years."

"An excuse," he snorted. "My wife said the same thing. But I convinced her to marry me anyway."

Adam shook his head. "I'm not looking to get married again."

"You should be. If you want children while you're young enough to enjoy them, and a beautiful wife to keep you happy, you'd better start planning. Otherwise the years just pile up."

"I think I've got some time yet," he said dryly. "I'm not certain I'm cut out for marriage."

Marsden's glance was pitying. "Just because you made a mistake when you were young doesn't mean you'll do it again. And while we're on the subject, running off to San Francisco was a damn fool thing to do. What took you so long to come to your senses?"

"I had a business to take care of down there," Adam replied blandly.

"Huh? So where is it now? You sure moved back with no problem." He climbed into the cab and slammed the door before Adam could answer.

The old coot, Adam thought in exasperation. He'd moved back because the truth of the matter was most of his business came from the Seattle area. Carving a niche for himself in San Francisco had been a tough battle. He'd fought it and won. Sort of. But coming home had always been in the back of his mind, and it had proved easier than he'd ever dreamed possible.

Why had he stayed away for so long? Adam mulled that over as the elevator bore him skyward once more. Because of Jenny. He'd left his life with her behind him.

No regrets. No uncomfortable moments. A complete break.

Except, was she really the reason? The break-up had been terrible, draining, depressing and almost soul-consuming—for a while. But then it had been over. A weight of responsibility was lifted from his shoulders. He was free! So why had he run away?

Never one to delve too deeply into subconscious motivations that could only drive you crazy, Adam pushed to the back of his mind the niggling thought that he was on the verge of some ego-shattering conclusion. What did it matter anyway? He'd left. Now he was back.

Kerry dunked her teabag in her cup, flushed with success. John Marsden had turned out to be a pussy-cat! She'd laid out her strategy clearly and succinctly and expected him to haggle over every point. Instead he'd shrugged and said, "I think you're right. Let's leave the real estate and concentrate on the stocks. I've made a fortune but I might be too vulnerable now. What do you suggest?"

What do you suggest? Kerry could scarcely believe those words had come out of his mouth. And she'd suggested plenty. She didn't consider herself the most flamboyant or aggressive investment adviser, but her judgments were generally sound. If a client wanted to take a flyer on a speculative stock or piece of real estate, she always asked him how much he was willing to lose. Some investors were flagrant gamblers. Others were misers. John Marsden, the supposed conservative, was a little of both.

"Adam is looking for you," Rachel said from the open doorway.

Kerry grimaced as she tested her tea. She'd burned her tongue yesterday and didn't feel like doing a repeat performance. "Tell him I'm taking a break and gloating."

"Your meeting with Mr. Marsden went well?"

"Five stars."

"Oh, goody. This is the time for you to suggest you need your very own secretary. Someone responsible and personable. With years of experience." Rachel's hands were folded in prayer. She gazed beseechingly at Kerry. "Someone who doesn't want to work for Randy Ron anymore."

Kerry laughed. "I wouldn't have enough work for you by myself."

"Hey, I'm great at looking busy. I can shuffle papers with the best of them. And check out my harried look." Rachel sighed hugely and glanced around distractedly, biting on her lower lip.

"Adam won't be fooled."

"Speaking of Adam, you know he doesn't have a personal secretary. He's using Ellen, and she's already overloaded with Sam and Carver. If you don't have enough for me, maybe I could help out the boss man?"

"And who will Ron use?" Kerry asked dryly, sensing she was getting to the crux of Rachel's sudden interest in moving. Her complaints about Ron Tisdale had been relatively minor up until today. "He's going to need someone to be his secretary."

"Kay could do it," she said eagerly. "She likes Ron, and she's not all that busy. In fact, I kind of mentioned it to her, and she said she'd be more than happy to help him, too."

Rachel's blue eyes were wide with innocence. Normally Kerry got a kick out of her machinations, but this time she felt impatient. Ellen, whom Kerry had chosen to field Adam's calls and help with correspondence, was a wonderful right-hand woman for any C.E.O. or business owner. She was also forty-five with an equally wonderful husband and three teenage children. Rachel was twenty-four, single, with long legs generally surrounded by very short, yet tasteful, skirts.

Jealous? Kerry asked herself. Afraid Rachel might take your place in Adam's affections if you turn him down?

If you turn him down?

Kerry was astounded by her thoughts. She had no intention of getting involved with Adam. He was just restless and looking for someone new. Soon he'd stop this ridiculous chasing and get back to being her friend.

I want you. And you want me.

Kerry's pulse fluttered. Rachel was looking at her expectantly. "I'll mention it to Adam," she finally said.

"Thanks, Kerry. You're the greatest!"

Anytime, she thought dryly as Rachel practically did cartwheels out the door.

She sipped her tea, telling herself it was just as well. Let Rachel run interference between her and Adam. She sniffed. Go to the San Juans with him? For an entire weekend? She'd have to be out of her head!

"There you are," he said behind her, and Kerry jumped, nearly spilling her tea. "So how'd the meeting with Marsden go?"

Recovering herself, she said, "You walked him out. Didn't he tell you?"

"Actually he gave me advice on my love life," Adam drawled. "He wasn't all that specific about the meeting. But from the satisfied look on your face, it appears you're not as irritated with either him or me anymore. Went well, huh?''

''Did you tell him to agree with me?'' Kerry demanded suspiciously, her good mood evaporating. ''Because if you did, so help me I'll—''

''Kerry, for pete's sake. Marsden only listens to business advice if he thinks it's worthwhile. It wouldn't matter what you, or I, or even Almighty God said if he didn't agree!''

''You might have influenced him a little bit. I don't like being manipulated.''

Adam shook his head in disbelief. ''How in the world could you be manipulated? Your defense mechanisms are working twenty-five hours a day! I can barely get close enough to you to even look you in the eye. Marsden listened to you because your advice was sound. Period. And I, for one, am as happy as hell that he thinks you're the person to handle his account. It's one less problem.''

Kerry wasn't certain how to answer. Just what did he mean by all that? ''You're right about Marsden,'' she said stiffly. ''I'm being too sensitive and ridiculous.''

''And it just kills you to admit it, doesn't it?'' He grinned.

''Yes, as a matter of fact.''

He draped an arm familiarly over her shoulders, and Kerry had to force herself not to turn into a stone statue. She could smell his after-shave and feel the curve of his hip. ''The San Juans are out?''

She nodded.

''No chance you'll change your mind?''

She shook her head.

''I can be good,'' he said, and the thread of laughter in his voice didn't escape her.

"I'm sure you can," Kerry said dryly, sliding him a look. "But actually, I already have plans. Marla and I are taking her twins out Saturday afternoon." A small lie, but one she intended to make good on. "I can't back out now."

Adam slowly withdrew his arm. "In that case, how about dinner Saturday night?"

"Oh, Adam, don't you have something better to do? I mean, give it up. It's not going to get either of us anywhere. I want to stay friends, and you're just...messing everything up!"

"You're the one who acts like I'm some kind of deranged lady-killer. Relax, for God's sake. I want to be with you. I want your company. What's wrong with that?"

Kerry stared into his gray eyes. This close, she could see the streaks of blue that softened their intensity. A woman could drown in eyes like his. "I'm not sure. Give me time to figure it out."

"Leave Saturday night open. Please."

She took a sip of tea. Space. She needed more space, because he was driving her crazy and totally destroying her common sense. "Rachel wants to be your secretary. She asked me to ask you. Kay can fill in for Ron. Oh, God, Ron! He wanted to talk to me!" She made a move for the door, but Adam grabbed her arm.

"Ron can wait. Besides, what's all this got to do with the price of tea in China?"

"Is it all right if Rachel's your secretary?"

"Yes!" For once Adam looked as if he were at the end of his rope. "Why are you so scared of men, Kerry?" he demanded. "Or is it just me?"

Kerry opened her mouth, prepared to argue, but then she stopped short. "It's just you."

"The hell it is," he muttered, now thoroughly angry. To Kerry's shock, his hands cupped her face. She glanced anxiously toward the door.

"Adam!"

"You're not being honest, Kerry."

"All right! You make me feel things I don't want to feel! Yes! I'm attracted to you! Who wouldn't be?"

A look of triumph swept over his face.

"But I won't have an affair with you. Period. I'd be committing emotional suicide to trust my feelings to someone like you! So let me go, Adam. Please."

"I can't," he said seriously.

Kerry wrenched herself free and walked out of the room, heedless of the tea that sloshed over her hand and onto the carpet. She didn't feel anything but fear.

Chapter Nine

I made a mistake. I can't work for Adam. The Marsden account is fast becoming a major problem, and Ron is out for blood. It's just a matter of time before he confronts Adam and then the you-know-what will really hit the fan. And that's not the worst of it. Adam absolutely will not listen to me about the insanity of taking our relationship a step further! He insists we have dinner together tonight. I suppose I should be glad he's given up on the idea of running away to the San Juans together, but I don't trust what's on his mind....

Kerry shaded her eyes with one hand, watching Jason and Melissa riding around and around in a circle atop the Shetland ponies in the grocery store parking lot. The pungent scent of horse dung mixed with the equally powerful and more pleasant smells of cotton candy and popcorn. A hot-looking clown held a large bunch of silvery helium balloons in one hand. Somewhere to Kerry's left a child cried and screamed incessantly. Coming off a sugar high, she decided. She could relate. She felt miserable, tense and cranky herself.

Marla fussed in her purse. "Where's my lipstick?" she demanded irritably. She'd been irritable all afternoon. It was catching.

"You think someone here's going to notice your lips?"

Marla snorted at Kerry, her expression hidden behind a pair of expensive white sunglasses. A white and gold tube of lipstick mysteriously appeared in her hand. Carefully, Marla laid a thin sheen of frosted pink on her mouth.

Her younger sister had always been more fastidious about her looks than Kerry had. It was a fact of life, one that Kerry had long since ceased to wonder about. Marla was simply made that way, and it was okay. Kerry wore makeup, but if she forgot her lipstick, or to mascara her lashes, or apply blush to her cheeks, it didn't bother her much. She was what she was. Marla was the beauty; Kerry the smarter older sister.

Or so she'd like to believe up until Adam Shard had reappeared in her life a few weeks ago. Her lips twisted. Smart? Hah! If she was so smart she wouldn't be suffering sophomorish tingles of excitement every time she thought about tonight.

Kerry groaned aloud, hating herself.

"What's wrong?" asked Marla.

"Nothing."

"Oh, come on. You've been like a bear with a sore head all day."

"You haven't exactly been Miss Merry Sunshine yourself."

Marla wrinkled her nose in response.

Kerry squinted across the parking lot at Marla's twins, almost three years old and as alike as night and day. Jason was auburn like Marla; Melissa had straight brown hair like her father. Both of them held the reins so tightly you'd think they expected the Shetlands to suddenly break free and race toward the open prairie. Fat chance.

"I hope they're having a good time," Marla worried.

"The time of their lives."

"That sounded suspiciously sarcastic."

"No, I'm serious. If they're not having a great time, they're scared to death. It amounts to the same thing, I think."

The pony ride ended and Jason and Melissa were pried from their mounts. Jason wanted to get right back on.

"Go again! Go again! Go again! Horsey!" he cried.

"Not now, honey," said Marla, clasping his chubby hand. But not before he managed to knock Marla's sunglasses off her nose. They went flying toward the blacktop, bouncing hard, one bow breaking off with a snap.

The ride home was accomplished with Jason intermittently screaming for the horses and kicking at Melissa. Kerry sighed with relief as Marla pulled into her driveway.

The Courtenay home was a sprawling ranch with a triple-car garage and a back deck and yard to die for. Kerry helped unsnap the twins from their car seats and led them into the house.

"Forget what they tell you about the terrible twos,'' Marla advised an hour later when she'd finally put the kids down for their nap. "It's the threes that are killers,'' Marla added, kicking off her shoes and joining Kerry at the kitchen table.

"Mmm.'' Kerry pushed one of the glasses of iced-tea she'd poured while Marla made her last trip to the kids' bedroom toward her sister. She knew better than to offer any kind of comment. She didn't have children, so her advice would be scorned.

"Thanks. And thanks for helping with the kids. They wear me out totally.''

Marla pulled her sunglasses from her purse and gazed sadly at the broken bow. "I can't show these to James. He didn't want me to spend the money for them in the first place. I'll never hear the end of it.''

"Since when does James not buy you everything you want?'' Kerry asked lightly.

"Oh, I don't know. Since...'' She didn't finish. Instead she touched her fingertips to her lips as if to prevent words from spilling out that she might regret.

The hair on Kerry's skin lifted. "Marla?''

"It's just tough right now with the twins so demanding. It seems like we're both looking for excuses to escape. James is golfing with a friend of his today. The weather's perfect for it.''

"Are you going to cry?'' Kerry asked softly.

"Uh-uh.'' She shook her head slowly from side to side, her chin stiffening with resolve. "I'm going to toss out this iced-tea and have a glass of wine. How about you?'' She got up from the table, poured her drink in the sink and pulled out a bottle of wine from the refrigerator.

Kerry shrugged. "Sure, why not?" She sensed Marla really needed to relax. She was wound as tight as a spring. "Tell me what's really going on with you and James," she urged quietly once the glass was placed in front of her.

"Like I said before, we're not on the verge of divorce. It's nothing serious." Taking a deep breath, she smoothed back her hair, then shook her head. "We're just not communicating well these days. Enough about my problems. Tell me about Adam."

Kerry rolled her eyes. "Oh, Marla, you're a broken record!"

"You should have gone to the San Juans with him," she declared for the third time since noon. "Why are you being so stubborn?"

"I told you. I don't want to get involved with Adam."

"It's probably perfectly innocent."

Kerry choked on a laugh. "I may not be sophisticated around the opposite sex, but Adam has been very clear about his intentions."

"And why shouldn't he be?" she asked, switching tactics. "I mean, look at you. I'm surprised it took him this long to wake up."

"What are you talking about?" Kerry narrowed her lashes warningly.

"You got beautiful," said Marla with a bittersweet smile. "Mom always said you would, but I never wanted to believe it. I was always jealous."

"Oh, for heaven's sake."

"It's true. You're the only one who doesn't seem to notice. You can bet Adam notices, though." Marla swallowed deeply from her glass, then swirled the wine reflectively. "You're crazy not to take a chance with him. I would."

"You can take my place at dinner tonight, then," Kerry muttered sarcastically.

Marla's face broke into the first real grin of the day. "You *are* having dinner with him tonight, then? You haven't chickened out?"

"I don't know what I'm going to do," replied Kerry, exasperated. "Stop pushing."

"I just think you ought to be more daring, Kerry! What's the worst that could happen?"

"I could lose Adam's friendship, that's what!"

"So? Look what you could gain!"

Kerry closed her eyes, shook her head and groaned, at her wit's end when it came to her younger sister.

"You're thinking about it, aren't you?" Marla said, a little breathlessly. "I can tell you are!"

"All right, look. There's a small itsy-bitsy part of me that notices him that way, all right? But I've been burned before, and I'm not going to get burned again."

"Why not?"

"Why not?" Kerry repeated, aghast.

"Yeah, why not get burned again? At least it's living. Feeling! At least your eyes are open!"

Kerry was flabbergasted. This was where her philosophies and Marla's veered in opposite directions. "Because I don't want to, that's why! It wasn't great the first time I got dumped! Adam and I are working together now. This is not the time to do something stupid."

"If I could do something stupid, I would," Marla whispered in a voice suddenly shaking with pent-up emotion.

They were in far deeper waters than Kerry had realized. "What in the world's going on with you, Marla? Don't try to fob me off again."

She shook her head, working to bring herself under control. "I just feel...bad sometimes. I look at you and think what it would be like to be so happy and carefree."

"Carefree?" Kerry sputtered. That was the last word she'd ascribe to her situation!

"Yes, *carefree*. You've got a man who's only interested in you."

"Now there's a leap of the imagination. You obviously don't know Adam very well," Kerry objected dryly.

"I do know Adam. As a matter of fact, I talked to him this week."

"You did? When?" Kerry stared at her.

"When I called the office to talk to you. You weren't there, so I asked to talk to him."

Kerry was absolutely stunned. "So, what did you talk about?"

A smile spread across her lips. "You, actually. I promised you'd be there for dinner tonight."

Kerry pushed back her chair. "Marla, stay out of this. I'm warning you—"

"Oh, shut up, Kerry! It's you who makes all the noise about how unfaithful and irresponsible he is! Come on. Give him a chance! It's worth it."

"Do you hear yourself?" demanded Kerry. "You're telling me I should have an affair with my best friend!" She wanted to clap her hands over her ears and run out of the room. As much as she hated to admit it, the gist of Marla's arguments was exactly what she wanted to believe!

"That's exactly what I'm telling you. You'll waste the best part of your life trying to play it safe."

Kerry replied automatically, "Better safe than sorry."

"Better *sorry* than emotionally dead!" she retorted. "You be there for dinner tonight, Kerry. Otherwise you'll never forgive yourself."

It was seven-thirty by the time Kerry arrived back at her apartment. Her mind was on stall. Adam had asked her to be at his place by eight. She would never make it in time. She shouldn't go anyway. Oh, hell! She wanted to be with him!

Scurrying inside the door, Kerry barely took time to rip off her clothes before dashing into the shower. She scrubbed hard and fast, working the soap into a lather. She felt frustrated, and it wasn't all because of Adam. Marla's husband, James, had arrived home in a foul mood. He and Marla had barely spoken six words while Kerry had been there, and she'd felt a nerve-prickling sense of dèjá vu. Her own parents had acted much the same way during the worst moments of their marriage. It made her scared for Marla. Scared for Marla's children. Something was very wrong.

She towel-dried her hair, then blasted it with the blow-dryer. After tossing on her chenille robe, she padded out to the kitchen. Seven-fifty. She had to call Adam and tell him she'd be late.

That was when she saw the note that had been shoved beneath her door. She snatched it up, and read

I'll be back at eight.

Adam.

P.S. Get an answering machine.

"Yeah, right," Kerry muttered, but she recognized the spark of desire starting to smolder. Damn it all. What was she going to do?

With a growl of self-disgust she raced to the bedroom, brushing her still damp hair until it crackled. In the middle of applying some light makeup she noticed her hand was shaking. Swearing beneath her breath, she laid her palms flat on her dresser. Calm down. Count to ten. Don't be such an idiot.

But glancing at her reflection she saw the lights dancing in her eyes, turning ordinary hazel into something mysterious and inviting. Her cheeks were tinted a faint pink. Her mouth looked full and tremulous. Kerry pinched her lips together, appalled. Oh, my God. I'm crazy. I am completely out of my mind!

The doorbell chimed and she gasped.

"Just a minute! Oh, holy—" She bit off the epithet and hurried to the door.

She tugged her bathrobe close to her throat as she threw open the door. "I'm not ready," she told Adam. "You'll have to give me a few minutes."

"Whatever you say."

He was in faded black jeans and a soft cotton blue shirt with gathered sleeves that made him look a little like a buccaneer. The collar was open and offered Kerry an unrestrained view of his tanned throat and a tuft of crisp chest hairs.

"Just a minute," she muttered, hurrying back to the bedroom. She felt like an idiot! It's just Adam, she reminded herself as she pulled on a pair of white cotton pants. Just Adam.

She threw on an aqua tank top and covered it with a white blouson overblouse. Then she slipped on sandals, grabbed her bag and returned to the living room.

Adam was standing in the center of the room. Though she didn't want to, she noticed the way his jeans hung low on his hips, the breadth of his shoulders, the thickness of his hair.

"What are you frowning about?" he asked.

"You'd never understand." Kerry headed for the door. "Okay, Mr. Shard. Let's eat."

He took her to his condominium on the southeast shore of Lake Washington. Fleetingly Kerry thought about how successful Adam had become. He'd received a substantial inheritance when his parents died, but Kerry suspected he'd never touched that capital. His business had already been flourishing.

"You know, you could have been a terrible snob," she remarked as they walked up the front steps of his town house.

"Where'd that come from?" He produced a set of keys and unlocked the door.

"I was just remembering high school. All the girls chased after you because you were rich and good-looking."

"I wasn't rich." He swallowed back a laugh. "But I've always been good-looking."

"And humble," she added dryly. "Your family was upper middle class. Close enough." Kerry threw him a smile. "*Now* you're rich. And successful, too. It must be a terrible burden."

Adam studied her for a moment. "It's never cut any ice with you, though, has it?"

His condominium was elegance personified. Rosewood furniture gleamed. Fan-shaped, frosted-glass wall lamps were scattered along the entry hall and lighted the short corridor to the kitchen. A mahogany staircase curved to a gallery that surrounded the upper floor completely.

Kerry's gaze lifted to the sparkling brass and clear-glass chandelier lit by at least fifty flame-shaped bulbs. "Now that's subtle."

"Ostentation is a prerogative of the nouveau riche." He grinned, tossing his keys on a tiny, ornate table near the foot of the stairs.

"Who said that?" demanded Kerry, following Adam as he headed for the kitchen.

"I did. You should have seen my place in San Francisco. It was a hovel. I decided to live it up."

"Oh, my God. This is enough to make every proletarian hair on my body stand on end!" Kerry gazed out the windows to the sweeping view of Lake Washington. In the dying twilight the purple water moved, stretching toward the horizon. Faintly, against the opposite shore, she could see a ragged skyline of trees and lovely waterfront homes against a fading blue sky.

"Proletarian, eh?" Adam pulled a bottle of champagne from the refrigerator and uncorked it with two deft twists. He filled two glasses nearly to the brim and balanced them carefully in one hand as he swept up the bottle with his other hand. He walked to the dining room where Kerry stood transfixed, her gaze on the vast lake. "You look pretty successful and upper crust to me."

She gently took one glass from his strong fingers. Champagne. Her chest tightened involuntarily. "I've already had a glass of wine today. My headache's sure to start as soon as I take another sip."

"As long as you keep drinking, you're okay. It's when you stop that it hurts." He clinked his glass against hers. The soft musical ping sounded loud in the quiet room.

"If that's an excuse to get drunk, forget it. I've got too much to do tomorrow."

"Like what?"

"Like appease my new boss. He gave me a new account a few weeks ago, and it's hard to keep up."

Adam stopped, his glass halfway to his lips. "Is that right?"

"Oh, I'm not complaining," Kerry said hastily. "But some of the others around the office are."

"Ron." Adam grimaced. "Don't worry, I'm taking care of him."

Kerry didn't like the sound of that. "I was half joking, Adam. What do you mean?"

"Forget it. Come on. I've personally prepared a terrific meal for us and I want to serve it on the balcony before it gets completely dark."

Kerry was instantly distracted. "You cooked it?"

"I haven't lived alone all these years without learning a thing or two."

"You're putting me on!"

"You told me not to laugh at your cooking skills, don't laugh at mine. Sit down out there," he ordered, pointing toward the French doors and the balcony beyond. "I'll bring it to you."

Kerry managed to close her mouth and do as she was told. Her pulse raced. Her lungs felt tight. This was how it had been with Ryan, she remembered with a pang. Every minute had seemed so important. Only this, *this*, was a thousand times worse!

Her hands shook slightly as she sat down at the glass-topped table in front of a straw placemat flanked by gleaming gold and silver flatware with an engraved *S*.

She'd seen the flatware when she'd had dinner with Adam and his parents eons ago.

She heard the soft chime of the microwave timer and smelled luscious, tangy scents. "So you're into budget gourmets, too," she called. "Quick, nutritious and microwavable."

"Didn't I say I made this myself?" he threw back.

A minute later he brought out a large wicker tray. A glass bowl filled with a familiar looking asparagus salad sat on one side; two china plates on the other. Kerry frowned. Wasn't this just like the asparagus salad she'd ordered last week? The one the caterers had delivered?

Adam brought out two more bowls, a smug smile on his face. Kerry's eyes widened in disbelief. *That* was the chicken and apple dish! And that one was just like the vegetable medley she'd ordered!

"Well?" Adam asked, raising innocent brows as he refilled her champagne glass and sat down across from her.

A brisk gust off the water tossed her bangs in front of her eyes. Kerry's eyes danced, and she stared down at her plate, fighting back laughter.

"What do you think of my cooking?"

She thought of Marla's insistence that she have dinner with Adam. Marla had talked to Adam last week. She'd probably recommended the same caterer!

"You...really made...all this?" she managed to choke out.

"Worked my fingers to the bone."

"You shouldn't have."

"Is there something wrong?" Adam demanded, growing wise.

Kerry collapsed into laughter. She pressed her hand to her mouth and fought back choking gasps. Tears burned her eyes. She glanced at Adam.

Twisting his glass between his fingers, Adam grinned somewhat sheepishly. "You know, don't you?"

"God! Adam!" she gasped. "This is what I was going to serve *you*!"

His gaze was utterly blank.

"Did Marla suggest your caterer?"

His jaw dropped. "Marla!" he yelled in betrayal.

Kerry laughed harder, shaking.

"Your sister talked me into this caterer!" be bellowed. "She said he was the best in the business!"

"And told you to fob it off as your own cooking!" Kerry gasped. "That's what I was going to do until you got sick!"

"You were?"

"Yes!" Kerry screeched in delight.

Adam started to chuckle. The more he thought about it, the funnier it was. Finally he threw back his head and roared with laughter. "That does it! We've got to pay Marla back."

Remembering her sister's problems, Kerry slowly sobered. "Let's wait on that. She's so worn out by the twins she probably wouldn't appreciate it." Forking up some of the chicken dish, Kerry added around a mouthful of food, "This is good, though. I should know. I've eaten enough of it."

"Serves you right for trying to trick me."

The corners of his eyes creased with humor. He lifted his glass to her in a salute, and Kerry noticed the sensual curve of his mouth. Her throat tightened uncomfortably. There were qualities Adam possessed that she truly loved. He was the kind of man who was easy to fall in love with. If she were willing to risk her heart, she would do as Marla suggested and fall into a relationship with him with her eyes wide open.

He met her gaze, his expression turning serious. In the flash of a heartbeat the mood changed. Goose bumps rose on Kerry's flesh. She attacked the meal with an energy and appetite she didn't feel, then ended up pushing her plate aside, barely touched.

"More champagne?" Adam asked casually.

"No. Thanks."

A yellow jacket buzzed threateningly above the table. Adam swatted it away, then thrust his own plate to one side. "I think I need something stronger."

"Like what?" Kerry shoved back her chair and followed him into the kitchen. The last thing she wanted was another drink, but she felt nervous and restless. Afraid.

It was ridiculous.

Adam was reaching to a high cupboard above the tile counter, his shirt straining against his shoulders. "How about brandy?"

The pesky yellow jacket shot into the kitchen, buzzing between Adam and Kerry. Kerry involuntarily stepped backward, then clamped her hand to her mouth in horror as the bee landed on Adam's shoulder and walked toward his collar.

"Don't move!" she commanded. "The yellow jacket's on your back!"

Adam turned to stone. Kerry swept her hand across his collar, then shrieked, "Oh, my God. Adam, I knocked him inside your shirt!"

"What?"

Adam was unbuttoning the front of his shirt as fast as he could. Without thinking, Kerry yanked the sleeves down his shoulders, turning back the fabric. The yellow jacket appeared, struggling in the folds of cloth. Kerry jerked her head backward as the bee zoomed toward her, before zigzagging toward the other room.

"Well," Adam bit out, twisting his neck.

His back was frozen, his arms, still entrapped in his sleeves, were at his sides. Every muscle of his back was taut and rigid. Kerry stared at the smooth planes of skin. There was strength in the definition of each muscle, a sinewy power that was fascinating, irresistible.

"Damn it all, Kerry," he said with forced patience. "Where's the yellow jacket?"

She let go of his shirt, suddenly aware of how warm his skin was, how springy and vital the back of his hair. "It's gone. It's okay."

Adam slowly turned to face her. "You're sure?" he asked suspiciously.

She nodded, gesturing vaguely toward the French doors, feeling slightly faint. "It headed that way."

The hair on his chest arrowed downward, dark but not heavy. Kerry fixed her gaze on the base of his throat. She swallowed hard.

At first Adam was too distracted to notice Kerry's odd silence. But when he looked into her eyes they shone with naked need. Desire flamed through him even though he didn't trust what he saw. He'd wanted her too long and too badly to believe the truth even when it stared out at him from the shadowed depths of wide hazel eyes.

"Kerry?" he asked, lifting her chin with one finger, feeling her skin quiver beneath his hands.

Kerry's pulse quickened. She saw the swift change that crossed his face, heard his intake of breath.

"Help me get this off," he said thickly, holding out his wrists.

"Your . . . shirt?"

"Unbutton the cuffs."

"No, Adam." Kerry retreated, hand to her mouth. But his fingers clasped her free hand, dragging her toward him. Her palms connected with the warm skin of his chest, her fingernails curling into the crisp hairs.

She met his gaze and saw herself reflected in his eyes. Swallowing, she glanced down in bemusement at his cuffs. As if from a great distance, she saw herself undo the buttons. His hands and wrists were deeply tanned and masculine. She'd never noticed before.

He smelled good, too. Some kind of spicy cologne mixed with his own earthy scent. She filled her lungs, listening to his even breathing.

When the cuffs were free, Adam yanked the shirt completely off and tossed it heedlessly on the floor. Slowly he reached for her, his fingers spanning her waist.

"I can't do this," Kerry said, pulse tripping.

"Just let it happen." His fingers gathered the hem of her white blouson overblouse, ready to slide it up her torso and over her head.

"Adam . . ." she protested faintly.

She felt his hands warm against her rib cage, holding her just beneath her breasts, his thumbs stroking her skin. "Do you know I've wanted you for years?" he said in a possessive voice that sent a thrill down her spine.

"Adam . . . please . . ."

"But it was so clear what you thought of me when I kissed you that first time that I never had the courage to ask again."

He gently, firmly, pulled the blouson over her head and dropped it on top of his shirt. Kerry's nipples stood taut and erect against her aqua tank top. "You didn't want me then. You don't want me now," she said.

"If this isn't wanting," he countered soberly, "I don't know what it is."

Kerry's heart lurched, then lurched again when his hands caressed her shoulders and neck before cupping her face, his thumbs gliding softly over her quivering lips.

"You want me, too."

Kerry couldn't lie. She couldn't speak.

His head bent downward, his mouth finding her with unerring accuracy. His breath was sweetly scented and warm and his mouth tasted of champagne. Kerry's lashes fluttered closed in spite of herself. What was one kiss? One simple kiss.

The image of her father in another woman's arms flashed across her mind. She could see it as clearly as if it were a moment ago. She could feel the anguish as if it had just happened.

"Kerry," murmured Adam in a tortured voice.

The image vanished. This was now and this was *Adam*! All her good intentions dissolved beneath his passion. His arms tightened around her. Her breath expelled in a rush.

His mouth was hot and wet and demanding. Desire surged through her veins. She clung to him, shaken. His hand slid convulsively down her spine, molding her to him, pressing her thighs against the hard pressure of his. She couldn't breathe!

"Adam," she protested against his lips.

"Shhh. Don't say it." She felt one hand move toward her breast. Her skin tingled with expectation. She wanted to wriggle and move, aid him in touching her. She shifted instinctively, moaning with both fear and pleasure when his hard fingers finally possessed one heavy, quivery breast. Adam caressed her through the thin cotton shirt, his breath quickening. "I don't want to wait anymore," he urged tensely.

He kissed her again, his tongue making little stabbing forays into her mouth, a precursor to his intentions. Kerry went limp with emotion. She didn't want to fight. She wanted everything he had to give her.

Adam groaned at her submissiveness, clasping her so tightly her breath squeezed from her lungs. "Kerry," he murmured, his fingers tugging on the hem of her tank top, pulling it free of her pants.

The cool air against her skin was a dash of sanity. "Not here!" she cried wildly. "Not like this."

Adam's eyes were dark with suppressed emotion. "What do you mean?"

The memory of her father was too vivid. "Not here in the kitchen."

"Oh, Kerry. You little Puritan." Adam laughed beneath his breath, gathered her into his arms and swept her off her feet. She clung to him as he headed for the hallway. Pressing her face into his neck, she blocked out her fears for the future. Grab your happiness now. Take it. Stop playing it safe.

He set her on her feet inside his bedroom. The room was dim, lit only by the shadowy light spilling down the hall from the kitchen. Adam didn't give her a chance to change her mind. He pulled her hard against his chest, kissing her mouth, shaping it with his lips, thrusting his tongue inside in a way that made her head spin. She sensed his growing desire and responded instinctively, opening her mouth to allow him greater access, sliding her hands around his waist, digging her fingers into his muscled skin.

"Oh, God," he murmured, pulling the tank top over her head. When she stood in front of him, naked from the waist up, she nearly panicked from embarrassment. But then he said "Kerry" in a voice so full of need that she slid into his arms and pressed herself to his chest, squeezing her eyes closed.

His belt buckle dug into her soft skin. She glanced down and Adam slowly released her. And then she did the unthinkable. She unclasped his buckle, the soft jingle loud in the quiet room, then pulled down his zipper, the sound sending a sharp thrill through her body. The intimacy of it shocked her. She wanted him so badly she ached.

She stopped, unable to go on. She wanted to explore all of him, but she wasn't that brave. She was ridiculously inexperienced! At this crucial moment she couldn't even remember what it had been like with Ryan. Certainly nothing like this!

Adam took the initiative. His thumbs hooked the waistband of her cotton pants and pulled them and her panties to the floor in one swift movement. Kerry's first instinct was to cover herself. This hadn't been the way it was with Ryan!

Adam pulled her to him, his mouth near her ear. He kissed her softly over and over again, the touch so soft, the sound unbearably erotic.

"Tell me you want me," he whispered.

Kerry shook her head.

"I can feel you want me. Why won't you say it?"

"Because I'm afraid."

"Of what? Me?"

"Yes."

Adam made a sound of disbelief, pulling back to look into her face. "Why?"

Kerry inhaled shakily. He had no clue to her history. She'd never been able to tell him a single word. But if she were ever going to be honest, this was the time. "I had a bad relationship once. When I was in college."

"That weekend you came to see me."

His perception surprised her. "Just before that. And then . . . you told me you were going to marry Jenny."

"That was all a long time ago."

"It doesn't seem that long ago to me."

"It does to me," he assured her, sinking down on the edge of the bed, drawing her to him. Kerry was anxious to climb underneath the covers, but Adam had other ideas. He drew her down on the bed beside him.

"Help me," he said thickly.

Kerry reacted instinctively, rolling him onto his back, burying her face in his stomach. Adam sucked in a breath and laughed. "I said help me, don't kill me."

"What do you mean?" she asked blankly.

"With my pants." He pressed her hands against him and Kerry touched his hard hips. Her breath came in gasps. What she wanted to do, she didn't dare, but he seemed to be asking her to!

"I—"

"Go on." His chest rose and fell.

Kerry pulled off his clothes, examining his maleness with unabashed curiosity. She ran her hands over his skin and his intake of breath made her bold. She touched and caressed and suddenly found herself flat on her back, trapped hard against the mattress, Adam's hands encircling her wrists.

"I can't wait. I'm sorry," he muttered, thrusting against her.

Kerry's whole body stiffened. Now she remembered what it had been like with Ryan. She closed her eyes, but instead of feeling him force a passage she wasn't ready for, she felt the caress of Adam's hand, kneading her skin, demanding a response, his hips hard against hers but waiting.

Waves of heat pulsated throughout Kerry's body. She opened her mouth in amazement and met his marauding tongue. When he entered her, she was wet with desire. He thrust deeply inside her, and Kerry gasped.

"God, Kerry," he groaned, and within seconds she felt the sweet warmth of his climax.

He slumped against her, his mouth against her throat, tasting her skin. She lay quiet, more amazed than disappointed. Her body felt on fire, waiting. She was as tense as a bowstring. It hadn't happened for her, the magic everyone talked about, but she didn't care.

But when Adam suddenly shifted to rest his weight on his palms, she sucked in a shaking breath, dying for something she couldn't quite name.

"You see that?" he said, smiling. "You see what you do to me? I don't have any control."

"I bet you say that to all the girls."

"Don't be flip, Kerry. Not now."

Kerry pulled away from him, turning on her side, aching. She hadn't meant to be flip, but she needed to protect herself. His fingers grasped her chin, forcing her to meet his all-knowing eyes, but Kerry struggled away, embarrassed.

With supreme ease his hands grabbed one shoulder, pulling her onto her back. "Where do you think you're

going?'' he demanded, thwarting her continued efforts
to escape.

"Home."

"Home!" he snorted. "Not yet!"

"Adam, let me up," Kerry demanded.

"No." His mouth trailed alongside her neck, one
palm gently rubbing across her breast.

Kerry froze. "What are you doing?"

"Making love to you."

Softly, slowly, his fingers set her on fire. She moved
restlessly, moaning. When he joined with her a second
time she was hot and anxious. Shifting his weight, his
hips pushed hard against hers. Kerry sucked in a breath.
Desire ran like a molten river through her veins. "I blew
it," he murmured near her ear. "I'm sorry. This one's
for you."

Kerry stiffened beneath him.

"This time I promise to act like an adult," he added
thickly.

"Adam . . ."

But he was already moving within her, slowly,
rhythmically, tortuously sweet. This was outside Kerry's experience. She refused to relax, but he kept coax-
ing her, moving in a way that had her responding in
spite of herself. He bent his head to her breast and
sucked one nipple. Her head fell back and she moaned;
a tightness was coiling within her. Her fingers dug into
his shoulders. Sweat dampened her skin.

Pressure built. Her hands slid to his buttocks. His
mouth moved to hers, his tongue teasing her lips. She
pulled him to her.

"Good?" he muttered.

She nodded vigorously, crying out as the unbelievable happened and a wave of pure pleasure swept over her. She clasped him hard, shuddering, and was rewarded by his own groan of desire.

"God, Kerry, what do you do to me?" he said through his teeth just before the pulsating heat of his own response.

Chapter Ten

Adam Shard and Kerry Camnen, 9 yrs., after the big fight scene.
Kissing Kerry at my wedding, 1980.

Kerry read the backs of the photographs and smiled at Adam's third-grade penmanship in comparison to his college script. "Where did you find these?" she asked, tucking the sheet firmly around her breasts.

"Don't you dare tell me you've lost yours."

"No. I'm just not sure where they are. You spelled my name wrong."

"That's what I thought it was at first. Camnen. Give me a break, I was only nine."

As if to make sure she realized he was nine no longer, he nuzzled his lips against her ear. Kerry twisted her head away. "Stop it!" she said with a laugh, slapping at him ineffectively. She'd grown more self-conscious with each passing minute. Not so Adam. He'd flipped back the covers, turned on the bedside lamp, then walked buck naked down the hall, returning with his wallet and the two pictures. Now he lay stretched out beside her beneath the covers, one hand tenaciously curved around her stomach even though she held the covers around her like a straitjacket.

"I've been meaning to show them to you for days," Adam admitted, "but you haven't exactly been approachable. You've avoided me like the plague this week."

"I have not."

"Have too."

He grinned unabashedly. Kerry dragged her gaze away from him, upset that her heart still beat hot and heavy. What was the matter with her? She glanced back at the photo, smiling at the sight of herself and Adam at nine, bloodied and beaten and proud of it. But the second picture was of Adam kissing her at his wedding reception. Thinking of it made her skin feel cold. Champagne and passionate kisses.

"Where did you find them?" she asked.

"In an old box of memorabilia from high school and grade school. I also found the letter you wrote me after I left for San Francisco right after my divorce."

"Really? You kept it? Why?"

He smoothed back a strand of sweat-dampened hair from her forehead, following up with a light kiss. "Because you've been on my mind."

His soft seductive voice chased a shiver down her spine. But the mists of passion had receded and Kerry was once again thinking clearly. "I'm not sure this was a good idea," she said, plucking at the comforter.

His grip tightened possessively. "It was a great idea."

"I just don't want to lose your friendship. No, don't tell me it can't happen, because it can!" Kerry added when Adam opened his mouth to argue. "But I'll admit this was... was..."

"Was?" he prompted when she couldn't seem to find the right word.

"Wonderful. But—"

"Shhh." He gathered her close, ignoring her automatic protests.

"I don't want it to happen again. And now, I really should get home."

"I'm not going to let you go."

His tone was merely conversational. Not bullying, not even worried.

"You sure as hell are."

"That was the first time you'd ever reached a climax, wasn't it?"

"Oh, God, if you're going to dissect everything, I really am leaving!" She thrust furiously at his arm but he tightened his grip, one leg clamping down on hers to hold her immobile. Kerry's eyes flashed fire, but Adam's were lazy with amusement.

"This guy from college. He's the only one you've been with, isn't he?"

"I didn't exactly want to repeat the experience."

"You said you'd had a *few* relationships," he reminded her. "But you lied."

"I lie about a lot of things," Kerry declared.

"Well, don't lie about this: could you be pregnant after tonight?"

What amazed her the most was his merely curious tone. No, she couldn't be pregnant. She hadn't been that out of her head! But she had the strange feeling if she told Adam she could be, he wouldn't really mind. "No. It's not the time of the month I could get pregnant."

"You're sure?"

"I might be foolish, but I'm not crazy! Now get your leg off me. I'm leaving."

"Why are you always fighting me? I swear, Kerry, there must be something you're not telling me. You overreact about everything that has to do with sex."

Kerry looked straight into his blue-gray eyes. Would he understand her deep-rooted fears about totally trusting a man? Trusting him?

Staring at her, Adam clasped her wrist and brought it to his mouth. He kissed the center of her palm, his tongue lightly stroking her.

She could see where this was heading. Though her heart kicked into overdrive she attempted to twist her hand from his grasp. "I've really got to go."

"Why? Tomorrow's Sunday. You can spend the night."

"Here? With you?" She laughed shortly. "No way. I'd never get any sleep!"

"That's the idea."

"Please, Adam. Let me go."

His eyes darkened, and his lips tightened. She thought he would argue, but he said instead, "You sure as hell make me feel possessive!"

Thinking he was giving in, Kerry wriggled beneath his leg and pushed at his thigh. She gasped when he suddenly climbed atop her, pinning her down. "I can't let you go," he said simply.

"Stop it, Adam. It isn't funny."

His tongue found her nipple. Kerry bit into her bottom lip and glared at him. Humor creased the corners of his eyes. Lightning leaped beneath her skin, and her mouth trembled. "There's a part of you you refuse to face," he said softly, so softly that she shivered. "You're an adventurer. It's your fault, you know, that I lost control the first time. The way you were touching me when I only wanted you to help me off with my pants . . ." Something dangerous smoldered in his eyes. "I want you to do that again."

"I'm not an adventurer."

"The hell you're not," he growled, his hands sliding up her rib cage to caress her breasts. "Stop fighting and just give in."

And she did.

Adam lay awake in the darkness long after Kerry fell into a fitful sleep. Her back was curled against his. His hand lay against her hip. There had been other women in his life, but he couldn't recall a time he'd felt such pleasure. When had another woman laughed and joked with him in bed? When had she wanted to explore him in that sensuous, innocently curious way Kerry had?

Never.

He didn't understand what prompted Kerry to pull back all the time, however. Sure, she was afraid this would ruin their lifetime friendship. He could admit that was a legitimate worry. But there was something else, some kind of self-preservation instinct that reared up whenever she let loose. She must have iron control of her emotions. How had she learned that? When? And why?

As much as he detested anyone who ranted and raved and exposed their "deepest" feelings at every available opportunity, he couldn't help but wish Kerry would let him see hers. He had the same sensation he'd felt for years: she wouldn't let him see the real Kerry Camden.

Kerry stirred in his arms, her lashes fluttering. Adam had expected to feel let down after being with her; it happened often enough with other women. This possessiveness was new and not entirely to his liking. It was probably because it was Kerry, he rationalized. She'd been the most important woman in his life for most of his childhood and adult years. It was natural to feel protective.

He ran his hand over her flat stomach, smiling as she protested faintly in her sleep. What if she had gotten pregnant? In the heat of passion he simply hadn't considered contraception. Most thirty-two-year-old single women were equipped to take care of that. But he'd rapidly figured out there was no way she could be preventing conception by artificial means; she wasn't active sexually!

The thought of Kerry pregnant with his child filled his senses. Remembering Marsden's advice, he wondered if maybe the old man was right. He didn't want to have children without marriage, but he wanted children. And he wanted them with Kerry.

For an insane moment he wished she were already pregnant. That would solve the dilemma once and for all. He would demand she marry him. She would have to comply.

You're losing it, Shard.

Her rounded bottom shifted against him. Adam felt the first stirring of desire and ruthlessly clamped down on it. Good God.

"You're too old to be reacting like this," he said aloud.

"Adam?" Kerry's eyes blinked open.

He buried his face in her lush hair, inhaling deeply. "Unless you're in an amorous mood, go back to sleep," he said in a pained voice.

Kerry gazed at him uncomprehendingly, then a smile tugged at her mouth. "I always read that it wasn't that easy for a man to—"

"Well, forget what you've read. Obviously the author never met you!"

Sunday passed in a blur. Kerry tried over and over again to make Adam take her home, but he simply wasn't willing. Truth to tell, her protests were pretty feeble. She didn't want to leave. They spent most of the day in bed. She learned to her delight and chagrin that Adam had absolutely no hang-ups about sex. He made her enjoy herself and forget her embarrassment. He made her see what she'd been missing in her life. He made her realize how addictive he could be for her.

Sunday evening she told him good-night at her doorstep. Firmly. She also told him she needed time to think. This wasn't what she'd wanted to happen, she explained reasonably. It was all too soon, too fast and too much trouble.

He stepped inside, kicked her door shut and kissed her, hard. That had been the end of that conversation.

And now...?

The jarring ring of the telephone brought Kerry fully awake. She was in her bed. At her apartment. The warmth of a male arm around her chest assured her Adam was beside her.

Squinting through the darkness at the clock, she realized it was five-thirty in the morning! Who would be crazy enough to call her so early?

Groping for the phone, she felt Adam's hand slide familiarly down her hip. Her pulse fluttered. Was she mad? she wondered now. They'd known each other for years, yet she felt such incredible intensity.

The telephone shrilled again and, horror-stricken, Kerry saw Adam reach for the receiver. "Don't you dare!" she hissed in his ear.

He laughed silently against the pillow. "Chicken," he muttered as Kerry swept up the receiver.

"Hello?"

"Kerry! Thank God you're home! I tried to reach you all day yesterday!"

Marla's voice was just short of hysterical. Kerry sat up in bed, tugging her comforter around her. Adam yanked it down, exposing her breasts. Kerry flushed, skewering him with a mock glare she couldn't quite sustain. "I was busy," she apologized, struggling to pull the comforter back up.

Adam's brown hand curved around her breast.

"Kerry, you won't believe what happened. James left me. Saturday night."

Kerry's blood froze. "He left?"

"He left me! Left me for another woman!" she cried. "I knew we were having problems, but I never guessed. You'd barely gotten out of the driveway when he confessed the truth. He's been seeing her for months. They meet at her place." Her words came faster and faster, nearly incoherent with sobs. "She's divorced. They have *fun* together. They go dancing. They *talk*! My God, Kerry, he acted as if it were all my fault that the kids take up so much of my time!"

"Marla..." Kerry felt sick.

"He wants a divorce. He wants to live with this other woman. Kerry, I hate her and I don't even know her!"

Images from Kerry's past blinded her. She saw her father with his lover. Heard the laughter. Felt the rage.

Marla was crying openly now. "I called and called you," she sobbed piteously. "But you weren't there."

"I know. I'm sorry. I was with Adam."

Sensing her distress, Adam leaned up on one elbow, regarding her soberly. She couldn't meet his eyes. She felt hot and stifled. She had to get out of the bed with him. This was too personal. Too close. "Marla," she said in a shaking voice, pushing back the covers easily now since Adam had given up the game.

He watched silently as she reached for the chenille robe lying in a heap on the floor. Climbing out of bed, she thrust her arms through the sleeves and cinched it tightly around her waist. "Do you want me to come over?"

"Can you? What about work?"

"I'll ask the boss for time off." Her eyes met Adam's.

"Oh, God. I don't know what to do. I've been a walking zombie. The kids have been awful. They don't know what's going on. Melissa's been crying and crying, and Jason's throwing things."

"James hasn't been back at all?"

"He called me yesterday," she said bitterly. "To make certain I hadn't committed suicide."

"I'll be right there, Marla."

She replaced the receiver and stood for a moment beside the bed, unable to hold Adam's questioning gaze. She felt such fury toward James Courtenay she was afraid it would spill out in a poisonous venom, burning Adam in its wake. The bastard. The selfish, adulterating bastard.

"What is it?" Adam asked soberly.

"Marla's husband's left her for another woman." Her voice was harsh and accusatory. "If he were here I'd strangle him with my bare hands."

She thought about how Marla had called Adam and set him up with the caterer and hurt filled her lungs. She wanted to bury her face against Adam's chest and flail her fists against him at the same time. It wasn't fair! It was never fair!

"Are you going to be all right?" Adam asked, frowning, swinging his legs over the side of the bed.

"Me? It's Marla who's in trouble!"

"You're as white as a sheet."

"Don't come near me," she warned, backing up. Flushing, she added lamely, "I've got too much to do. I'm going to be in the office late today. I'm sorry. You're just going to have to understand."

"I do understand," he said, his voice trailing after her, full of bafflement as Kerry raced to the bathroom.

She closed the door behind her, leaning against the panels, fighting back angry sobs of fury and misery. James Courtenay should be drawn and quartered. Her fists clenched. He had a wife and a family! How could he? How *could* he?

She caught her reflection in the bathroom mirror. Her eyes were wide and sunken. Adam was right. She was deathly pale.

If nightmares could come true....

Kerry took a shower, scrubbing herself so thoroughly her skin hurt when she was finished. She tugged on her robe once more and returned to the bedroom.

Adam was leaning against her dresser, shirtless but in his jeans. His ankles were crossed, but he was far from relaxed. "Is there a chance that Marla could be mistaken?"

"Mistaken?" Kerry raged.

"I'm just asking."

"He *told* her he was in love with someone else! He wants out of the marriage!"

"Ahhh. I see."

Problem sauntered into the bedroom and jumped onto Kerry's dresser. Adam absentmindedly petted him, his gaze focused on the woman in front of him, unsure how to deal with her.

"The man has two children," Kerry added through her teeth. "He's just dumping them all!"

"It sounds pretty damning all right, but maybe there's more to it than you know," he responded, feeling his way. Kerry's reaction was so swift, so overblown, he could tell something else was at work.

Kerry viciously yanked her clothes from her closet. "I know that when a man cheats on his wife there's no excuse. And he's a father cheating on his children, as well! So don't try to pass the blame. It doesn't work that way!"

He made the colossal mistake of crossing the room and laying his hands on her shoulders. Kerry froze, clenching her teeth together. "You're probably right, but—"

"Probably?" She shrugged his hands away, glaring at him with misdirected fury.

"You've got to be calm for Marla. You know that, Kerry," he added tersely. "Why the hell are you acting like an avenging crusader?"

"Because somebody has to. Women always get taken. They're the ones left to pick up the pieces! I'm sick of it. Just sick of it!"

"Kerry." Adam was shaken. More than anything he wanted to pull her into his arms and comfort her, but she wasn't going to let him.

"I've got to go," she said, blindly pulling her clothes off the hanger, trying to get dressed. "Oh, God. Marsden's coming in today. Could you—"

"Yes, I'll take care of everything," he cut her off.

Kerry finished pulling on her clothes. She left her hair wet, searching distractedly for her purse.

"Let me drive you to Marla's. You're in no condition to do it yourself."

"No, Adam. I want to be alone."

"Let me help."

"You can't." Her smile was taut with misery. "You can't. Goodbye, Adam."

A cold foreboding filled his chest. She was walking away from him. She'd found her excuse to leave and she was rejecting him. Again.

There had never been a longer day in Adam's life. Minutes were hours. He was distracted and uneasy, his mind on Kerry. He'd found something this weekend, something he wanted badly. Emotions he'd thought dead or nonexistent were unfurling inside him, awakening after a long, cold hibernation. He wasn't going to let her slip away again. He'd done that once before.

The tip of one long, gnarled finger tapped against his shoulder. "Something on your mind, son?" John Marsden asked with a twinkle in his eye.

Adam dragged his attention back to the man seated on the conference room couch. "A few things. Never mind. Where were we?"

"You were about to tell me how you're getting on with your prettiest employee."

Adam laughed. "I was not."

"Where is she today?"

"She had some personal business to take care of."

Nodding thoughtfully, he said, "Well, I want to make a couple of changes, and I want to get the ball rolling today." He gave Adam a shrewd look. "Can you bring yourself down to earth long enough to help me out?"

A deep flush crept up Adam's neck. It wasn't like him to be so self-involved that he neglected his work. "Just tell me what you want and I'll try to talk you out of it," he said with forced cheerfulness. Marsden chuckled, drew his chair closer to the desk, and lit his pipe.

An hour and a half later they were finished. Adam glanced at the clock—3:00 p.m. He wished Kerry would call.

"I guess that's it," Marsden said, climbing from the depths of the chair. "I'll see you Saturday morning then, bright and early."

"Saturday?"

"The boat, Adam. You said you'd come."

Adam had completely forgotten his promise. "I'll be there," he told his friend as they walked to the door. He realized ruefully that he'd been planning to spirit Kerry away to the San Juans this weekend, as he'd wanted to last weekend. That trip would have to be postponed again.

"Bring Miss Camden, too, if you like," Marsden added with a straight face.

The old reprobate. Adam's lips twisted into a grin.

"Have you been thinking about what I told you?" he asked as he walked toward the door.

Adam crossed the room in three swift strides, twisting open the knob. "About marriage?"

"And children." A momentary shadow passed over his craggy features. "Don't let the time slip away from you because it might not happen. My son's gone, but I have memories." He patted Adam's arm, as if embarrassed he'd brought up the subject. "And I've still got Mary Lou."

Moved, Adam asked, "Is your wife going on the boat with us?"

"I named the damn thing for her. She'd better!"

As he stepped through the doorway, chuckling, Adam saw Ron Tisdale marching down the hall in their direction, his face red and stiff with fury. He shot a glance at Marsden, straightened comically as if at attention, uttered a greeting, then swept on toward Adam.

"Could I speak to you a moment?" he demanded tensely.

Out of the corner of his eye Adam saw Marsden look back and shake his head in commiseration. Ron was too intense and arrogant for the man. Marsden wanted someone smart, efficient, with a sense of timing, but also with a sense of humor. Kerry.

"Something the matter?" Adam asked, closing his door.

"Kerry's not in today, she was supposed to have a meeting with Marsden."

Adam was rankled. Kerry's business wasn't Ron's concern. "I know. I took care of him for her."

Ron stopped short, his mouth a pugnacious line of anger. "You gave her the Marsden account because you're friends! Now she can't even follow through. I think you owe me an explanation."

The guy certainly didn't lack courage. A fool's courage, to be sure but courage nonetheless. Adam decided to be just as blunt. "John Marsden didn't like the way you handled his account. Whether he's right or wrong doesn't matter. He doesn't want you as his investment adviser. He quit this company once because he felt you bungled his investments. I gave him to Kerry because she's more qualified than you are, and she seems to have a better handle on how to deal with John's personality.''

Rage flared Ron's nostrils. The color faded from his cheeks, leaving them gray and withered looking. ''You gave Kerry Marsden's account because you're sleeping with her!''

There was a soft rap on his door. Adam was cold with fury. He didn't bother heeding the knock. ''Ron,'' he said succinctly. ''Clean out your desk.''

The door opened and Kerry stood there, looking confused. ''I'm sorry. I didn't hear anyone.''

Ron's hands were shaking. He balled them into fists and marched to the door. Kerry moved to one side, her brows furrowing at his demeanor.

''He just fired me,'' Ron told her as he strode past her. ''Looks like you're the favorite once again. And we both know why, don't we?''

Kerry's eyes were huge. She gazed questioningly at Adam. ''What did he mean by that?''

All Adam wanted to do was drag her into his arms. Wishing life weren't so complicated, he drawled, ''He accused me of giving you the Marsden account because we're sleeping together.'' The blood drained from her face, and Adam lost patience. ''For God's sake, Kerry, I didn't tell him about this weekend! That was just a mean guess on his part. He probably doesn't even believe it. Give me a little credit, hmm?''

She held up her hands. "You see why this can't go on. Rumors have already cropped up about us. If the truth comes out, I don't think I can take it."

"I bought this company because of you," he said flatly, realizing as the words formed that it was the absolute truth. "Because I wanted to be with you, to work with you. J. & K. had a great reputation, but I never thought they'd sell to me. If you hadn't worked here, I wouldn't have even made an offer."

Kerry looked confused. "But after this weekend..."

Adam waited, as tense as strung wire. "I wouldn't trade this weekend for anything."

She strode jerkily across the room to stand by the window. Sunlight fell on her hair, turning it to burgundy flame. "I can't do it, Adam. I can't work with you, and make love to you—" She stumbled over the words, as if they were nearly impossible to speak. "And be your friend, too. Something's got to give."

"You're looking for an excuse to end this relationship before it's even begun." Adam was outwardly calm, but inside he was seething with emotions too complicated to name. Primitive emotions. Like a man out of another century, he wanted to force her to his will. Show her he was right. John Marsden's ideas on marriage and children sounded less and less farfetched, yet he sensed he was damned close to losing Kerry.

"I can't do it all, Adam. I'm not made that way. I've been thinking today. Thinking a lot." She threw him a swift, troubled look. Adam's blood ran cold. Uh-oh, he thought. Here it comes. "Maybe we should take a deep breath and step back."

"I can't." He walked up behind her, wanting to kiss her neck, the soft hollow behind her ear. "I want you right now."

She shivered involuntarily. "The timing's not good for me. It's not good."

"Look at me," he urged, placing his hands on her shoulders and twisting her around. She resisted, but he felt the tremor that ran through her narrow shoulders. She glanced up, looking so vulnerable and feminine that Adam had to forcibly restrain himself. "Can you really give up what we shared this weekend?"

She drew a tortured breath, paused, then shook her head. "No."

Adam was weak with relief. "Well, then?"

"Not yet, anyway. But later I will. I'll have to."

Impatience made his voice harsh. "Why, damn it?"

"I told you before, I can't be involved with someone like you. I mean, I am, for now; I know that. But it's only temporary."

"What do you mean, someone like me?" he demanded.

Her smile was fleeting. "I know you, Adam. This won't last between us. And if you're honest with yourself, you'll admit I'm right."

"So this is just an affair for you?" he demanded, shocked by how much her words hurt. "Because if you felt something more you'd end it right now, right? Before it could get out of hand?"

She hesitated. "That's right."

"You little liar," he snarled. "If it didn't mean something to you, you'd never have gone to bed with me in the first place!"

His fingers gripped her shoulders so tightly they hurt. Kerry was too upset to think straight. She just wanted him to leave her alone. "It doesn't mean anything more to me! I'm not that foolish."

His intercom buzzed. Rachel's fresh, young voice sounded as if it were from another world. "There's a call for you, Mr. Shard. She says she's a friend of yours from San Francisco. Katherine Forrester."

Kerry's gaze zeroed in on the intercom. Adam could almost read her mind and he swore silently, furious with her for believing what she wanted rather than what was the truth. "Tell her I'll call her back."

"Okay." Rachel hesitated a moment before clicking off.

Silence followed. Kerry's eyes were full of "I told you sos." Grinding his teeth together, Adam said, "Katherine's a business associate."

"Like I'm a business associate?"

"I knew you'd make the most of that." He dropped his arms and strode away from her. Knowing he was damning himself, but too angry to dissemble, he stated flatly, "If you mean, did we have a relationship, the answer's yes. Once. Years ago. Now it's strictly business."

"I need a few extra days off," Kerry said in a faint voice. "James has moved out all his clothes. Marla's in pieces. The kids are wrecks."

"Take the whole damn week off. Whatever you want." Adam's tone was blistering. "Escape."

"I can't talk to you about this," she murmured, heading blindly for the door.

"You're scared to death about caring even the littlest bit for me. I know Marla needs you, but you've welcomed this chance to get away from me, to avoid facing your feelings. So go. I won't stop you."

All day, with Marla's crumbling marriage so potently evident, Kerry had rehearsed what she would say to Adam. She'd known before she'd made love to him that their time was doomed; Marla's problems had simply put those thoughts into focus. But hearing Adam tell her to leave wasn't what she'd wanted after all. Protecting her heart wasn't as easy as she'd thought. She ached inside.

"I'll be at Marla's if you need me. Rachel's got her number."

Adam nodded briefly.

"Did you . . . take care of Marsden?"

"I think I've taken care of everything, Kerry. Tell Marla I'm sorry she's having such a difficult time, and if she's able to listen, tell her it does get better."

Does it? Kerry regarded him uncertainly, but Adam had closed himself off from her. Quietly she left his office, her muffled footsteps sounding terribly lonely in the empty hallway.

Chapter Eleven

*I knew this would happen. I knew it! One week-
end with Adam and poof! I lose all my brains.
They just leaked right out of my head. A friend of
mine once told me lust makes you stupid. Well, she
was right. How can it be that Marla's utterly miserable over a man, and all I think about is Adam?
What kind of sister am I? She thinks I'm being
wonderful, taking care of the kids, fixing meals,
running interference for her and James when things
get really rough. But it's Adam I think about.
Adam I want. I don't trust myself anymore. If he
crooked his little finger, I'd follow.*

Kerry sat on a bench, exhausted, watching Jason and
Melissa have fun on the playground. Jason could barely
crawl onto a two-foot-tall wooden platform; Melissa

couldn't at all. This created a fight, and Kerry had to step in.

"That does it, kids," Kerry muttered. "We've got to go back."

It took all her energy to corral them into the car and buckle them into their safety seats. Jason impudently unbuckled himself, glaring at Kerry.

"Do it again, and you'll forfeit that ice cream cone I promised you," Kerry muttered, refastening it. Jason's pudgy hand moved to the buckle, and Kerry met his gaze squarely, daring him to test her.

He pulled back his hand and looked at the toes of his shoes.

Kerry smothered a smile. I'm going to make a terrible mother some day, she thought as she climbed behind the wheel, then was struck dumb by how suddenly, achingly she wanted her own child. Adam's child.

Oh, God, I'm in trouble.

The park was only two miles from Marla's house. Kerry drove by rote, so miserable her arms seemed held down by weights. Pulling into Marla's driveway, Kerry felt her low spirits ebb even lower. For three days she'd hidden her own feelings and presented a cheery face to Marla. She'd even refrained from murdering James whenever the worm showed his adulterous face. But it was wearing on her. She couldn't take the indecision. Throughout her life Kerry had met obstacles head on and made choices. Why Marla couldn't make a choice now was beyond her. As far as Kerry could see, divorce was the only option. How could you hang on to a man who didn't want you?

The twins had fallen asleep on the way back. One by one Kerry carried them to their beds. The house was silent, only a faint breeze stirred up the sweet heavy scent of the bouquet of yellow roses on the dining table. Kerry had bought the flowers, needing something fresh and beautiful to admire while she sorted through her own self-doubts and Marla's ragged emotions.

"Marla?" Kerry called softly, quietly closing the door to the twins' room. Fear prickled along her skin. Where was she?

Visions of disaster filled her head. She walked rapidly down the hall, searching each room. The back of Marla's head showed above the outdoor chaise longue. Calling herself an overimaginative fool, Kerry slid back the screen door. "Marla?"

A sigh sounded. Marla's head lolled to one side. Kerry moved around to the front of the chair. She picked up her sister's wrist and checked her pulse. She couldn't help herself.

Marla's lashes lifted. "Whad are you doin'?" she asked sleepily.

"Nothing." Kerry felt sheepish. Her sister was just taking a nap. "The kids are asleep in their beds."

"Thanks for taking them to the park. Did they have fun?"

"Up until World War III broke out." She told her about the fight.

Marla sighed, gazing reflectively across the cedar deck to the line of firs beyond. "James called while you were gone. Now that everything's out in the open, he's really pressuring me for a divorce. Can you believe it?"

Kerry grimaced. "Divorce, huh? He wants this woman that badly?"

"He seems to. She must be really something," she said, a catch in her voice.

Kerry's heart broke. Marla was trying so hard to be fair. "Are you going to fight the divorce?"

"Yes."

Kerry didn't answer. She felt it was a lost cause, but she wasn't her sister.

Marla reached for the glass of iced-tea on the table beside her. She took one small sip, collecting herself. "I know you'd opt for divorce if it came down to it," she said, unable to hide the bitterness in her voice. "You're strong, Kerry. But even though you probably can't understand this, I love James. I can't give him up. And I have the twins to think about."

Kerry shot her a sideways glance. "You still want him even though he's treating you like dirt? How can you stand knowing he's been sleeping with some other woman? I wouldn't put up with it. I couldn't."

"Have you ever been in love, Kerry?" Marla cut in. "Even once?"

"This isn't to do with me," Kerry began gently, but Marla shook her head vigorously.

"Yes, it is! I'm trying to explain how I feel, and you just won't listen. I love James. I think this affair is just a temporary thing. I hate it. It makes me crazy, and I want to kill him! But I know, deep down, if I stay rational and don't give him any ultimatums, it might just go away."

"Marla, listen to yourself. That's the most masochistic thing I've ever heard. The man wants a divorce!"

"That's what he says today, but Kerry, he broke down on the phone. He knows how much he's hurting me. He just needs time to get himself together."

"I can't listen to this." Kerry paced to the far end of the deck, angry. How could Marla delude herself so completely?

She felt Marla walk up behind her, heard her deep sigh. "There's not right or wrong, you know. I've been giving this a lot of thought, and I know what I want."

"There is a right and wrong. James was wrong to cheat on you. He's even more wrong to be seeing this other woman with you knowing about it. For God's sake, after Dad's infidelities how can you stand to be with that kind of man?"

There was a deep, silent moment, as if the earth itself had paused to take a breath. They had never discussed their father before. "James isn't like Daddy."

"You could have fooled me!"

"Daddy cheated on Mom for years with all kinds of different women. James just wants this one woman."

"Today. But what about next month? Maybe there'll be somebody new. A different one. Somebody *better*!" Kerry was too incensed to be amazed at how much Marla knew about their father.

"That's not how James thinks," Marla insisted.

"It's how they all think!" Kerry lashed back.

"You're wrong. You've got a warped sense of perception about men."

"*I* have!"

Marla was growing angry, too. Her cheeks flamed pink, and her eyes glittered. Distantly Kerry realized she resembled her sister more in anger than at any other time. But they disagreed totally on men.

"All right, Kerry, I've had it. I've listened to you put down men for years. They're all bad. They're all out to take advantage of you. You can't trust them. They should be blasted off the face of the planet."

"That's not how I feel—"

"Isn't it? The only one you've ever cared about is Adam, and it looks like you've blown that, too!" To

Kerry's startled look, she added flatly, "I'm not blind,
you know. I can see you're absolutely miserable. And
every time you call the office you just leave a message
with his secretary. You don't even talk to him."

Kerry was amazed that Marla, who'd seemed to be
sunk in total depression, had been so aware.

"He called while you were gone," she went on.
"Right after James did. I was a mess, and he calmed me
down. He told me to take one step at a time."

Kerry couldn't contain her surprise. "Trust Adam to
be original."

"See what I mean?" Marla yelled. "As soon as we
get down to real emotions, you say something flip and
clever and meaningless!"

"Well, what am I supposed to say?" she yelled back,
upset.

"Just say what you really feel for once!"

Marla strode back to her lounge chair and sank onto
it, spent. Kerry immediately felt guilty for letting her
own problems add to Marla's burden. "I'm sorry," she
murmured, sitting on a chair by the table. "Let's not
fight."

Marla nodded and closed her eyes.

"Why did Adam call?"

"He wanted to talk to you. Something about fishing
this weekend with Mr. Martin."

"Marsden." Kerry's heart lifted before she remembered she couldn't see him anymore. But the memory of
being wrapped in Adam's arms, of him thrusting into
her, the wetness of his tongue, the seductive scent of his
cologne, the roughness of his whiskers against her flesh,
made her throat close with pure longing.

"Are you going to tell me what's going on with you
two?" Marla asked wearily. "Or are you too afraid?"

Kerry picked up Marla's glass, helping herself to a swallow of diluted iced-tea. "We slept together last weekend."

She couldn't have said anything to astound her sister more. Marla sat bolt upright. "You did? You and Adam?"

"Yes."

"Well, that's...wonderful! No wonder you were gone all day Sunday. You were with Adam!"

Kerry nodded, squinting against the bright sunlight. She was uncomfortable with this topic. She'd never been able to get into the nitty-gritty kind of girl talk other friends she knew seemed to eat up.

"Was he at your place Monday when I called you?" Marla asked perceptively.

Kerry nodded again.

"Well, that's great, isn't it?" she asked.

"No. It's already over. I...ended it."

"Oh, Kerry." Her voice was full of compassion and a kind of resigned disapproval.

"Unlike you, Marla," Kerry said wryly, "I can't set aside my pride and let a man walk all over me. It's not worth the humiliation."

Marla's nostrils flared. "And what's Adam done to walk all over you?"

Kerry hesitated. "He hasn't done it yet. I'm just getting prepared."

"Good Lord!" Picking up her drink again, Marla shook her head. "I don't know which one of us is the bigger fool, but if I had to put money on it, I'd pick you. You're in love with him, and you won't even give yourself a chance. At least I'm honest about what I want. But not you. Oh, no, not Kerry Camden. Keep lying to yourself and you'll get what you're asking for: a lifetime of loneliness!''

Kerry unlocked the door to her apartment and was met by hot, breathless air, and a lonely, yowling cat. "Did you get locked inside?" she teased, scratching Problem's head.

The Siamese trotted after her as she walked into the kitchen to pour herself a glass of water. Problem's bowl was low on water, too, so Kerry refilled it, but the cat merely purred and rubbed her legs.

"Miss me?" Kerry pulled Problem's lanky body into her arms. "Between Mr. Little and myself, I don't think you've suffered too much. You're just lucky he offered to feed you at all. He must like you more than he lets on."

Problem started squirming so she set him on his feet and let him out. With a disdainful flick of his tail he sauntered toward Mr. Little's property.

Glancing anxiously toward her neighbor's sliding glass door, Kerry half expected the man to race out, broom in hand. But Problem appeared safe for the moment, his nine lives still intact.

Kerry leaned on the balcony rail, heat soaking into her head, making her feel itchy. It was Friday afternoon; too late, really, to go into work. Besides, Marla's situation made her feel drained and lethargic. Her sister clung to the kind of hopes that should have died long ago.

"But not me," Kerry said aloud, her eyes closed against the beating sun, wishing she didn't feel so miserable over doing the right thing.

She'd called Adam back to ask him about the fishing trip, but he'd been too busy to answer in anything but monosyllables. At the end of the conversation he'd begged her to join him, however.

"I want you to come," he said in that intense, sexy way that made the hair on Kerry's arms stand on end. "Please."

"I'll . . . think about it."

The truth was, Kerry was torn. She wanted to be with him. She wanted to drag him off to bed and make love to him. She wanted it all. But sooner or later she was going to pay the price. Adam had never said he loved her. In fact, love didn't even enter into it. And as far as having a future with him, she knew Adam wasn't interested in marriage again.

And are you?

Kerry sighed, running her hands through her hair. Two weeks ago, she would have said no. But that had been before she'd faced her attraction to Adam. Now the thought of being married to him made her feel weak and afraid inside, like when you wanted something you knew you couldn't have.

Yet she could have him for a little while. If she were willing . . .

"Oo-ooh," Kerry muttered in frustration, striding inside and reaching for the kitchen phone. She punched out the office number and asked the receptionist to be transferred to Adam.

"Mr. Shard isn't in right now," Rachel's voice rang over the wire. "If you would leave your name and number—"

"Rachel, it's Kerry."

"Oh, hi, Kerry! How's your sister?"

"Surviving." Kerry had been forced to reveal something of Marla's problems to explain her own absence from work. "Just barely."

"I hope things work out."

"So do I. Do you know where Adam is?"

"No, he left early. He's got that fishing trip with Marsden tomorrow. Maybe he had to get ready."

Kerry grimaced. Of course he would be out when she needed to talk to him. "Er, any news about Ron?" she asked, not really wanting to ask, but feeling she ought to know.

"He came and talked to Adam yesterday. I don't know what was said, but Ron seemed a little more subdued when he left. You know, Kerry," she added in an admiring tone bordering on hero-worship, "Adam is amazing. He really knows how to handle people."

For some reason Kerry couldn't bear for Rachel to sing Adam's praises to her. "He's one of a kind," she agreed, and hung up a few moments later.

Flopping down in front of the TV, Kerry searched for something just short of thought provoking and one step up from mindless. Impossible. She turned off the set in disgust and tried to block out her thoughts. She knew some of the things Marla had accused her of were true. She was too careful when it came to matters of the heart. Yet the thought of suffering the same fate as her mother, and now her sister, was enough to give her nightmares.

If Adam was a different kind of male, she might be tempted to trust to fate. Contrary to Marla's remarks, Kerry was fully aware there were lots of men who were loyal, faithful and honest with their wives. And yes, Adam possessed some of those qualities. But she would be a worse fool than even Marla claimed if she believed she was the one woman who could make him happy. She didn't overrate her attributes that much.

The doorbell rang and Kerry sprang from the couch as if caught in some nefarious act. Swearing under her breath, she unlatched the lock.

Adam stood on the other side. "Hi," he greeted her. He wore a polo shirt and a pair of khaki shorts, white socks and sport shoes. He looked so much like the Adam of her youth that Kerry was momentarily speechless.

"What? No snappy comment? Not even a hello?"

"Hello, Adam. What are you doing here?"

"I came to see you." His gaze skated over her from head to foot. Kerry wore a pair of jeans with holes at the knees and a red tank top. She realized with amusement that she also looked as she had when she'd been a teenager.

."Come on inside, if you can stand the oven," she invited, closing the door behind him. "This place is unbearable when it's hot."

"How's Marla?"

"A little better considering James wants a divorce, and she's not giving it to him. She thinks he'll change his mind and want to be with her later on, so she's holding out."

"Hmm."

Small talk abruptly ground to a halt, and they stood facing each other, feeling uncomfortable. Now that he was here Kerry couldn't think of a thing to say.

Wiping nervous palms on her jeans, Kerry asked, "What do you think she should do?"

Adam's mouth twisted wryly. "Just because I've been divorced doesn't make me a marital expert." He shrugged, moving his shoulders as if to ease some inner tension. "But it does seem like he's rushing it. A few days ago she didn't even know there was another woman involved. I think they should wait a while just to let the dust settle a bit. Don't you?"

"No. If a man treated me like that, I'd never want to see him again," Kerry answered calmly.

"Even if you loved him?" Adam regarded her with a kind of detached curiosity that nevertheless made her feel he was really listening for her answer.

"The *L* word, Adam?"

His lashes lowered thoughtfully. "Your memory is way too long," he said with a grimace.

"You're not saying you've changed your philosophy?" Kerry smiled.

To her surprise, he didn't immediately answer. Instead he walked to her sink and poured himself a glass of water. "It's too damn hot," he muttered.

"I called Rachel and she filled me in a little on what's been happening this week. I feel like I kind of ran out on you, especially with Ron leaving at the same time."

"It didn't matter. It was a slow week in a lot of ways. By the way, Ron came back and apologized."

"Apologized?" Kerry stared at him in disbelief.

"Grovelled is probably closer to the word," Adam said with a relish he couldn't disguise. "He wanted his job back."

"Did you give it to him?"

"Hell, no. He's got an attitude problem I don't need. But I offered him three month's severance pay, and he left peaceably." Adam looked sideways at her. "He seems disinclined to make any more tasteless remarks about you and me."

Embarrassed, Kerry glanced around, feeling the potency of his gaze even when she couldn't see it. "Well, that's a relief."

"Mmm. I'm going to level with you, Kerry. I've been thinking about us all week." He laughed shortly. "I can hardly think of anything else."

Kerry swallowed. She heard the drip, drip, drip of the faucet in between her heartbeats.

"I've come to some conclusions, and they've been hard ones to admit. There's something between us that won't go away. It's always been there. And I want to explore it. I want to take it to the end."

Kerry darted a glance back at him. "What end?"

"I don't know. I'm not ruling out anything. There've been women in my life, I can't deny it. But none like you. None so enduring." Grimacing, he shook his head. "I ran off to San Francisco after I got divorced and I always thought it was because of Jenny, because I needed to escape from what we'd shared, but now I'm not so sure anymore. I think I might have been running from you." His jaw slid to one side, and he frowned. "Does that sound crazy?"

Kerry's nerves tightened. "A little."

Adam regarded her soberly, his eyes that seductive shade between blue and gray. She focused instead on his mouth, which was a mistake. The shape of his lips had always intrigued her.

He swore softly. "Oh, hell. I don't want to talk." In one swift stride he pulled her into his arms, his hands sliding around her back, his face somewhere near her ear. Kerry pressed her palms against his chest, inhaling sharply at the feel of his lips tugging on her lobe. "Don't stop me," he ordered, his breath tickling her ear.

Her senses reeled. She clutched his shoulders, longing to be possessed, fighting her attraction, losing...

As if she'd verbally conveyed her feelings, he hauled her even closer, his masculine angles filling her feminine curves. She was starved for the feel of her skin rubbing against his, and her soft moan was willing and eager.

"Tell me you want me," he ordered thickly, one hand tangling in her hair.

"I want you." Her voice was breathless.

"Well, it's about time," he growled.

There was no more waiting after that. With impatient fingers Adam stripped off her garments, then waited tensely as she did the same for him. Her hands were slower, clumsier. Groaning, Adam closed his eyes, as if it were a painful endurance. Then they were naked and she slipped into his arms. Somehow they made it to the bedroom, and Kerry knew she would always remember the sweet wrestling of their limbs and the rustle of the comforter beneath her back, the smell of Adam in her nostrils and the taste of him on her tongue.

With her heart pounding in her ears Kerry didn't battle her feelings. She let her fantasies take flight and dismissed the voice that told her she was in dangerous waters. When she felt Adam slip inside her, his hips grinding lovingly against hers, she urged him onward, touching and caressing and demanding, until he laughed in her ear.

"Slow down. You're making me crazy!"

"Good," she answered firmly and ignored his advice completely.

She felt the sweat on his shoulders, the muscles that glided beneath his skin like oiled satin, the hard thrust of him deep inside her, pushing her upward, upward, upward. She clenched her teeth together against an almost intolerable pleasure. The wave of pure sensation that poured over her made her cry out in ecstasy, wringing an answering moan from Adam as he reached his own climax.

Afterward Kerry lay gasping for breath. So much so, in fact, that she felt the silent laughter that rippled through Adam's heavy body.

"Why didn't we do this years ago?" he asked.

"Because I was smarter then. Now I've lost all sense."

He braced himself on his elbows, staring into her eyes so closely there was nowhere to hide. "Sometimes you make me feel so alone," he said with a poignancy that reached inside Kerry's soul. "Why do you do that?"

She couldn't answer.

"I love you, Kerry," he said.

Her lips parted. Shocked, she was certain she'd heard wrong. "What?" she whispered.

His gaze drifted from her troubled eyes to her mouth and back again. "I want a life with you. Children. Marriage. I want it so bad I can taste it."

"Why?"

His voice gentled. "Is that so hard to believe? We're good together, Kerry. We always have been. We could make each other happy. It would work. I got to thinking about you being pregnant with my child, and I can't get it out of my head. Marry me. I want you."

Kerry was almost afraid to look at him. Her heart beat frantically. This wasn't what she'd expected. She was afraid. Afraid of believing him as she'd believed Ryan, as she'd believed her father. But he meant what he said, at least at some level. His eyes didn't lie.

She licked her lips, unwittingly drawing his attention to them. He sucked her bottom lip in an utterly sensual gesture, releasing her only to allow her to answer.

When she couldn't, he asked in a quiet voice, "Do you love me?"

She laughed, seeking to diffuse the tension. "Adam, I've always loved you. You know that."

"I don't mean like a *brother*," he pointed out impatiently.

"I know."

His fingers cupped her chin, forcing her face in his direction. There was a blue flame of anger in his eyes. "I didn't want to fall in love with you, but I have. Maybe I've always been in love with you. There's been something there for years. But you don't give anything, Kerry! Sometimes I think I'm wasting my time, but then I tell myself you couldn't make love to me like you do without feeling something!"

"Of course I feel something." Her voice quivered.

"What?"

She inhaled sharply. "You're scaring me with this conversation, Adam."

"Am I?" He swore under his breath. "What is so difficult about facing your feelings?"

"Well, maybe it's easy for you, but it's not for me!" She tried to slide off the bed, but he yanked her back, rolling onto his back and pulling her across his chest. Her hair fell down around them like a silken black curtain.

"What happened to you, Kerry, that made you so cautious? I *know* you. No, don't shake your head. I do know you, in a way that you refuse to even acknowledge! It scares the hell out of you every time I get close to the truth. What the hell is it? I deserve to know!"

"You deserve to know?" She tried to twist her wrists free of his hands, but he held her tight.

"Yes!"

"All right, here it is: I don't trust men. Period. Ask Marla."

"You trust me or you wouldn't be here right now, like this, with me."

"My father cheated on my mother," she said through her teeth. "Marla's husband's cheating on her. Did you ever cheat on Jenny?"

"No. I told you I didn't."

"If you'd had to stay married to her the rest of your life, would you have?"

"That's a stupid question. We got divorced because she knew we couldn't work it out."

"Oh, yeah? Well, how can you say you'll never cheat on me?"

Adam's breath came out in a rasp of frustration. "I'll never cheat on you, Kerry, and you know why? Because you'll never give me a chance!"

They glared at each other. Kerry knew she was being ridiculous but she couldn't help herself. She realized suddenly, potently, that she did love Adam, loved him more than she'd ever loved anyone in her life.

Witnessing the emotions crossing her face, he waited, watching her closely. Her heart beat painfully in her chest. This was the moment, she sensed, when she made her choice. Either trust Adam enough to take a chance, or turn away.

"Come with me tomorrow," he said urgently. "I want you with me."

She drew a breath. "I can't. Marla..."

"Marla can live without you for one day. Call your mother. She can be with Marla."

"She won't come. It would be too much for her."

"Then let Marla stand on her own two feet for one day. Just one day."

In his eyes she saw the kind of need she'd always wanted to see in a man. The kind of vulnerability and open pain she was afraid to reveal to herself. Her heart responded. Her breath quickened. Kerry's lips parted. *I love you,* she thought, her face naked with emotion.

"Say it. Just say it," he urged.

Her hesitation was too long. There was a roaring in her ears, a tidal wave of fear that she was following in her mother's and sister's footsteps.

From a long distance away she heard him say bitterly, "It's not in you, is it? I never realized until now that you didn't feel the same. God, what a joke. I've suffered from loving you for years, and you don't even feel the same way." With a muscular twist he was out from beneath her, pulling on his clothes.

"Adam . . ." Kerry's voice shook.

He glanced back, his shirt in his hands.

I love you, she thought again, throat dry, working up the courage to lay bare the emotions she'd kept hidden for most of her lifetime. Perspiration broke out on her skin. Her stomach clenched.

When she said nothing, he turned and left without another word.

Chapter Twelve

I'm meeting Adam's boat at the pier. Last night was the worst night of my life. He asked for a plain, simple answer and my throat just closed. Oh, Lord, just thinking about the look on his face makes me feel sick. I'm going to tell him the truth today. I love him. And I want him. And if he's serious about marriage, so am I. I'll risk it. Being careful doesn't make me happy. It's time to take a chance.

The sun was so bright, the smell of the sound so dank and intense, that Kerry was sure she would faint. Pinpoints of light danced across the water, mocking her. Adam. Oh, God, Adam. I can't bear it if you're gone.

"Ms. Camden?" The Coast Guard representative glanced her way, cutting the fuzz from his walkie-talkie with a flick of his thumb on the button. "The *Mary Lou*'s been found."

He'd appeared almost magically, as if some divine presence had known she would need an answer. He'd told her that a Coast Guard ship had received the relayed S.O.S. and been dispatched from its dock. It hadn't passed this pier, but it most definitely was answering the *Mary Lou*'s mayday call.

"Survivors?" Kerry asked in an unnatural voice.

"Don't know yet. A life-flight's been sent from Seattle Memorial. That's where any survivors will be taken." He turned to the captain of *Camille's Folly*. "You were the one who took the call?"

Kerry didn't wait to hear more. Dizzy, she stumbled back toward her car on rubbery legs. The doors were locked and she jerked on the driver's door twice before realizing what was wrong. Reaction struck. She fell against the hot roof, burning her arms as she buried her face against them, certain she was going to be sick.

It could have been eons later when she opened her eyes and looked around again. She breathed deeply three times, clearing her head. She dug through her purse for her keys. The interior of the car was stuffy, the air so hot it hurt her lungs.

She'd heard of channeling one's energy but had never fully understood what it meant until she made that drive to Seattle Memorial Hospital. Sweat poured off her temples and ran in rivulets beneath her arms. She drove with intense concentration, repressing her emotions to a tiny burning core.

Seattle Memorial sat on a hilly rise, the closest hospital to the sound. Still, it took Kerry forty minutes of fighting traffic and road construction and furnace-heat before she pulled into the white-lined parking lot near the emergency door.

She walked slowly, forcing herself to move forward, her knees so unsteady she didn't trust herself to stop for fear she'd fall. Above the door was an impersonal sign: Emergency in plain black letters.

She stepped inside. The place was as quiet as a tomb. Where was everyone?

"Can I help you?" the woman at the reception desk asked.

"The boat accident . . . I'm here to see if . . ." Kerry couldn't go on.

"Please sit down, ma'am," the woman said swiftly. "The helicopter hasn't landed yet."

"Hasn't landed?" Kerry blinked. "But that can't be. It's been over an hour since I left."

"Sometimes it takes time," was her response.

Numb, she sank down in a chair. The pandemonium she'd been expecting began happening by degrees. She'd been first on the scene, she realized. Treated to the news before the rest of the world. Hushes, excited whispers filled the room. She recognized one of Seattle's news station reporters.

Her stomach heaved and she rose slowly. "The women's restroom?" she asked the receptionist faintly.

"Down the hall and to your left. Here. Let me show you."

Kerry followed, the gray-tiled floor seeming to heave and buckle beneath her feet. She made it to the restroom and into a stall before retching violently.

He can't be dead, she told herself reasonably, washing her face at the sink. She took another deep breath and hazarded a glance at her reflection. Pale as death with black circles around her eyes. Automatically she pulled a tube of lipstick from her purse and colored her lips for lack of anything better to do. Tears of fear gathered in the corners of her eyes.

She dropped the lipstick into her bag, pressing a hand to her trembling stomach. The smell of the restroom sickened her. He can't be dead.

In the waiting room the crowd sat in quiet clusters. Eyes followed Kerry's progress to a chair in the corner. She knew there was something she should do to help. Someone she should call. But until she knew about Adam...

She heard the whir of the helicopter. All talk ceased. The air was filled with expectancy. The phone rang at the desk. Several doctors appeared, then disappeared. No one explained anything.

The reporter walked to the desk. Kerry was in earshot of snatches of conversation.

"Three people were brought in," a serious-faced intern revealed.

"Alive or dead?" The reporter's pen was poised over a notepad.

"One dead, two alive."

"Do you have names yet?"

"Not until we tell the next of kin."

"What about the ones who are still living? Men or women?"

"Men. They're all men."

The reporter scratched madly on his notepad. "Were there any others? I understand four people were on the boat."

"I don't know anything more."

Four people? Kerry knew of Adam and John Marsden and the *Mary Lou*'s captain who had already been reported as dead. That report had been made by a woman passenger. Marsden's wife? Oh, God, how she wished she'd paid more attention when Adam had talked about this boat trip!

He is not dead, she told herself fervently, lashing herself with guilt. Oh, Adam, I love you. I love you. God, give me the chance to tell him.

"He insists we give him a local," the barrel-shaped nurse said shortly, her chin thrust forward with injustice.

Dr. Anthony regarded Adam with tolerance. "We're going to have to put you under. You may have nerve damage in that arm."

"You can fix it with a local."

"We can, but we'd rather not." He looked skeptically down into Adam's face. "How strong's your stomach, young man?"

"Strong enough."

Adam lay on a gurney in one of the recovery rooms next to O.R. They hadn't taken the boat accident victims through emergency since the helicopter had landed on the roof. But he'd be damned if they'd put him out now. His distrust of doctors and nurses and fear of hospitals in general ran right back to the time in high school when he'd been so sick with the flu.

He wanted out.

"Any word on John Marsden?" he asked as the nurse began cutting off his shirt. His left arm throbbed and burned. Glancing at it, Adam understood why they'd wanted to put him out. It was a bloody mess. The explosion from the engine had sent pieces of wood flying like shrapnel. He'd been thrown face-first to the deck, dazing him. Seawater boiling from the hull had sloshed into his eyes and nose, wakening him. The rest was a surreal nightmare. Marsden was knocked unconscious. His wife was stricken with fright.

The captain was dead from the onset.

He felt the jab of a needle as a minor discomfort. The nurse glared down at him, angered that she'd lost authority.

Adam was too tired to care. He closed his eyes. Thank God Kerry hadn't been there. If something had happened to her...

"We're going to give you a general after all, Mr. Shard." The doctor's voice sounded wavy and distorted. "Because you're going under all by yourself."

Kerry must have fallen into some kind of trance. Her muscles suddenly jerked awake, and she gasped, trying to get her bearings. She blinked. Outside the windows she saw the news van. Inside, the emergency room had grown quiet with dread.

A doctor appeared, looking briskly efficient. He glanced around, and Kerry realized he was about to make an announcement of some sort. The newspeople went to work, their man holding out his microphone for the doctor.

"The three people brought in by life-flight from the *Mary Lou* were Mr. John Marsden, Mr. Adam Shard and Mr. Giles Wilkes, the boat's captain. Mr. Wilkes was dead on arrival. Mrs. Mary Marsden, also a passenger, was brought in by the Coast Guard and has been admitted for shock and exposure, but she's in good condition."

Kerry climbed to her feet. Fear filled her heart.

"Mr. Marsden is in critical condition. He sustained head injuries and we're still checking the extent of those injuries. Mr. Shard is in the operating room to repair damage to his left arm."

Hope surged through Kerry, and a relief so vast she felt faint. She dropped her head to her knees as the doctor finished his interview, then shakily she stood and went to him. Just before he turned away, she grabbed his arm. "I'm sorry, but I'm a friend of Adam Shard's. When will I know how he is?"

"When he's in recovery."

"And when will that be?" Kerry asked, hands trembling uncontrollably.

"Fairly soon."

"Do you know how serious his injuries are?"

He gave her a long look and gently pulled her to one side. "No. I'm sorry. You'll just have to wait and see. That's what we do."

It was nine o'clock and the skies had deepened to a bluish-gray, nearly the same shade as Adam's eyes, Kerry thought miserably when she decided she could wait no longer. "I need to know about Adam Shard, one of the boat accident victims," she told the woman at the desk.

"You'll have to wait—"

"I won't. I won't wait."

The receptionist examined Kerry's determined face through eyes that had seen it all. With a sigh, she said, "Dr. Anthony will be down soon."

"Who is Dr. Anthony?"

"Our surgeon on duty."

"Can I wait for him somewhere else?"

"I—" The line rang and she picked it up, but her eyes were on Kerry. When the call ended, she said, "Just a moment." After punching out a number, she asked into the receiver, "When will Dr. Anthony be available?" A pause. "Because there's a woman here who's very worried about one of his patients—a Mr. Shard." Another pause. She glanced up at Kerry. "Are you related to Mr. Shard?"

Kerry drew a breath and prayed she wouldn't be struck by lightning. But she wasn't going to be deterred. "I'm his sister."

The receptionist relayed the information and suddenly Kerry was whisked into the inner sanctum. Dr. Anthony came striding toward her, still in surgical greens.

"We didn't know he had a sister here, ma'am," he said by way of introduction. "Your brother's fine. His left arm was severely lacerated, and it took a few stitches to put him together, but the nerves look fine and there're no broken bones. He was lucky."

Lucky. Reaction turned Kerry's legs to water. "I—I need to sit down."

"Come along to your brother's room. I'd like you to fill out some forms. He's still in recovery, but we'll bring him in soon. He didn't want us to put him under, but we had to."

"Adam doesn't like hospitals."

"No patient does. Sandra!" He turned to a young nurse at the medical station. "I need some patient forms for this young lady. She's one of the boat accident victim's sister."

She'd been prepared for the injuries to his arm, but they hadn't told her about the bruises and lacerations on Adam's face. The whole left side was swollen and covered with some kind of yellow antiseptic. He looked as if he'd been beaten up by a band of thugs.

Just like in the third grade.

Kerry sat in absolute silence, hardly daring to breathe. She'd been given a second chance, and she felt humble. What had she been fighting against for so long? She couldn't even remember now. She loved him and always had. From the moment he saved her—and the frog—from those sixth-grade bullies.

Even with the bruises, she was painfully aware of how sinfully long his lashes looked against his cheeks, how sculptured his nose was, how sexy his lips, how thick and luxurious his hair. Oh, Adam. I've been given a second chance. I promise you, I won't blow it this time. I'll tell you exactly how I feel.

There was a familiar smell in his nose. Hospitals. Adam slowly lifted his lashes, disoriented. Oh, God, he thought. That's right. They put me under.

He recognized the woman standing by the window the same moment he realized he was still under the influence of some kind of painkiller. His head was fuzzy, his arm was as sore as hell, and his mouth was as dry as cotton.

Kerry. He wanted to call out to her but didn't have the strength. Vaguely he remembered that she didn't love him and sorrow made him weak. His eyelids fell. His last conscious thought was that he didn't want her to be there when he woke up.

Sunlight was beaming across his face. Adam groaned. Pain shot to his skull from his arm.

"Mr. Shard? Are you awake?" asked a brisk feminine voice.

Do I look awake? he thought in disgust. "No."

"Dr. Anthony will be in to see you in an hour."

Adam opened his eyes. It was somewhere around midday. Where was Kerry? "Wait! Can you tell me about John Marsden?"

"He's still in critical condition. I don't know anything more. Oh, your sister had to run an errand. She said she'd be back soon."

Adam narrowed his gaze at her, confused. "My sister? I don't have a sister."

The nurse frowned at him, then shrugged and walked through the door, more interested in finishing her duty than easing his mind.

Now what was that all about?

He lay back and stared at the ceiling. The past twenty-four hours were in fragments. Had Kerry been here last night? He could almost remember seeing her in his room, standing at the window, her black hair like a dark cloud.

But that had to be imagination. They hadn't left on the best of terms Friday night. His lips twisted. Well, she probably would come to the hospital as a friend. Not a lover, a friend. Sucking air between his teeth, he squeezed his eyes closed. The pain of her rejection was a thousand times worse than the pain in his arm.

Dr. Anthony appeared. Adam remembered his trim gray hair and glasses. "How are you feeling?"

"Not bad. A little fuzzy still."

"We want to keep you here until tomorrow, maybe Tuesday."

Adam laughed. "Dream on, Doctor. I'm leaving as soon as someone shows me where my clothes are. And I want to know about John Marsden. And where's Mary Lou, his wife?"

"She's with him. He's had a rather severe concussion and we're keeping a watch on him."

"But he'll be okay."

"We don't expect any complications."

Doctors. They always hedged their bets. Marsden could be doing handsprings in the hall, and they'd only admit he was making progress.

But it was an enormous relief. Adam hadn't realized how worried he was until now, when he could feel his muscles unwind. Still, the room was close and his ears buzzed. "You didn't tell me where my clothes are."

"They're in the closet, but my recommendation is that—"

"I don't care what it is," he muttered tersely. "I've got to get out of here."

Light footsteps turned into his room and Adam looked up to see Kerry standing in the doorway. Her hair was pulled back into a braid, her eyes purple with shadows.

"You're awake," she said in an unsteady voice.

"Ah, Miss Shard. Maybe you can talk some sense into him. He insists on leaving today, but I strongly advise against it."

Adam worked hard to keep his feelings under control. He was too weak. Whatever drug they'd pumped into him was working on his emotions, lifting them to the surface. If he didn't watch it, he'd break down in some embarrassing way. What the hell was wrong with his hearing? "Miss . . . Shard?"

"Your sister's been here most of the night." The doctor patted Kerry's arm in a friendly way before he left.

Kerry walked to his bedside. Her perfume was as light and soft as spring, cutting the thick dull air. Her eyes were sober, a deep forest green, flecked with brown and surrounded by dense lashes. She flushed a becoming pink. "I lied. I was afraid they wouldn't let me stay if I told them I was just a friend."

He understood finally. "So, you're my sister?"

She nodded, smiling faintly.

She wore the aqua tank top and white pants he remembered sliding off her smooth skin that first night they'd slept together. He ached inside. His throat tightened, and he felt suffocated. So this was what love was. Real love. He wasn't certain he could survive it.

Touching his bandage, Kerry shivered a little. Adam's gaze followed the path of hers. Around the fringes, his bandage was brick-colored from his blood.

"I don't do well with blood," Kerry admitted.

"You never have."

Their gazes locked. "You don't do well with hospitals."

Adam swallowed and glanced away, narrowing his eyes on the view outside the window.

"You scared me to death," she said in a low voice. "For a while I was afraid . . ." She exhaled and bit her lip.

"Afraid you'd lost your best friend?"

Her brows drew together at his mocking tone. "Well, yes."

He couldn't take this. He wasn't up to it. Better to cut it off now, before he suffered more humiliation. "Kerry, you were right, and I was wrong. Getting involved ruined our friendship. It's not the same anymore and I'm sorry."

Her eyes were huge dark pools. He noticed the ravages on her beautiful face and realized belatedly that she'd spent a sleepless night on his behalf. "You're sorry?"

"I wish we'd left things the way they were. We can't go back, we can't go forward. Looks like we're in purgatory."

"Why can't we go forward?" she asked in a small voice.

He clenched his teeth until his fillings hurt. "I don't love you, Kerry. I was...wrong."

He looked her straight in the eye and lied. It was simple, really. Maybe if she felt he didn't care as much as he did, then they could have an affair, or a friendship, or something. Later. When he was ready. When everything didn't hurt so much.

His breath caught. Brimming in her eyes were huge tears. He'd never seen her cry before.

"I came to...the pier yesterday...to tell you—" she covered her mouth with her hands and closed her eyes; two tears slid over the hills of her cheeks "—I love you. I thought I'd lost the chance, and then at the hospital...I wasn't sure if—"

The rattle of the medicine cart echoed in the doorway. A cheery young nurse entered like a typhoon, destroying the moment. "Dr. Anthony said you're thinking of trying to leave us. I need to check you out, if that's so."

Kerry abruptly turned toward the door.

Adam flipped the covers back, furious. "Kerry, wait!"

She walked away in fast, efficient strides, never looking back once.

Marla's house was bearable only because she'd propped a fan on the kitchen counter and cool air kept everyone from being really cranky. Kerry sat on the couch, too upset to want to go home and face her own company. The last day and a half had wrung every possible emotion from her. She was so happy Adam was all right she wanted to cry, and so miserable that his love had been an illusion she wanted to die.

You have no one to blame but yourself.

She'd known from the beginning that Adam couldn't love her. He'd *told* her he didn't believe in love! So why had she listened when he'd said three meaningless words? Why had she reached to the bottom of her soul and told him how she felt rather than let it lie?

Jason walked into the living room. His T-shirt was too short and his belly hung out, giving him the look of a belligerent prize fighter gone to seed. A scowl was plastered across his baby face. Kerry looked at him, forcing a smile. "What is it, tiger?"

"'Lissa hit me."

"You've hit her a time or two, haven't you?"

"No!"

"I don't think that's quite true. I've seen you hit her."

The conversation wasn't going the way he wanted it to. For a moment he stood in defiant indecision, then he climbed onto the couch and buried his face in Kerry's neck, crying as if his heart would break.

For Kerry it was a surprising moment. Jason so rarely showed need for affection, especially from her, that she hardly knew what to do. Hugging him close, she rubbed his back. "Hey, it's not so bad." He sniffled louder, for effect. Kerry smiled against his hair. She had to resist the desire to squeeze too hard, to ask for the love she herself craved. Her eyes closed. Her heart hurt. She inhaled deeply the smell of dirt and chocolate, and the clean baby scent that lingered through all. Tears burned. "Oh, Jason," she murmured, a catch in her voice.

His blue eyes looked at her, huge and round. "You sad?" he asked in empathy.

"Very sad."

"Why?"

She couldn't talk. Jason lay his head against her shoulder and she wept silently, brushing at the tears, unable to stop their flow.

Marla stopped short at the entryway to the room. She didn't say anything, merely lifted her brows to ask if Jason was bothering her. Kerry shook her head. It felt wonderful to have someone in her arms who gave and received love so willingly.

Jason lasted about thirty seconds. Patting Kerry's hair, he said matter-of-factly, "You feel better," and slid from her lap.

"Do you?" Marla asked after Jason had gone in search of his sister. She perched on the ottoman in front of the couch.

"I don't have any problems. I'm here for you."

"Kerry, stop it. I know you're miserable. I can't remember the last time I saw you cry."

Kerry's gaze dropped to her hands. If Marla kept this up, she was going to see her sister cry rivers.

"You haven't lied to me about Adam, have you?" she asked quickly.

"No. Oh, no. He's fine. He'll be fine." Kerry drew in a deep breath and exhaled heavily. "I...finally told him how I felt."

"You did?" Marla paused, sympathetic. "What happened?"

"He doesn't feel the same way."

"Oh, Kerry."

"It doesn't matter." Kerry glanced away, chewing on her lower lip. "I knew it would be this way. I was stupid to get involved."

"Maybe he's just not admitting how he really feels."

"Marla, I don't want to talk about it." Kerry sighed. "Really. You've got worse problems than I do."

Marla grimaced. "James is coming by this afternoon. I've asked him to hold off on the divorce, and he's agreed, at least temporarily. We're going to talk. Really talk."

Kerry struggled to pull herself together. "That's wonderful. That's just what Adam said you ought to do...." Her voice trailed off with remembered pain.

Squeezing her hand, Marla advised, "Don't be sorry you said how you feel. It might hurt, but at least he knows. You've hidden your feelings for way too long."

Kerry lifted her brows in reluctant agreement. "It never seemed like a good idea to let anyone get that close. They can really hurt you."

"Yeah." Her lips twisted. "I know. But I have two wonderful children, and I wouldn't change things, even knowing what I know now."

Kerry left Marla's when James arrived. He looked terrible. He might be the villain in this drama, but his choices weren't making him completely happy, either. Had her father felt like that? Kerry wondered. She'd never credited him with emotions stronger than lust, but maybe it had hurt him a little to give up his family.

She drove home aimlessly, stopping by the park where she'd taken Jason and Melissa. It was still hot but a light breeze had kicked up, making the air feel fresher, more bearable, more Seattle. Kerry thought over everything that had happened since Adam had blown back into her life. She hadn't been the same since he'd walked across the threshold of her office.

She'd been so frightened, so suspicious. Adam had accused her of being an adventurer at heart, but Kerry had closed her ears, wanting to keep her safe, ordered world intact.

I know you, he'd said in a tone that suggested deep, private secrets shared between the two of them.

Kerry picked up a stone, plunking it into the duck pond, encouraging the whole flock of darkly feathered ducks to skim toward her, hoping for a handout.

Well, she knew him, too. And he'd run true to color in the end, rejecting her when the going got sticky.

But he did tell you he loved you.

So what? He probably says that to all the girls.

You know that's not true.

Oh, yeah? Then what is?

The ducks honked noisily, flapping their wings and fighting for position in front of Kerry. "Sorry, I'm empty-handed," she apologized, turning back toward her car.

She thought briefly about going back to the hospital, then headed home instead. She wasn't strong enough to face Adam, yet. She needed to work out some things first anyway.

At her apartment she pulled into the slot next to a luxury car and had to do a double-take before she recognized it. *Adam!* Throwing open her door, Kerry glanced to her balcony. There was no one there.

Kerry walked slowly up the steps, glancing backward from time to time. That *was* Adam's car. She was certain of it. So where was he?

She nearly jumped from her skin when her apartment door opened in front of her face. "Adam!" she shrieked.

"Kerry." He looked surprised, too.

Problem streaked outside, darting down the stairs.

"I was just letting the cat out," he explained.

"What are you doing here? How did you get in?"

"Your neighbor, Mr. Little, saw me sitting on the stoop and took pity on me. I guess he has a key to your apartment, because he let me in."

"Oh, right." Kerry shook her head to clear the cobwebs as Adam stepped aside, then closed the door behind her. For once the room didn't feel so bare. Adam's presence filled the empty spaces. "He was feeding Problem some of the time while I was at Marla's I'm surprised he let you in. He's so cautious."

Adam smiled faintly. "I think he decided after waiting three hours that I wasn't going to rob the place." He glanced at the sling on his left arm. "And I imagine I don't look like much of a threat."

Kerry met his amused gaze, resisting the urge to run her hand along his bruised cheek. The swelling had receded, and the cuts and blackening around his eye gave him a dangerous, raffish air. "You shouldn't have left the hospital," she said, turning away. "And you shouldn't have waited all this time for me."

"I needed to talk to you."

"I was at Marla's."

"I figured as much. But I also figured you'd show up here sooner or later."

Kerry glanced back uncertainly. She loved the way his hair smoothed dramatically away from his forehead, the lines of humor surrounding his eyes, the slant of his mouth. "What was so important that couldn't wait until you feel better?"

"Well…" He stretched, wincing a bit at the strain on his arm. "You told me you loved me in the hospital."

Kerry was shocked by his boldness. He really knew how to pour salt in a raw wound. "So?" she said, taking refuge in her favorite defense: flippancy and cynicism.

"So, I love you, too. And if you'd stuck around long enough, I would have told you again."

Kerry stood utterly still. "You said you didn't love me."

He sighed. "I was using one of your tactics, lying to cover up my true feelings."

Kerry shook her head, fighting back the surge of joy that threatened her common sense.

"Did you really think I would tell you I loved you if I didn't mean it?"

"But at the hospital—"

"Forget what I said at the hospital. I was really down, worried sick about Marsden, who, by the way, is getting better by the hour. I was still suffering the effects of the night before. I didn't mean it. You'd hurt me, and I wanted to hurt you back."

After that speech Adam sank down onto the couch, laying his head back and closing his eyes. Kerry was instantly filled with concern. "Are you okay?" she asked quickly.

"Yes, I'm okay," he answered with difficulty.

"I'm glad about John." Kerry hovered uncertainly. "You should have stayed in the hospital. This is crazy."

"No, I'm fine. Truly. Sit down."

Kerry perched on the edge of the couch; her eyes searched his face. He was pale beneath his tan. "Can I get you anything?"

He lifted his lashes until his eyes were two silvery slits. "I wouldn't mind hearing how you feel again, if you could manage it."

"Feel about you?"

He nodded, reaching out to stroke her hair away from her cheek. The look in his eyes was so tender that Kerry turned her cheek into his palm.

"It's hard for me to admit my feelings, but I've written them down for years, ever since we met."

"Written them down?" He frowned.

"In a journal," she said softly. "A diary, I guess. I started in the third grade and though there've been times when I left it for years, I've just recently been keeping it up again." She flushed, embarrassed to add, "You're my main subject."

"Really?" His lips curved.

"Yes, you egotist."

"Are you going to let me read it?"

Kerry thought of all the moments she'd recorded: her feelings after she'd caught her father with his lover; the misery she'd felt over Adam's marriage; the love she'd finally admitted to. Her most private thoughts and fears, all the emotions she'd kept hidden from the outside world, would be there on paper, raw, bare, unedited. It was the biggest risk she'd ever taken.

Without a word she went into the bedroom and found the spiral notebook, returning to the living room before she lost the courage.

She handed it to him with a shade of reluctance. "You're my friend," she murmured in a voice unsteady with emotion. "And the only man I've really ever loved. But even though I trusted you, I've always been afraid you'd turn out like my father somehow.'' Drawing a breath of courage, she added, ''When I was seventeen, I caught my father in the arms of his lover. They were at my house, my mother's house, drinking champagne and kissing. I told myself I would never trust a man. Any man.''

Comprehension slashed across his face. ''You never told me.''

She shook her head. ''But it's all in there.''

Adam's gaze turned to the journal lying in his palm. ''You're trusting me with this?''

Kerry lifted her shoulders, unable to speak. He reached a hand over, yanking her down beside him once more.

''I love you, Kerry,'' he said fiercely, cupping her chin, and kissing her with so much emotion that her limbs turned to water. She lay limp beside him, reveling in the taste of him. ''I've loved you from the moment you saved that poor frog!''

She laughed against his mouth. ''Oh, come on! No more lying, Adam. You did marry Jenny Sutcliff.''

''Only because she looked like you.'' Kerry pulled back, her hazel eyes wide and suspicious. Adam's blue-gray ones stared right back. ''Oh, I didn't know it at the time otherwise I wouldn't have done it. But that's why I married her. I wanted her to *be* you, because I couldn't have the genuine article.'' Softly he added, ''I told you, didn't I, that I never really loved her.''

''You told me, and I thought that meant you couldn't love anyone.''

''Maybe that's what I wanted you to think. I didn't really want to face my feelings, either. Your rejections hurt.''

She drew his mouth back to hers, rubbing her lips against his. "I only rejected you because the timing wasn't right, and because I was afraid. I promise I won't be afraid anymore."

"Then will you marry me?" he asked casually, his gaze traveling back to the blue spiral journal. Across the front Kerry's Diary was written in bold third-grade handwriting, the dot of the i a tiny circle.

Adam turned to the first page.

I met a new boy at school today. He's in the third grade in my room. He got hit by those mean sixth-graders. There was lots and lots of blood. He saved my life!!!! His name is Adam.

He slid her a sideways glance, amusement tugging at his lips.

"Yes," Kerry answered with love shining openly from her eyes. "I'll marry you." She glanced down at the page. "After all, you saved my life."

* * * * *

Silhouette Special Edition

COMING NEXT MONTH

#601 LOVE FINDS YANCEY CORDELL—Curtiss Ann Matlock
Yancey Cordell had every reason to be cynical about Annalise Pardee. Yet
the fragile new ranch owner inspired a strange kind of loyalty...and
evoked something suspiciously like love.

#602 THE SPIRIT IS WILLING—Patricia Coughlin
Thrust into an out-of-body experience, Jason Allaire landed the unlikely
role of guardian angel to adorable oddball Maxi Love. But would earthy
masculine urges topple his halo and destroy his second chance at love?

#603 SHOWDOWN AT SIN CREEK—Jessica St. James
LaRue Tate wasn't about to let the government commandeer her precious
prairieland. But when "government" fleshed out as handsome, rakish
J. B. Rafferty, she faced an unexpected showdown—with her own
bridling passions!

#604 GALAHAD'S BRIDE—Ada Steward
Horseman Houston Carder had a heart the size of Texas, with more than
enough room for sheltering delicate Laura Warner. But this particular
damsel seemed to resist rescue, no matter how seductive the Sir Galahad!

#605 GOLDEN ADVENTURE—Tracy Sinclair
The thrill of being romanced by a mysterious expatriate made it worth
missing her boat. Or so thought stranded traveler Alexis Lindley...until
she discovered the dashing adventurer was a wanted man.

#606 THE COURTSHIP OF CAROL SOMMARS—
Debbie Macomber
Cautious Carol Sommars successfully sidestepped amorous advances—
until her teenage son rallied his best buddy, who rallied *his* sexy single dad,
whose fancy footwork threatened to halt the single mom's retreat
from romance....

AVAILABLE THIS MONTH:

#595 TEA AND DESTINY
Sherryl Woods

#596 DEAR DIARY
Natalie Bishop

#597 IT HAPPENED ONE NIGHT
Marie Ferrarella

#598 TREASURE DEEP
Bevlyn Marshall

#599 STRICTLY FOR HIRE
Maggi Charles

#600 SOMETHING SPECIAL
Victoria Pade

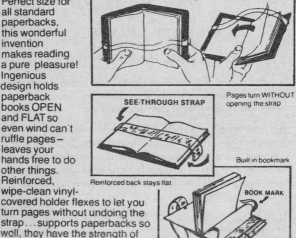